Eyes Guts
Throat Bones

Moïra Fowley

T0385346

WEIDENFELD & NICOLSON

First published in Great Britain in 2023 by Weidenfeld & Nicolson
This paperback edition published in 2024 by Weidenfeld & Nicolson,
an imprint of The Orion Publishing Group Ltd
Carmelite House, 50 Victoria Embankment
London EC4Y 0DZ

An Hachette UK Company

7 9 10 8 6

A CIP catalogue record for this book is
available from the British Library.

ISBN (Mass Market Paperback) 978 1 3996 0052 1
ISBN (eBook) 978 1 3996 0053 8
ISBN (Audio) 978 1 3996 0054 5

Typeset by Born Group
Printed and bound in Great Britain by Clays Ltd, Elcograf S.p.A.

www.weidenfeldandnicolson.co.uk
www.orionbooks.co.uk

Eyes Guts Throat Bones

About the author

Moïra Fowley is the author of three critically acclaimed YA novels, and a part-time witch. Her short story 'Such a pretty face' from *Eyes Guts Throat Bones* won the 2023 Irish Book Awards Short Story of the Year. Half-French and half-Irish, she lives in Dublin with her girlfriend and her two children.

EYES

GUTS

Interval

THROAT

BONES

What would you give
for a treat like me

On the twelfth day everything started to smell like sweets.

We'd already lost the Murdocks – the two children burrowing into a pile of dead leaves late on the third day.

You said you thought they were making a den for themselves and smiled until they started eating the earth. I thought maybe this was a thing children did, until I saw your grimace. I'd never really understood children, didn't know how to reconcile their loud, chaotic, sticky messes with my own well-ordered childhood. You loved children, as though extreme youth by itself was enough to trigger your affection. I didn't see the appeal. They weren't quite people yet, were they?

Get up outta that, the dad – Greg, maybe, or Gary – said. *Stop yizzer messing.*

But the children stuffed leaves into their ears and mouths, down their pants. Dirt to their foreheads, clumps of it in their hair. Worms and woodlice curled from between their lips. The mother – Anne, maybe, or Alison – started to scream.

A few of us hushed her. This was before. If it'd been even a few days later half a dozen hands would have clamped over her mouth in seconds.

Alison and Greg grabbed their children by the armpits, tried to hoist them up from the soggy ground underneath the tree, but they were rooted, wouldn't rise. Their eyes shone, their teeth masticating leaves and mud, their little fists still stuffing earth and insects and deer shit down their gullets and up their noses. Wet, choking noises; shining eyes.

STOP THAT, Gary yelled, and yet more of us made shushing sounds. The children's panting and scuffles, the high, desperate keening coming from Anne's throat. I looked to the front of the line, to the leaders, to those who'd been walking the longest. They exchanged sombre glances, shook their heads. The first few started to move on, more quickly than before.

You watched the Murdocks pull at their children, stick fingers into their mouths and noses to scoop out the mess of mulch and spit, to quell the strangled noises behind their smiles. You took two steps towards them but Bet stopped you with a raised arm.

Keep walking, she said. *You know the rules.*

I angled myself between the two of you. I said, *Don't worry. We know.* I took your elbow and you followed.

The Murdocks stayed behind, the children now mostly mud and mulch, bright eyes laughing, small bodies stopped by tight-packed mouldy leaves.

When I turned back – we were still turning back, then – Greg was covered in a greenish fur, hunched in front of his children like a mossy boulder. A shape a lot like Alison was growing into the ivy vines on the tree her children sheltered under.

We hadn't talked about children in months, but after the Murdocks that old conversation circled us like the midges that clouded with the sunset, whined around our faces on tinny wings, impervious to the slaps that made our ears ring.

When we made camp we lit citronella and sat close, our hushed voices around the fires no louder than the insects.

Maybe I started it. Sal had a bit of whiskey left and she passed it around. I suppose we were all a bit shaken. When I closed my eyes I could see brown mulch between milk teeth. My own throat felt choked.

I think I said, in an attempt at buoyancy, *Aren't you glad we didn't end up trying for a kid, before all this.*

You spat your mouthful of whiskey into the fire – dragon spit, high, hot and hissing – and didn't say a word to me until two days later, after Johnny.

★

Five years ago, winter. Snow up to the windowsill. You wanted to light a fire but we only had peat briquettes, no firelighters. You tore the sports section out of the paper, twisted it into long newsprint plaits like the cheesy puff pastry things you'd just pulled out of the oven. We were drinking hot whiskeys with honey, cloves stuck in the lemons like coffin nails. We hadn't seen another soul in five days apart from through the living room window. The country practically shut down. Shops ran out of bread as people stockpiled. Schools and colleges closed. Children screamed in delight through the estate, snowballs flying past the windows.

You took the whiskey bottle by the neck, blocked half the hole with your thumb and sprinkled the twists

3

of newspaper with single malt Jameson. After that, the fire lit fast.

We sat on the floor in a fort of cushions and blankets, the fire blazing, the darkness outside brighter than normal winter dark, waning moon reflecting on white ground. In the untouched snow of our garden, the neighbours' kids had made a couple of snow-women. One was taller than the other. One had short, spiky stick hair. They were holding stick hands. Their shadows stared in through the open curtains at us, cold mirrors.

You laid your head on my shoulder and watched the whiskey-sprinkled fire. *Do you ever think about kids?* you asked.

You mean, about having them? I said.

You laughed. *No, I mean eating them.*

No, I said. *I've never wanted kids.*

You were quiet so long I thought you were sleeping. When you spoke it was so low the spits and crackles of the fire almost drowned out your words. *What if I did?*

I pretended I hadn't heard.

★

Johnny was the eldest of us, which didn't mean he was the slowest. He'd been in the army as a youth, then worked as a gardener until well after he'd started collecting his state pension. He identified every edible plant and fungus we added to our rations, knew the best way to treat insect bites and nettle stings. He was a bachelor, not mourning anybody in particular. He was in turns taciturn and jolly, and I liked him.

On the sixth day, when we'd put maybe a hundred kilometres between us and the Murdocks, he started to slow. He raised each leg as though it weighed twice what it had the day before, and the imprints his feet left in the spongy ground grew deeper.

Sal doubled back to check on him, which spoke volumes about his value to the group. Sal didn't double back for just anyone.

It's nothing, Johnny barked. *Keep walking.*

Sal raised an eyebrow but didn't argue. She joined Bet up front, walking sticks beating back overhanging twigs and vines.

We were further up the incline so could see it when it happened: the moment Johnny went to raise his right leg and it refused. He tipped forwards, straight as a plank of wood, and landed face-first in the moss. Those closest to him hurried to help but he grunted at them to get back. Voice muffled. Earth and moss and leaves.

One of the young lads – Aiden, maybe, or Adrien – nudged Johnny with the toe of his hiking boot, rolled the old man over on his back with some difficulty. Johnny stared, unblinking, up at the sky between the trees, his body suddenly so heavy he sank as we watched into the damp ground. The only part of him that wasn't solid gold were his dentures.

When we made camp that night nobody spoke. You hadn't said a word to me for days so this didn't make a huge change. But when Bet called lights out, instead of rolling away from me in our shared sleeping bag, you curled into my back like a comma and cried into my hair.

I miss you, you whispered. *I miss you.*

I said, *I'm right here*, but pressed against my back I could feel you shake your head.

Four years ago, spring. A shower of cherry blossoms drenching the pavement. Your hair was growing out. It fell into your eyes, and you kept blowing air up onto your forehead from pursed lips. Pink petals falling on your shoulders.

The market had opened and I carried a canvas bag full of organic beetroot, leafy greens, boxes of early strawberries, cut flowers. We'd shared a crêpe from the little van and I could still taste the lemon and sugar at the edges of my mouth.

On your phone, a picture of your niece, a baby. Rolls and folds of baby skin. Round cheeks and sparse hair, a gummy smile.

Couldn't you just take a bite out of those thighs, you asked me. *Isn't she just the most beautiful thing.*

You are the most beautiful thing, I told you. You, with cherry blossoms on your shoulders and lemon sugar on your tongue, hair falling into your eyes. You laughed and told me you loved me.

That night, naked in bed with the covers kicked off, tongues tasting a lot less like lemons, you told me, *I'm going to marry you someday.*

I traced the dip of your hip, your waist. *I wouldn't put it past you.*

We'd be happy, you said. *Wouldn't we?*

We're happy now.

You laughed. *Can't you picture it, though?*

Picture what?

You made a screen of your two hands, stretched your arms so I could see our imaginary future from where I lay naked beside you. *You and me*, you said. *Buying fresh fruit at the market. Our little children sneaking berries from the bag so that by the time we got home the basket would be empty, their faces pink and giggling.*

If you want to have all the food gone by the time we get home, I said, *we should just get a dog.*

You're allergic, you reminded me.

I'm allergic to kids, I said.

You didn't laugh. *Just think about it*, you said.

Okay, I conceded, just so the conversation could close, just so it could be you and me again, naked in bed, with no imaginary berry-faced children between us. *I'll think about it.*

★

After Johnny, one of the other women – younger than us, early twenties maybe, the look of an art student about her – disappeared into the woods and didn't come back. We couldn't call too loudly through the trees. We'd learnt that, at least. Two days beforehand we'd lost Melissa; we knew what happened when we could be heard.

You'd liked Melissa. Enough that I could feel a sharp splinter of jealousy under my nail. She was in her forties, divorced, her son in tow. He was older than the Murdock children had been, less indecipherable. He didn't speak much, stayed close to Melissa, often walked holding her hand, which you told me was unusual in a boy his age. You said he must have seen some horrible things.

We have all seen horrible things, I said.

You liked the boy, too, tried to engage him in conversation, showed him how to tie knots the way you'd learnt

7

in Girl Scouts, seamed long grasses with a thumbnail for him to blow into, making a sound like a quiet bird.

You're good with him, I heard Melissa tell you one evening. *You'd make a great mother, you know?*

I looked away quickly because I knew you'd look right at me, could feel your gaze heat the skin of my left ear.

You whispered low but it carried. *It's too late for that, now,* you said.

It's not too late, Melissa answered. *Women have always had children as the world ended.*

That evening you were almost cheerful, gathered the small group of children around the fire and taught them a game that seemed too complicated for people so young. It was an almost silent game, but for the giggles – the children hadn't giggled in days – and involved a series of gestures that bounced the game back and forth around the circle. Crossed arms to block it, fingers pointing to pass it on, palms pushed up to send it to the other side of the circle. The adults watched with rare smiles. That night, there were fewer nightmares.

In the morning when we packed up camp, Melissa's son was gone. Tucked into his sleeping bag in his stead was a wolf cub, lanky and grey. When Melissa tried to catch it the wolf streaked into the woods and she stood at the edge of the clearing and screamed a name the cub surely no longer recognised. The forest fell silent.

Move out, Sal hissed. *Now.*

We left anything we hadn't yet packed behind.

You took Melissa's arm and whispered, *He'll follow, don't worry, he'll follow from the woods.*

Melissa tried to speak but her voice flopped out of her like a fish, fell flapping to the ground. Melissa stumbled, tripped over her own legs. Legs fusing together to form a fin.

Your look of horror was so familiar. So was the way Bet came and unclutched your fists from Melissa's jerking form.

Keep walking, Bet said. *You know the rules*.

Melissa couldn't walk. We left her behind to dry-heave fish into the bushes. When I turned around – I was one of the only ones who still turned around – a small, grey wolf had nosed out from between the trees, was tearing into the still-flopping fish with its sharp teeth.

*

Three years ago, autumn. Crisp leaves, trees on fire. You'd brought me *home*, you called it, brought me to where you grew up. Back then, it was mostly fields of sheep, the winding river leading to the beach, sea dotted with surfers in thick wetsuits, flat feet in soft rubber boots balancing on their boards.

Now, there were no more sheep, no fields, and we'd walked for weeks without seeing a river, although we thought we could hear water, sometimes, thick and churning, far away. Even the rainwater we collected when we made camp tasted sludgy, earthy, smelled just like the trees.

Three years ago the trees were hard bark and bright leaves and you brought me to the river where you went fishing with your grandparents as a child. We sat on the bank and shared a thermos of tea, chocolate digestives. You told me stories of you and your brother and sisters slipping into the water, accidentally letting the cows out of the field across the river, climbing the trees up on the hill by the mobile home campsite, sneaking into the playground with the seesaw you could fly off at the top if you didn't hold on.

It sounds like a childhood from a book, I told you. *The Secret Seven or something.*

Wasn't your childhood like that? you asked.

My childhood was books about childhoods like yours, I answered. Ballet and violin, neatly parted hair, the same diets as my mother. My tidy body in well-pressed clothes in the mirror; other children outside the windows.

Later, done fishing, and having caught nothing, we picked wild blackberries from the bushes along the river, fed them to each other and kissed them out of each other's mouths, faces stained purple as though we'd been gobbling live things, bloody-lipped. You pressed me up against a stile hidden from view and unbuttoned my jeans. I came at the beckon of your berry-stained fingers.

That night, in the bed of the B&B, after a pub meal of steak and chips, too much bad wine, I said, *I'd do anything in the world to keep you.*

You smiled, you stroked my hair. *I know,* you said.

In the morning you had the number for the IVF clinic already saved in your phone.

★

On the tenth day our group was halved. It happened all at once. We were walking through the endless sameness of damp and mud and low-hanging vines between slick-glistening trees, two dozen of us, or thereabouts, led by Bet and Sal, the thwack of their sticks and the squelch of their boots our marching metronome. Our supplies were dwindling, the packs on our backs so much lighter than when we'd started. The wind in wet leaves and the constant grumble of empty stomachs. Then the sounds changed, the constant footfalls knocked off kilter. It took a few moments to realise this was because almost half of those footfalls had stopped.

Not again, you breathed, and I reached for your hand. It was only Bet and Sal and the Callaghans in front of us. Behind us, the Murphy sisters, a burly man who called himself Hawk, and two of the young lads. Behind them, nobody.

One of the young lads started swearing softly, retraced his steps for a few metres, turning in wide circles to try to see between the trees. A crunch; an awful, tiny cry. The young lad went white, lifted a foot. On the heel of his boot, a splash of bright blood, bits of gore dripping from the sole.

Don't move, he whispered, frantic. *You'll step on them.*

The other young lad and the sisters, who'd been about to join him, stopped. The young lad bent one hand to the ground and scooped up two small people. Barely the size of his pinkie finger, now, and shrinking fast. I thought I recognised the parents of some of the children you'd been playing the gestures game with around the fire. The tiny figures clutched each other, grew smaller and smaller. Around us, the forest went quiet.

Bet didn't have to say the words. The young lad dropped the tiny parents beside their bite-sized children and the other tiny figures who had been part of our group, and he, like the rest of us remaining, turned to keep walking.

That night there was no fire. The wood wouldn't take. There were no games to play. You didn't go to comfort the remaining children, crying hungry in their tents, the other adults, the young lads. Your face was thin and pinched. I took you in my arms and gave you the last of the food I had left. You broke it in half to share, and you kissed me with dry, cracked lips.

I would do anything, you said. *To keep you.*

I whispered into your hair, *I know.*

★

Two years ago, summer. Parisian street hot in the sunlight. Leafy boulevard, the metro entrance arching overhead. You had your hair tied up in a silk scarf and I told you you looked French. You laughed and said French women didn't have freckled, sunburnt noses.

The round, iron table we sat at side-by-side over-looking the street was filled with food: a plate of oysters, a bucket of mussels in white wine sauce, bowls of skinny chips, scallops in brown butter, white bread rolls.

I had always loved watching you eat. You did it with such abandon, neck arched, eyes half-closed, an almost erotic act. You loved food, and through your enjoyment I learnt to love it too. After years of restriction, my mother's pursed lips when she spoke of *sugar* and *carbs* and *bad fats*, I learnt to love the foods I'd never eaten growing up: real butter melting on thickly sliced sourdough toast, creamy pasta with crispy bacon, fat chips, apple pie. I grew into my breasts, my hips, and I loved how you held me, how you begged for the weight of me on top of you in bed, pressing you, gasping, into the mattress.

12

We climbed the steps of the Sacré-Cœur, calves aching, stomachs protesting. From above the city was sparkling and so were your eyes.

I'm going to marry you someday, I said.

I wouldn't put it past you, you answered. Still, you were surprised when I took out the ring.

That night you swallowed me like an oyster, like a buttered scallop. I thought I knew your hunger. Your hunger for my body. Your hunger for my love. Your hunger for the happily ever after you'd dreamed up in your plump and messy childhood.

I thought, why not give you what you wanted? What was just one morsel I couldn't yet stomach compared to a lifetime of your hunger? If this was what it took to keep you, I would help to put a child into your hungry belly.

★

After that you got hungry. We all were, our stomachs echoing in their bone cages, but for you it was something else. I saw it in how your eyes roved over the children. I saw it in how you licked your lips. At night in our tent you pressed your teeth against my flesh. It was difficult to stifle my moans.

In the morning, the young lads' tent was empty, their pillows filled with pearls. We pretended not to notice that the two large bullfrogs by the smouldering fire had human hazel eyes. We told ourselves the young lads were the pearls.

Bet dashed the frogs' skulls against a rock and Sal stuck them on a spit. That afternoon, we walked faster and for longer, the groan of our stomachs quieted, a spring of energy in our step.

When the paunchy middle-aged man who called himself Hawk stumbled over a tree root and fell into the wet, sucking forest, we didn't hesitate. We threw ourselves on the patchy old bear who blundered out from between the trees in his stead. The smell of slow-cooked meat filled our no-longer-empty backpacks, clung to our clothes for days.

The Murphy sisters started to pitch their tent close to ours when we made camp, took to greeting us warmly in the morning. The youngest had finally stopped crying. You didn't ask where their parents were or how long ago they'd been lost; maybe you already knew. Maybe you'd already befriended these girls, the last sweet teens we'd ever see.

You told me the eldest reminded you of yourself at her age – sixteen, I thought, maybe, or seventeen – tough and spunky, spark of mischief in her eye. It was difficult to see mischief in the low, green damp of the forest, but it was true that the older sister was stronger than the younger, got on with things. It was she who swung her whole body off the bear's neck, dragging it down so Sal could drive a pointed stick through its eye to its lumbering brain.

She watched us, the oldest Murphy sister, appraisingly. She asked, *Do you think things will ever be the way they were before?*

You placed a hand, unconsciously, on your belly, fuller now than it had been. I could see you thinking of Melissa, of how she had said it wasn't too late.

You said, *No. But life goes on, even if it looks different to the way you'd hoped, or thought.*

It was the younger Murphy sister who crumbled, late in the afternoon of the eleventh day. We thought, at first, that she'd started crying again. Her face crumpled, her hands made fists. The older sister stopped, tugged at the arm of the younger. It broke off at the shoulder, stiff and gritty in the older sister's hand.

The muggy air around us suddenly smelled like baking, yeasty and sweet. Each droplet of drizzle from between overhead leaves landed like little craters on the younger sister's skin. Sugar dissolving. The last piece of her to turn to gingerbread was her hair, and each strand scattered slowly into crumbs.

No, breathed the older Murphy sister (the only Murphy sister, now).

Sal had stopped, turned back. *Keep walking*, she said. *You know the rules.*

Bet snapped a finger off the younger Murphy sister.

The older sister shrieked.

The rest of the bear meat would last us another week at most and we hadn't had anything bread-like in months. The Callaghans opened their backpacks to stuff the hard biscuit inside but the remaining Murphy girl picked up her stiff sister and hissed at the lot of us. The forest fell silent.

Sal said, *We have to move,* and Bet led the way.

The Callaghans followed, the baby reaching around in its tight-wrapped sling, desperate for a taste of gingerbread, that dry hardness that you told me was good to soothe teething gums.

You stood, unmoving, staring at the girl you'd said so resembled you at that age. Your look was fierce but hers was feral. Yours was hungry but hers was starved. In the handful of seconds I held your attention, taking you by the elbow to pull you on, the eldest Murphy had melted into the forest with her sugared sister, and was swallowed up by the trees.

★

One year ago, spring. Muggy skies. The drizzle had started, although we didn't know yet that it wouldn't stop. The tall, damp trees had started to grow. They didn't yet block out the light. They didn't yet cover the country. But they were there. Growing. Transforming. Consuming.

We had booked a sweets cart for the wedding. The kind with striped awnings, jars of bonbons, little plastic scoops in rainbow hues to dip into dolly mixtures.

You said your nieces would be our taste-testers, although I thought children became hyper after eating sweets, grimaced at the thought of sugar-filled toddlers destroying the white seat backs of the wicker chairs, puking over the floral arrangements. But you were so happy, enticing the children over early with lollipops and liquorice until you were the centre of a flower made of tiny chubby petals, your nieces in pastel dresses ready to bounce up the aisle before us, showering the path in confetti.

At five in the morning, the last women standing, we bid goodnight to our more stalwart partying friends, our drowsy, drunk family, and filled our arms with sweets, sat up to greet a murky green dawn with sugar on our fingers.

You fed me strawberry gummies and I barely bit them, swallowed them the way we'd eaten oysters in Paris. That slick slide down our throats in tandem, the deep kisses that followed.

16

Let's have a baby, you said, and there was no world in which I could refuse you.

★

On the twelfth day everything started to smell like sweets. The swamp scent of the forest turned hard and sugary, a chemical bite to the warm air. My mouth watered. We kept stopping, turning, twisting our faces to catch the source of the smell.

Keep walking, said Sal, but even she could sense it, licked her lips and seemed surprised to taste the salt.

You said something, softly. I inclined my head to hear you better but you didn't repeat the words I thought I'd heard you say: *We'll know it when we see it.*

When we made camp that night you asked me, *Are you still glad we didn't try for a baby before all this?*

How couldn't I be? I asked, gesturing at the tent walls around us keeping the forest out. *What kind of a world is this to bring a baby into?*

I keep thinking, you said, brushing the tangles from your hair, tying it back into a plait like Sal's, thick and ropelike, yours now newly streaked with grey, *that if we'd only had another month. If we'd only made it to the appointment.*

I said nothing.

You think we dodged a bullet, you said.

I repeated Melissa's words, although I knew there were no IVF clinics any more. *It's not too late.*

It's not too late. You said again what you'd said to the eldest Murphy sister. *Even if it looks different to the way I'd hoped, or thought.*

We were woken by one of the Callaghans' screams. I had never been able to tell them apart, besides the baby. Both parents were bald and bearded, wore lumberjack shirts under a large backpack and a baby carrier, respectively. Both spoke mostly to each other and not often to us, although you approached them frequently, offered to rock the baby to sleep when its parents' eyes were drooping, heads nodding late into the night. If the baby had a name I didn't know it, although I'm sure you did.

Maybe it managed to get its hands on a morsel of the youngest Murphy sister. Maybe it had somehow reacted to that sweetness. When the Callaghans emerged from the tent to the rest of us watching – surrounding them, but at a distance, cautious, now, ready to leave anything we hadn't packed and keep walking – the baby wasn't flesh and fat, sparse hair, gummy mouth. All of it was falling apart. The flushed brown of its face paled and cracked like cement before the weak sun shone on the still-packed crystals, just about in the shape of a small child. The smell of sweets was in the air but the baby was all salt. Slowly, before our eyes, it disintegrated, white and shining. Out its parent's arms it poured to the damp ground, the pile of salt soon translucent, dissolving into the mud and moss. Soon after, the Callaghan parents dissolved into puddles of their own. Only the last of the dust of the finest salt crystals lingered in the air.

Bet and Sal and you and I packed up the rest of the camp and kept walking.

The smell of sweets followed us for days.

On the fifteenth day, we awoke to find twin rose bushes growing in the remains of Bet and Sal's tent. One red, one white, the topmost branches intertwined. You took my hand and we breathed in the scent of candied flowers, crystallised sugar glinting in the drizzle. They may have looked like salt but they were so sweet.

On the seventeenth day, we walked into the clearing, and saw the house.

★

Gabled roof of biscuit brown, the gutters icing ridges. Ice-cream wafer shutters at the windows. Long tongue of liquorice leading us in the door. We took off our boots and our socks slid on the caramel-lacquer floorboards, their shine reflecting the spun-sugar sofas, the cocoa-bark table, the hard candy stove readied for roasting.

We'll know it when we see it, you said. And you laughed and laughed.

★

Into the house came the children. I didn't know them at first, but you did. You recognised them right away, welcomed them with open arms. Two mounds of mud and mulch, smelling of damp dead things, earthworms in their ears and woodlice between their teeth, eyes still shining. They came first, tracked muck over the shiny floorboards. A lone, scraggly wolf cub skulked in later, when the sun went down. In the darkness, tiny children, each no bigger than a thumbnail, climbed over each other to reach the low front steps and clamber across the threshold. Not long after them came the gingerbread girl, brittle biscuit fists full of salt.

The stove fire burning. A sweet feast on the table. Two empty plates.

I shut the door behind them. You opened your wet mouth wide.

Come in, little children, you said. *Come inside.*

Flowers

The first time we kissed it rained flowers for a week, beautiful and biblical until the gnats and the worms and the clumps of black soil landed in everybody's hair.

The priests had a field day. Billboards sprung up outside the town's three churches: GOD LIVES, MIRACLES ARE REAL. As if they hadn't ever properly believed it to begin with. As if they too had been looking for proof all along.

The hippies all thought it was some eco-magic. Mother Earth talking to us at long last. But the Earth has always had flowers (even if they don't ordinarily fall from the sky) and we knew this wasn't anything miraculous. Just two girls falling in love. Nothing magical at all.

Mam says she knew the day that girl came to town that she would be trouble. There were crows all crowding up the telephone lines, sign of sudden change. When she opened a fresh packet of Brennan's sliced white bread that morning there was a little mouse inside. Perfect tunnel chewed through the whole pan.

'Unwelcome guests,' spat Mam, and she threw the mouse at our cats. She isn't cruel, my mam. She just gets what's going to happen and doesn't have much patience for the meantime. Besides, cat food isn't cheap.

Before that girl arrived the whole town was a meantime. For fewer than two thousand souls there were two schools, two shops, three churches, three sports pitches and five pubs, which really speaks for the town's priorities. We got our books from the county mobile library, twice a month on Tuesdays. We waited for the bus to bigger towns in the rain rather than shelter in the little wooden shed beside the bus stop. That's where the statue of the Virgin Mary is. It's more important that she be kept dry.

I knew one day I'd cut my hair, wear big boots and crop tops with words splashed over the chest like I'd been ripped open and the words were my heart. I knew one day I'd have friends who'd stomp in the pit at concerts with me, who'd throw themselves fully clothed in the sea, who'd tattoo hearts and stars on our thighs with India ink, who'd read aloud with me on rainy days. I knew I'd fall in love with somebody and the world would open up to greet us. I knew one day I'd live somewhere where nobody cared that that somebody would be a girl.

But in the meantime my hair was straight down past my shoulders, parted in the middle, the same way it'd been since I was five. Weekdays I wore my school uniform and on weekends I wore my sister Orla's old jeans and Mam threw out any t-shirts I ripped up or wrote on. In the meantime the only person I knew who went to concerts was Orla and the only person I knew who had a tattoo was Mr McGahern, the school caretaker. In the meantime my friends would have rathered watch a GAA match than read aloud, and the most adventurous they got was going to see a Saturday matinee in Mayo Movie

World. In the meantime I'd no idea what it felt like to be in love but I'd a fairly solid notion about how this town would feel about it when I did.

'Just keep your head down,' Mam said. 'Give them what they expect.'

My mam's always known I'm not what they expect. Too restless, too wanton, too wild, too used to longing. I want so much it cuts my breath sometimes. I'll never be satisfied. She says she knew it from the day I was born, a small red squall, never quiet. She knew it from how salty her milk became to feed me, from how the fairy cakes she baked for my birthdays rose twice as high. From how I'd cry enough to salt the soup every day after school. From how even the classical radio station would start playing Sinéad O'Connor the second I walked into the room. From how my clothes would all mysteriously dye themselves black and purple in the wash, how footballs deflated in my fingers, how my father's hair went grey before I turned five.

Years ago I'd've been called a changeling but in the year of our Lord 1995 I was just a mess of a girl.

A mess the new girl walked right into on the second week of the summer holidays when she followed her grandfather into the market in the main hall of the biggest church in town.

My mam was selling her roses to the hippies. 'Good for love,' she whispered, out of earshot of our neighbours or the priests. 'One small spoonful of this in tea to ignite true passion.' She slipped a small vial to the hippies under the palm of her hand. Motherwort, peppermint and angelica, if I had to guess. The women'd be coming to her for pennyroyal in the next couple of months.

'They sell condoms in the supermarket in Castlebar,' my sister Orla said in an undertone as the hippies left the church. One of them nodded silently in her direction. Maybe they wouldn't need Mam's pennyroyal after all.

Orla was back from college for the summer and getting in Mam's hair. Every morning when Mam woke up she'd unwind her long brown plaits and brush out Orla's chewed-up biros, her lecture notes, stray beads from her many bracelets, the clinking change she kept in her pockets. They fought all day like a pair of housecats, all hiss and no claws. Mam's admonitions kept getting stuck in Orla's throat. Every night before bed Orla'd cough out crickets and corrections, scatter them out the back door before chugging a blend of lemon and honey hot water to ease her throat for the following day. It had only been two weeks and already we all knew it was going to be a long summer.

The hippies left in their cloud of rose and incense and out of that cloud she emerged, hair blown all blonde into her eyes from the breeze outside and big boots biting at the bottoms of her cut-off jeans.

I watched her make the rounds with her granda, trailing half a step behind him, hands in her pockets, as he greeted the farmers, the primary school headmaster fundraising for the under-10s Gaelic football team, as he bought some of the clams Rory McDonnell's boys drove out past Westport to dig for, and some of Mrs Leary's soda bread. I knew her granda'd never come to my mam's table but we were set up right next to Mrs O'Rourke and her granda's always been partial to one of the widow's apple tarts.

She smiled at everyone. That's what got me. At first glance she looked as if she might actually be happy to be here, in this echoey church hall filled with camping tables covered in vegetables and ugly cakes and snap judgements. The neighbours saw her too-short jeans, her messy hair, the leer of her lips and they knew her better than I did. City kid, they stage-whispered to those few who didn't, single mam, made of notions. Shower of pins on her denim jacket. Probably vegetarian. Worse than the hippies, the neighbours thought. Thinks she's too good for us.

At closer look her smile was a slice of lightning.

The first time we looked at each other was a tornado. Twists of wind crashed through the church doors and set Mam's roses flying. Tables overturned, glass shattered, eggs smashed across the floor. Everyone either fell or took cover, except the two of us. Only souls left standing in the wake of the storm.

The town shook itself, laughed nervously. The neighbours righted the tables, counted the vegetables, cleaned up the eggs.

Mam said, 'Tess!' sharp as teeth. My name's an easy one to hiss but this was cut glass rather than a snake.

I looked away from the new girl for a second and Mam held something up, stabbed it in my direction. A mouse tail. Tiny, thin and grey, it lay right across my palm like a scar.

Unwanted guests.

But when I looked back at her there were petals from my mam's roses in her hair and she was laughing. And she was still looking at me.

The first time we spoke it caused a landslide. Stones skittered across the road beside us and whole chunks of earth slid with them. Half the street was swept away.

Shopkeepers rushed to the road, grabbed at the signs outside their shop doors so they wouldn't be carried off in the rubble. Buggies overturned and small children forced their feet to hopscotch over uneven pieces of pavement. Parents threw out their arms to balance them. Old ladies crossed themselves, flattened their backs against the steadiest walls. They didn't see us hidden in the archway between the church and the florist, her leaning up against the cold wall, shoulder to stone, me twisting my fingers together with nerves.

She asked my name.

'Tess' turned part of the footpath to pebbles.

'Emer' broke car windows so that glass sparkled in the gutters.

She asked how long I'd lived here (my whole life), I asked how long she was staying (all summer) and the roads unwound like ferns before us.

When we'd talked so long the pavement was cracked and unsteady all along the street, what was left of the road sprouting tufts of dry earth that flew into car windshields like tumbleweeds, she blew me a kiss to say goodbye. A single petal fell slowly from the sky.

There was a small cluster of hippies in front of the house when Mam and I got home from mass on Sunday. They did that sometimes, lured by the thatch on the roof, the red door, the roses, the herb garden around back. Glimpses of Mam in her dungarees with her hair in a silk scarf, tailed by five cats. Most days she just shooed them away, but sometimes she'd sneak one into the front room for a tea leaf reading at fifty quid a pop.

The town mostly ignored the hippies because they

were tourists passing through and they boarded in the O'Malleys' B&B and they bought the Aran jumpers and apple tarts and Mrs Gorman's knitted baby booties even though to my knowledge none of the hippies ever had any babies, not that they brought with them anyway. It was fine to be different if you weren't from here. Even Mam got more leeway than the real locals, though she'd lived in town for over twenty years. Her daughters, however, counted as local born and bred, and were expected to act like it.

No slogan t-shirts, no ripped jeans, no – heaven above forbid – lesbianism. The year before, Young Rory (as distinct from Rory, his father) had left town fast after the GAA lads found him kissing a boy from the other team behind the clubhouse the night after a home match. Blood on the collar of his team shirt on the morning bus to Dublin. He hadn't been back since.

Orla stuck her head out her bedroom and hissed at the hippies, who scattered.

When we walked in the door Mam said, 'What have you done now?' and the mouse tail in my pocket twitched.

Orla shouted from upstairs, 'Did you catch fire in the church again, Tessie?'

Mam shook her head as if to dislodge a fly. Three of Orla's earrings fell out of her hair and clinked onto the kitchen table.

'They saw you on Main Street, when the road went,' Mam said. 'With that new girl.'

The council was already rolling in big cement trucks and men in high-vis vests, slopping grey sludge over the broken road.

'And?'

Twitch-twitch went the little mouse tail, a live wire, a lie-detector, an unwanted guest. One of the cats looked up at me hopefully.

'You watch yourself, Tess Delaney,' she said. 'And keep your damn head down.'

I kept my head down for three days and then there she was in front of the mobile library, arguing with the librarian about censorship. The side of the van gleamed in the sun and my reflection was watery and strange. She held up the queue of kids and recited a litany of book titles like a rosary.

The librarian shook her head. 'There isn't enough space, young lady,' she said. 'For those kinds of books. There isn't enough demand.'

She wanted to put in an order. She said, 'I'll create the demand. I demand!'

I felt a jolt of desire so strong it burst several of the books to flame. In the ensuing chaos she saw me. Like my mam said, I watched myself. In the hot shiny side of the van I watched myself take her hand and lead her away.

Out on the country road she asked me, 'How do you stand this place?' with enough of a laugh in her voice that I took it as city-kid exasperation.

'I don't,' I said, and she kissed me, and into my mouth she whispered, 'Then let's burn it to the ground.'

For a week it rained flowers. Enormous papery peonies and tiny violets, buttercup and sorrel. Daisies, already chained, landed on children's heads. Wild rose and iris drifted to join their earthy sisters. Chickweed petals shone on car windshields, foxgloves and poppies covered the pavements. The hippies raised their arms and danced in the fields. The priests proclaimed a miracle.

Her mouth was a miracle. Her soft, cool hands right on the bend of my lower back beneath my t-shirt. The miracle was her tongue, and mine. The miracle was this collision, in the back bedroom of her granda's farm.

When I came home Mam was banging the pots and pans in the kitchen and Orla, on the threshold, already half out as I walked in, declared the place a red zone.

'Storm's brewing,' she said, and she pulled the hood of her jumper up over her hair so the flowers wouldn't tangle in it. Her eyes were already watering. 'Fuckin' pollen,' she said.

Out the kitchen window four of the cats were fighting. I joined Mam at the counter and watched them. I thought at first that they were trying to catch the flower stems still falling from the sky, but the slick, wormlike thing they fought over was dead and grey.

'Another mouse,' Mam said. She caught my wrist and turned my hand over. Into my palm she pressed a freshly cut rose from the garden. One of the hippies' favourites, it was deep burgundy, the petals so thick they were fleshy. Open lips, thorns like teeth.

'If you don't keep your head down,' Mam said, 'those flowers'll fall in your face. Roses are pretty when you know how to handle them. Do you know how to handle her?'

My hands knew how to handle her, but I didn't say that to Mam. My hands knew how to grab her hips, how to cup the back of her neck, how to curl into fists with her hair inside them to pull her head back, expose her throat to my kisses. Her hands knew how to handle me too; knew how to handle the buttons on my jeans, the clasp of my bra, the elastic of my knickers, but I didn't say any of that either. Instead, I stuck the rose in a cup of water and slept sweetly to the soft sound of flower petals falling on the roof.

The following day I brought her the rose. She pressed it to her lips and licked it, eyes closed. She teased the petals open with her fingers. The thorns were so sharp they scored new love lines in our palms. We hid inside her wardrobe and cut each other's names into our inner thighs, rubbed ink into the raised red welts.

Rose thorns rained in people's eyes. Fat purple bluebells squelched under Sunday shoes. The more we kissed the more they came.

A man from the six o'clock news arrived in a van with a film crew, stood in the rain of tulips and daffodils in front of the second church (the church on Main Street was blocked by bulldozers still flattening the upturned road). The priest, Father Twomey, was interviewed, wore pale peachy face powder he must have borrowed from one of the old ladies, twin circles of blush on his cheeks.

'This is a miracle,' he said to the reporter. 'A sign from God. God created the natural world, and He is with us today.'

The reporter went on to talk to a meteorologist while the hippies watched with dirt and worms and greenflies showering their flowery hair, the locals huddled under umbrellas.

If God had made the natural world then God had made the mouse tails that warned of unwanted guests, had made the crows who cried on the telephone lines, telling of change. Had made the flowers and the earthworms and the landslides and the wind chill and the warm, wet flesh between her legs.

'By that logic,' she told me, 'God also made this town. Made the small minds in the large, dumb skulls that live it in.'

'I suppose,' I said. The air was sweet with the rotting flowers piled up along the pavements where they'd been swept. One of the Cunninghams' babies had been taken to hospital for eating an orchid. Mam burned rained-down lilies out the back of the compost heap by the armful in case one of the cats got at the poisonous stamen.

Emer watched with me from the back step, Mam shooting us dirty looks and muttering about uninvited guests, Orla in the kitchen cackling about there at least being no need for condoms. The two mouse tails in my pocket twisting together and apart.

'Let's get out of here,' she said, and we took a bus to the city and snuck into a concert in the Róisín Dubh, elbowed our way to the front by the stage and danced until we were more sweat than clothes. Close to midnight, we walked off the edge of the pier and into the water.

'Just imagine', she said, in the back seat of the delivery truck we hitchhiked a lift home from, 'if we came back and there was nothing there. No town, no pubs, no churches. No GAA pitches or shops. No dirty looks or turned-up noses. Just a massive crater where the whole town used to be.'

I was half sleeping, my head on her shoulder still smelling of the sea.

'Imagine that,' she said. 'No town, no backwards

culchies, just you and me.'

Mam was sitting at the table when I walked in. Outside, the flowers were still falling. Horseflies and caterpillars crowded the kitchen. The cats had thistle spines stuck in their paws. An evening wind had driven rose thorns through the bedroom windows, cracked the glass. They'd flown through my open wardrobe and ripped the bellies of my t-shirts, the knees of my jeans.

Mam looked tired, her hands cupped over something in the way she usually would a mug of tea. When she lifted the steeple of her fingers there was underneath the tiniest mouse I'd ever seen. The cats circled the table, limping.

'Throw it out into the garden,' I begged. 'Just let this one escape into the field.'

Bead eyes, pink nose, thin wire whiskers twitching. It was like a toy.

'I found it in the sugar packet,' Mam said. 'The one I got from the shop today. Not a hole in the outside.'

The mouse sat in the cup of Mam's hands, fearless as me and Emer in the delivery van, certain we'd get home safe.

'Look in the press,' said Mam. 'Open the packet of flour. The biscuits. The tin of mackerel.'

The wind blew in the broken bedroom windows with a sweet and rotting smell. I did as I was told. Inside the roll of chocolate digestives and the bumper pack of Rich Tea, in the unopened paper parcel of self-raising flour, inside the tin of mackerel I opened with a can opener, was a mouse. Four mice, alive, each as tiny as the last, each as fearless. Mam held out her hands for them, took them by the tails like an upside-down bouquet.

She said, 'Everyone feels like there are flowers falling

32

from the sky when they meet their first love. But that doesn't mean she's right for you. Look how many earth-worms and spiders' eggs are nestled in with the petals.'

And she threw the bunch of mice to the kitchen floor, and the cats.

By August the town was crawling with hippies. They filled the B&Bs and the campsite down by the river, they set up their canvas tents in muddy fields and slept in their vans. On days we kissed, when flowers fell, they danced, held hands. On days we argued, when the wind turned trees to ice, they sang and prayed.

Mam made a fortune. Every day another bunch of hippies knocked on the front door and even Mam, queen of keeping her head down, didn't want to turn away the crowd of crisp fifties in their earthy fists.

In my bedroom, the door open at Mam's command, Mam's scathing looks warming the floorboards beneath our bare feet, Emer said, again, 'Come with me.'

I said, again, 'You know I can't.'

The end of summer loomed like a church bell about to strike the angelus: long drawn-out noises heard all around the town that nobody could talk over.

I said, again, 'You could stay here, you know.'

And she, again, scoffed and talked about a lake big enough to drown the town so I would have nowhere to go but with her.

At mass that Sunday Father Twomey's sermon was about vagrants and promiscuity and public decency, but the town didn't scoff so much at the hippies, not now that the farmers at the market were selling twice the produce

33

they used to. Not now that Mrs Gorman's booties and the Aran jumpers in the wool shop were being shipped to Germany and America. Not since a bunch of hippies had helped her granda clear the mulch of rotten flowers from his wheat field in time for sowing and hadn't accepted a penny for their work.

Emer hated the hippies almost as much as she hated the town. 'Hypocrites,' she called them. 'Thinking this place is all flowers and wool jumpers, not even looking at the worms and the maggots underneath.'

'I don't know,' I said, thinking of my mam's words. 'I think they seem the same as any summer people, passing through.' I didn't say, *Like you*.

She didn't listen. She said, 'The town with their God, the hippies with their eco-magic. They have no idea. We should freeze it all solid. Break it into shards of glass.'

'I'd do that,' she said. 'For you.'

The town with its kids and cats and market, its priests and hippies and farmers. My mam and Orla. For her love, I thought, I'd let her.

On market day Mam's stall sold out of roses. A couple of the locals shuffled over looking for 'some of those herbs you have' for their tea.

'Wear a condom,' Orla called after them. Mrs O'Rourke crossed herself twice but across the church hall Rory McDonnell's mouth twitched into a smile and he gestured at his boys to mind that one, and take her advice.

It hadn't rained flowers in nearly a week and Mam was almost cheerful, counting up the money from the roses, the tinctures, the tea-leaf readings. Enough for a holiday.

'I can come and see you,' I told Emer, stroking the back of her hand with my thumb. 'Over midterm. Take a train and rent a hotel room. We could stay together.'

'We could stay together if you came with me,' she said. 'How does this arse-backwards town have you under its spell? We could just destroy it. Start over.'

'It's not a spell,' I said softly. 'It's just home.'

She wasn't listening. 'Kiss me,' she said. 'Let's burn this place to the ground.'

I still didn't think she was serious. When she kissed me, no flowers fell, so she kissed harder, bruised my lips with the force of her teeth. When I kissed back with equal fervour the trees didn't freeze, so I pressed harder against her, mouth to chest to groin to knees. In my pocket, seven severed mouse tails shrivelled.

Into my mouth she breathed a flower. Deep burgundy rose, petals thick as flesh. The floor shifted beneath us, rocking the back bedroom of her granda's farm. I froze in place mid-kiss and the slick of her skin stuck to the ice of me, tore when we tried to move. The wind spun in and circled us like a storm.

Let's burn this place to the ground, she'd said. Let's make a lake and drown the whole town. Let's sink it into a crater. Let's freeze it solid and break it into shards of glass.

The last time we kissed the town shuddered, the land around the back of her granda's farm breaking apart like a heart. The crack spread like a web from the farm to the town hall, from the church to the school, fissures running up the walls of houses. From beneath, the water rose. The tops of trees burst into flame. The far-off screams of our neighbours were stopped by the flesh of fallen petals, their flailing limbs frozen by sudden gusts of icy air.

When it was over the ground gulped like the gullet of the cat that caught the mouse it had been hunting.

Nature morte

Belleville is not the terminus. Only every other métro pauses there, green and off-white, siren ripping the air before the doors close, halfway, then shut. Little stickers at hip-height on the carriage walls show a pink rabbit with its paw caught harmlessly in the door: a cheery message of caution to children to keep their limbs inside the train. The doors close on the sound of the accordion player moving through the almost-empty carriages begging for change. The doors close and leave her standing here, on the strip of bumpy pavement warning of the drop to the tracks. Leave her standing here, clutching a shoebox, staring at the monster.

The air tastes metallic, smells of urine and stale sweat. The sound of the métro fades to a vague rumbling in the distance. Her eyes dart to the plastic seats, to the monster, then back to the exit, the flight of stairs. The next métro will not stop. The next métro will charge past the station. One small step at the right time and her body could be crushed against the white and green. Ribcage caved in, deep blow to the skull. Fingers severed by the scream of wheels on singing tracks. Blood and bits of brain. She steps off the bumpy strip and into the safety of the station, walks shakily past the monster.

On the seats – which are really just two bars to rest a waiting body against; a deterrent to rough sleepers – a man is sitting as if on a chair, his legs swinging two inches off the ground. The station is badly lit; she can't see his face.

Her hair is held up with a pencil and a paintbrush, has just about withstood the bumpy journey that jerked the passengers in their seats. She got on at Cambronne, an open-air station above the boulevard fifteen minutes from her favourite supply store. The 15th is a wealthy arrondissement, the métro stations cleaner and smaller than those underground. Cambronne reminds her of the stations in that new film she went to see last week, *Le fabuleux destin d'Amélie Poulin*. Bright, with fresh paint and intact advertising posters on the walls. A too-clean tourist-eye view. She went alone, bare legs goose-pimpling against the air-conditioned cinema seat, the elbows of the monster nudging the armrest beside her. She makes a mental note to tell her mother she's seen the film. Proof she's getting out of the apartment.

The man swinging his legs is humming tunelessly under his breath. When she passes by him, shoebox clutched to her chest, he stands up and takes a few steps towards her.

'You got the time, chérie?' His voice is scratchy like an old record. His nose is crooked. He has three teeth. She shakes her head mutely and shows him her bare wrist.

'Too bad, too bad.'

She makes to go past him.

'You not got one of those phones, then?' asks the man.

'What?'

'You know, a phone.' He mimes a mouthpiece. 'One of them phones that can tell you the time.'

'No, sorry.'

The man leans on one hip. 'And I thought all young people had them. I see kids with them all the time, talking into them, pushing these tiny buttons.'

She shrugs, turns towards the exit.

''Cause I thought to myself, I thought, that young woman looks like she's from a well-to-do family, if you don't mind me saying.'

She smiles politely. 'I suppose.'

'Yes, yes. And I said to myself, I said, Xavier, my friend, that young woman looks like she might have a watch. A watch, or one of those phone things.'

She raises her hands, empty. 'I'm sorry.'

'Oh, now don't be sorry, chérie. I just wanted to know the time.'

A métro rushes in, screeches to a halt and opens its doors. She and the man both turn their heads. Two figures step out of separate carriages. Heads bent, they walk briskly to the stairs.

'Well, there it is,' the old man says.

'Pardon?'

'I was wondering at what time it would come.' He swaggers into the métro, singing to himself. The siren screams out again and the doors close, leaving her alone on the platform staring after the man in the métro with the crooked nose. The métro stopped. No one was crushed beneath its wheels.

Not this one.

The monster tries to take her hand.

★

Outside the light is waning but the air is hot. The shops are closed, their shutters drawn, but the cafés and restaurants are still open and the streets are stretching into the kind of alive they only get at night. She prefers the 20th to the 15th, which is eerily quiet after dark. In Belleville it is never quiet. There is always music playing and people talking, shouting, dancing, living, at all hours of the day and night. It used to be Adeline's favourite thing about living there. The monster doesn't like it.

She lowers her head and keeps walking. Past the laundrette Jamel shouts out to her.

'Hey, Sophie! Tout baigne?'

She slows her walk. 'Yeah, I'm okay. How's it going?'

'Not too bad.' He pushes a stray curl out of his eyes. 'So fuckin' hot in there, it's like a sauna.'

'I'll bet.' Inside, Jamel's mother is still busy pressing suits and dresses.

'What's in the box?'

'Art stuff, mainly.' She looks down at the shoebox in her arms. 'Odds and ends.'

Jamel's mother calls from inside. 'I'll talk to you later, okay?' he says.

'Yeah.'

'Take care of yourself.'

'I always do.'

Jamel disappears into the steamy dry-cleaners.

Sophie crosses the street and walks up to the green door beside the deli where she works on weekends, school holidays, and in summer. The familiar smell of kebabs and paninis makes her mouth water. On a plastic chair outside the door Monsieur Molinet is lounging with the same beer he has been clutching all day. Adeline loved M. Molinet. She used to say that he was 'one of us', a people-watcher, a storyteller. Now all Sophie can see is a sad old man sitting in the same place all day every day, telling anyone who will listen that he is waiting for his wife to come home. Every night at half-past nine he returns to his apartment inside on the fourth floor to watch *Sunset Beach* on M6. Alone.

'Good evening, Monsieur Molinet.'

'Good evening, ma petite Sophie. How are you today?'

'Well, thank you. And you?'

'Oh, I find this weather very overbearing. My body doesn't appreciate the heat. I'm just waiting for Martine, she should be back any minute. She works very hard, you know. Long hours.'

'Yes.'

'And you are keeping up your studies?'

'Yes.'

'That's good. Education is very important.'

'It is.' She keys the code into the lock beside the door.

'It is,' says M. Molinet. 'Goodnight, Sophie.'

'Goodnight, Monsieur Molinet.'

The door closes softly behind her. The foyer is dark and cool. She reaches for the light switch. The wooden stairs creak as she climbs six floors, a reassuring sound only marred by the echoing creaks, a few steps below her, of the monster's measured pace.

She fits her key into the lock of the door to the right of the landing. There is a package on Mme Velázquez's doormat across the hall and a note is pinned to the lock of the Hammonais family's door opposite the staircase that says, *Françoise, your father and I have gone out to dinner. Simone and Manu are spending the night with Marie-Ange. There are noodles in the microwave. Don't forget to feed Tomate. Bises, Maman.*

Inside, the apartment smells musty. It catches the sun in the afternoon and heats up if Sophie doesn't close the shutters. Her sneakers squeak across the linoleum. The windows groan reproachfully when she opens them to let in the cooling evening air. She does not have to open the heavy wooden shutters on the outside of the glass, as she forgot to close them that morning. Her shoebox thunks onto the table and she slides her bag off her back with a sigh.

Sophie's apartment has two rooms: the main room onto which the front door opens, which is a living room with a small stretch of kitchen in one corner, and the bedroom. There are no chairs in the apartment because Sophie's grandmother, who helped her move in, said Sophie needed some 'space to breathe. The room's energy is already so cluttered, Sophie, you need a good dose of Feng Shui.'

Sophie's home has always been the crowded and noisy duplex in Bayonne beside the train station, but she humoured her grandmother and complied, telling herself she could buy chairs and a higher table once Mamie had left. She hasn't got around to it yet.

Sophie forages in the cupboards and finds broccoli, cream and a few pink potatoes, the kind you don't have to peel. She fries some breadcrumbs to put on top of the dish while the oven heats up. Absorbed in her task, she doesn't realise the phone is ringing. She runs into the bedroom as the answering machine clicks on.

'For heaven's sake, Sophie, give the machine a few more rings before it kicks in,' comes her mother's voice.

Sophie picks up the phone. 'Maman?'

'Oh, you're there.'

'Looks like it.'

'What?'

'Never mind.'

'Why do you have the machine on if you're in? Is there somebody you're avoiding?'

'No, Maman, I just got in. I forgot to turn it off.'

'Oh. You just got in? Were you out with your friends after class? I really think it's a good idea for you to go out more. It can't be healthy, cooped up alone in that apartment all the time. And those oil paints give off terrible fumes.'

Sophie tries not to let the exasperation colour her voice. 'I was out buying supplies,' she says, because she knows it is useless to lie to her mother. 'There's this great place in the 15th that has everything. They do student discounts. But I went to the cinema last week. I saw that film, you know, *Amélie*?'

'Oh, that's good.' The relief in her mother's voice is a heat haze through the telephone. 'It's so important to get out. Back to real life. You are eating enough, aren't you?' She asks this question every time she phones.

'Yes, Maman, I'm eating fine. Balanced nutritious meals three times a day. Plenty of fruit.'

'Oh, Sophie.' Her mother sounds pained. 'You're putting on your "I'm humouring you, Maman" voice. Don't deny it, God knows I use it myself enough to know.'

'I'm only joking, Maman.'

'I just want to make sure you're okay.'

'I'm fine, really.'

'I mean, there's a lot to adapt to. Your grandmother was very worried. You still living in that apartment, alone, after . . .'

Sophie is quick to cut her off. 'Maman, really, I'm fine. I'm comfortable here.'

'No, I know that. It's just, mentally, emotionally, it's a lot.' She pauses. She says, 'You could come home.'

'Maman.'

'Even just for a little while. The rest of the semester. You could catch up.'

'I'm behind already, Maman. I'd have to repeat the year.'

'Maybe that wouldn't be a bad thing, Sophie.' Sophie squeezes her eyes shut. 'Your flatmate,' her mother says. 'Your friend –'

'Maman, I'm sorry,' Sophie says shortly. 'I have to go, my broccoli's burning.'

'Oh. Okay. Well, listen, I'll give you a call during the week to talk.'

'That'd be great. Bye, Maman.'

'Bye, Sophie.'

Sophie lowers herself onto one of the cushions around the little table and takes off her sneakers. Her bare toes crack as she wiggles them. The room is almost the same as it was before. Bookshelves, TV, stereo, coffee table holding the computer with a blue-and-white beanbag in front of it serving as a seat, upon which the monster is now sitting.

Sophie had suggested getting a chair and a real desk, but Adeline wouldn't hear of it. She loved the beanbag and the cushions that served as chairs around the knee-height

44

dining table Sophie's grandparents had had shipped back after a holiday in Japan. She loved the futon in the bedroom, loved rolling over Sophie to land on the rug on the floor in the morning, Sophie grunting, half asleep, Adeline kissing her tangled hair. She loved that Mamie had insisted on decorating their apartment. She loved everything about Sophie's family.

'It's that sense of fitting in,' she used to say. 'Everybody knowing everyone else's business, constant communication, no matter where you are. You all love each other so much.'

Adeline had very little family to speak of. Her parents had been in their fifties already when they had adopted her, both only children, their own parents long-dead. Adeline's father had died when she was a child. Her mother had been in a care home for years. Adeline visited every weekend but month by month her mother recognised her less.

'You are my family,' Adeline had once told Sophie.

From the beanbag seat, the monster reaches out for her.

The smell of cooked potatoes and cream is getting stronger, so Sophie hoists herself up to go check on her meal. She sets the table properly, the way Mémé taught her, knife on the left, blade towards the plate, fork on the right, curve towards the table. She eats in silence, listening to the sounds coming from the open window. Her apartment faces the back of the building, in away from the street. Its windows open onto the little courtyard where the concierge grows herbs in plastic pots. She can hear the cars out on the street faintly, like a memory, and voices at varying volumes throughout the building. She thinks she can hear the sweet snatch of a song from a radio, somebody singing along.

She leaves the dishes in the sink to do later and closes the shutters so the mosquitoes won't get in, but leaves the windows open, for air. On the easel in the corner of the bedroom is a square canvas with the beginning of a new painting pencilled hastily, then abandoned. Her latest series, her professors tell her, is too much the same as the last. Empty métro stations, the lights above the advertisement posters harsh and white, the tracks gleaming. Neat, clean stations like Cambronne; art-filled, tourist-attracting stations like Rivoli; grubby, graffitied stations like Belleville. Her professors tell her this series of stations is perfectly good, but not what they are looking for from her. They say it with pity in their eyes, but pity won't pass her exams. They suggest she tries some natures mortes, instead.

The monster shuffles up to the canvas, head to one side. Sophie thinks she hears a voice come from its mangled throat, a click of the tongue with a kissing sound like Adeline used to do. A hint of orange flower in the air. Sophie snaps her head up, looks around the room. Nobody, she tells herself, there is nobody there.

*

For the first time in months Sophie does not dream of Adeline, but of her mother. Maman is speaking on the telephone to Sophie's father who is standing beside her.

'She is fading,' her father says. 'She is getting so old.' Sophie thinks he means Mamie or Mémé. Her mother takes the phone from his hand and speaks to him through it.

'Artists rarely live to be twenty-one,' Sophie's mother says. She means me, thinks Sophie. I will be twenty-one next month. Three days after Adeline.

Sophie's parents fade and are replaced by Monsieur Molinet, who in her dream is her European Art History lecturer. The classroom is the métro station at Cambronne. There is no train.

'No,' he is saying. 'There is nothing natural about this.' He holds up a photograph that is really her unfinished canvas. 'This is just another monster.'

She wakes up sweating, a mosquito bite beside her ear.

'Shit,' she says out loud, reaching behind her head to find what is digging into her skull. It is a broken paint-brush she forgot to remove from her bun last night. She is still wearing yesterday's clothes: paint-stained jeans and an oversized purple t-shirt, wrinkled and faded from too many washes, advertising last year's Paris Pride Parade. She opens the shutters to let in the fresh morning air. The monster has done the dishes.

Sophie shuffles barefoot and fuzzy-legged to the bathroom. The monster draws stick figures in the steam of the shower.

When she is dressed in denim shorts, a linen shirt, and the espadrilles her classmates tease her about, good-naturedly, calling her a plouc, telling her nobody in the city wears the raffia-soled canvas slippers her home region is famous for, Sophie pulls on her backpack, hoists the long, black plastic tube of rolled-up paintings by its strap onto her shoulder, and lets herself out of her apartment. She locks the monster in.

From the Hammonais' door comes the sound of

scratching, a plaintive mew. Françoise, the eldest girl, has forgotten to give Tomate his breakfast. He will have to wait until the whole family is home from work and school, this evening. Sophie has a spare key to the Hammonais' apartment, and they to hers, but she does not use it. The cat can wait a few hours.

At the front door of the apartment building Monsieur Molinet is setting up his plastic chair for the day.

'Good morning, ma petite Sophie,' he greets her.

'Good morning, Monsieur Molinet.'

'Another hot day, today, it looks like.'

'Yes.'

'Do you manage to sleep,' he asks, 'in the heat? Not me. I toss and turn. Martine has never liked it either. We dream of air conditioning.'

Sophie smiles a little. 'You're not the only ones, Monsieur Molinet.'

She closes her eyes, briefly, remembering suddenly that she has, again, forgotten to close her shutters. The apartment will be a hothouse when she returns. She has time to run up and shut them, and the windows, keep out the rising heat. Her bedroom would be cooler and she would sleep better that night. But that would mean letting out the monster.

M. Molinet has cracked open his beer. It is cold, now, condensation dripping from the glass neck. By evening it will only be slippery with the sweat of his palm.

'You have a good day in class, ma petite Sophie,' he tells her.

'I will,' she replies. 'You have a good day too, Monsieur Molinet.'

Sophie crosses the road before the laundrette, remembers

48

only then that she has dirty clothes in her hamper to bring. There is no washing machine in her little kitchen corner, only the oven, the counters, the fridge and the sink. Adeline used to fill a basin with soapy, boiled water and scrub their t-shirts and underwear by hand, wring them out and hang them from the bedroom windowsill. They brought their jeans and jumpers to Jamel and his mother, though, as they were too heavy to hang without fear of their clothes falling into the courtyard on top of the concierge's potted herbs.

Jamel is taking a smoke break when she walks by, kisses her cheeks twice.

'So when's the exhibition?' he asks, the smoke from his Gauloise curling with the steam coming from the door behind him out onto the street.

'I don't know that any of my stuff will be in the exhibition,' Sophie reminds him. 'But next month.'

'I'll be there anyway,' Jamel says. He extinguishes the last of his cigarette under his sneaker on the footpath. 'Where's your monster this morning?' He takes a stick of gum from his pocket, offers her another.

Sophie feels her face flush. 'No, thank you,' she mutters. 'See you later.'

Jamel shrugs and disappears into the steam. 'See you later.'

Several times on the way to the station, Sophie smells orange blossom in the air, sharp as longing. She turns her head, wishing she had a scarf to pull up over her nose, even a light silk one like those her mother wears. In front of the green signpost marking the stairs to the métro there is a cart selling crêpes bretonnes, the scent of spelt and burnt butter and orange flower. Sophie is reassured, tells herself this must be the source of the once-familiar smell, but takes deep breaths of the stale, hot air of Belleville station once she has descended the many steps, glad to find herself filled with the rancid smell of urine, overheated metal, and too many bodies in close proximity. Nobody here wears orange blossom perfume. Not anymore.

In the crowd of commuters Sophie is jostled against a man who smells like sour milk and unwashed clothes. He grabs her arm and rights her when she stumbles.

'Well, hello there, chérie,' says the crooked-nosed, three-toothed man. His face is very close and his breath is foul. 'Have you got the time?'

'Hey,' a businesswoman standing on the bumps at the edge of the tracks in stiletto heels says to him. 'Move over.'

'I don't have the time,' Sophie whispers. The man cannot hear her over the scream of the siren and the screech of the métro pulling into the station on hot, singing tracks. This one stops. Just before it does, though, Sophie's stomach heaves in panic. What if it doesn't? What if this one rushes past the station? She has visions of a body jumping, a torso slamming against the metal, a bent skull, severed fingers on the tracks. She has visions of the monster lying below her.

The train stops. Bodies shuffle forwards to the doors.

'Too bad, too bad,' the old man says. 'Thank you all the same.' He does not enter the train alongside her. She is standing unsteadily just inside the crowded carriage, angling the tube of paintings on her shoulder so it will not catch in the doors, when she hears the old man call.

'Say. Where's your monster this morning, chérie?'

The doors close, halfway, then shut. The siren rips the

air and the métro moves away.

The Saint-Germain campus of the fine-arts university is in the 6th arrondissement, a few streets from the banks of the Seine. Sophie exits the métro at Rivoli, although staying on the line to Saint-Germain-des-Prés would be quicker, and walks slowly across the Pont des Arts, looking out over the river to the museum, windows shining in the sunlight. Adeline would meet her here, sometimes, take the thirty-minute métro journey on a half-day from work, sit beside her on a bench in the square, crumbs from their sandwiches littering their laps, tourists milling around them, cameras dangling from their necks. When they left the pigeons would descend to pick at their leftovers.

Sophie stays on the bridge so long she is late for workshop. She has left her latest paintings on the professor's desk and knows what she will say. She knows that the professor will give the same small, patient sigh she has given when she has seen every new painting since Adeline. She knows that the professor will smile at Sophie with pity in her eyes, but pity will not display Sophie's paintings at the end-of-year exhibition. She knows the professor will say something like, 'I will be direct with you, Sophie,' before suggesting, again, that Sophie turn her hand to natures mortes, the way she used to.

'Maybe this is Sophie's nature morte,' Camille, her classmate and friend, suggests gently. 'A series that speaks to grief.' Sophie smiles thinly at Camille, grateful, but embarrassed.

'I understand,' says the lecturer. 'But, Sophie, I will be direct with you. These paintings do not seem to me like a series that speaks to grief.' She holds up the painting to the class, asking if anyone agrees. Heads nod. They like to give feedback. 'There is no truth here, Sophie.'

The door to the workshop room creaks open just before the end of the hour. The monster slips silently inside.

*

Sophie returns to the 15th arrondissement after class, clicks open the door to the art supply shop that does student discounts. A small bell above the door tinkles and cool air leaks out until the door swings shut again.

There are a few other people browsing the shop's narrow aisles. It is not far from the Champ de Mars and is frequented as much by tourists as it is by students. The monster walks around the shop, touching everything, smearing watercolour paper and canvases and individual tubes of oil paints hanging in rows by hue with old blood, reddish-brown. It is trying to say something but Sophie doesn't listen.

The shop owner, Mme Renaud, is speaking with one of her assistants, a young man with long hair pulled back, pirate-like, at the nape of his neck. They are talking about the film, *Amélie*, which both of them have seen in the cinema that weekend. Sophie thinks they may be mother and son.

Mme Renaud thinks the film was 'très nya-nya', so twee. Her son agrees.

'There is no true art in nostalgia,' he announces. 'Painting the present with the colours of the past is no kind of bravery.'

Amélie's mother dies early in the film, Sophie remembers suddenly, tube of dark crimson in the palm of her hand. Amélie is only a small girl. A tourist throws herself from the rose window of Notre Dame. She lands on Amélie's mother, whose name Sophie has already forgotten, and kills her instantly. Some people in the darkened cinema hall laughed. Sophie did not think it was supposed to be funny, but Adeline had always said Sophie did not understand dark humour. The monster had put its gory hand on Sophie's trembling knee.

Mme Renaud puts Sophie's purchases into a small plastic bag, which Sophie then adds to the shoebox of supplies in her schoolbag. 'That will be one hundred and twenty-five francs,' she says.

Her son corrects her. 'Eighteen euro and fifty-six centimes, please.'

'Oh,' Mme Renaud grumbles. 'I can never keep that nonsense straight.'

Sophie counts the change into the glass tray by the cash register.

Mme Renaud's son laughs. 'Come on, Maman, stop living in the past!'

*

It is Jamel's mother who is taking a smoke break when Sophie passes the laundrette on her way home. The steamy air coming from the open door is hardly more suffocating than the heat outside.

'Good evening, Mme Abitbol,' Sophie says.

'Good evening, Sophie,' Jamel's mother replies. She calls something in through the door to her son, then turns to greet the monster.

Sophie ducks her head and hurries on, more quickly than before, muttering a brief goodbye over her shoulder.

At the door to the apartment building, M. Molinet raises his warm beer when he sees her. 'Ah, there you are, you two!' he says. 'I saw from the courtyard that you closed your shutters, Sophie, that was a good thing to remember. It will be hot as an oven tonight. Especially with two of you in the apartment. I know how Martine suffers in the room with me.'

Two of you. Sophie forces out a 'Good evening, Monsieur Molinet,' before keying in the code and pushing open the heavy front door.

'None of us are likely to sleep well tonight,' M. Molinet calls through the door slowly swinging shut behind her.

On the sixth floor Sophie fits her key into her door. From the closest neighbouring apartment comes the sound of the youngest Hammonais children playing video games. Mme Velázquez, across the little hall, is leaving for dinner, her lips painted and her heels high. She pauses on the threshold to greet Sophie.

'You're lucky Simone Hammonais was sent home sick from school this morning,' Mme Velázquez laughs. 'Or your monster would have been locked in all day.'

The monster reaches around Sophie's frozen body and turns the key in the lock, pushes open the door. Mme Velázquez's heels echo down six flights of stairs.

The apartment is cool and dark. Sophie trips over one of the cushions, cracks her knee on the side of the low table. Under her fingers on the smooth, light pine are bits of brain and entrails, sharp shards of bone. She makes her way by touch along the bookshelves on the wall opposite the kitchen area, fingers fluttering the collage made of her sister's photographs. She knows the

54

people each picture contains without having to look: her parents and sister in their garden, she and her sister as children in a paddling pool, Sophie and her old friends from lycée on various school tours. Mamie and Papi in t-shirts and jeans, Mémé in bright flowing tunics studded with brooches, her fingers all rings. She knows the spaces in the collage where the pictures of Adeline used to be.

Sophie wishes she could say that the monster removed them, but it was her hands that took the photographs down and slid them under the futon with the dust and the dead mosquitoes and the little enamel cat, smiling, with one shiny, white paw raised.

Sophie avoids the TV, the stereo, and leans over the computer on the coffee table to swing open the windows and unlatch and push away the shutters. They are covered in gore and bright blood. They bang against the outside of the apartment wall. A small shower of white plaster flutters onto the concierge's basil and mint six floors below.

Again, the monster tries to speak but Sophie shuts the door into the bedroom and sinks onto the futon bed. Three fingertips, severed, lie like commas on the creased blue sheets. There is a sound like a ribcage breaking. Sophie pushes herself to stand on shaking legs and throws open the bedroom shutters, too. The light is soft and warm, tastes of evening and a mixture of sizzling smells coming from other open windows throughout the apartment building. Sophie can hear the monster in the kitchen, cooking dinner, like her neighbours.

On the easel in the corner of the bedroom beside the cluttered chest of drawers, there is a painting of the monster. It is old-blood-red and gore-brown, gut-yellow and vein-blue. It is bone-white in the spaces between. Its face is unrecognisable as a face, only a mess of brain and skull fragments. Its fingers are missing, blood pours onto the tracks. The canvas. Onto the canvas. Its ribs have caved in. Its limbs are twisted. It smiles. It whispers. It beckons.

Sophie throws open the bedroom door and asks the monster, 'Why did you do this?' She points a long, rigid arm at the easel, at the painting that did not exist on that canvas the night before.

'I did nothing,' says the monster. 'What do you mean?'

It chops spring onions with a small, sharp knife. Crushed garlic is already spitting in a pan of olive oil on the hob. Beside the monster's mangled hands a bunch of sun-ripened vine tomatoes sits on the counter, red as fresh blood.

'Why did you paint this monster on my canvas?' Sophie demands. 'You had no right.'

'I painted nothing,' says the monster. 'That was you.'

'No,' Sophie says.

'It was you,' the monster says again. 'Do you not remember? You drew her. I heard you, in the night. In the morning there was this painting. You locked me in the apartment with this painting of your dead girlfriend.'

The garlic begins to burn, small sections popping in the pan.

Sophie stops short. She can barely speak. 'This,' she says. 'This isn't Adeline.' Behind her, through the bedroom door, the painting of the monster grins. 'This is you,' she says in a whisper. 'This is the monster.'

The monster leaves the garlic to smoke and blacken in the pan. It walks slowly past Sophie into the bedroom. It stands a long time in front of the easel.

'If this is me,' the monster says finally. 'Why have you

painted me with her face?'

Sophie's reflection in the mirror standing on the floor is just as ravaged as the monster's.

'Why have you painted me with gore and blood?'

Blood on the tracks. Gore splattered on the strip of bumpy pavement at the edge of the platform.

Sophie presses her fists into her eyes. She runs her nails down her cheeks like tears. The monster reaches out its hands to hold hers.

'You think you are a monster for wanting me?' it asks. 'When she is gone? You think I am a monster to want to replace her?'

Fingers severed by the tracks. Chunks of gore on her pretty face. Belleville is not the terminus, Adeline knew this. One small step at the right time and her body was crushed against the white and green. Sophie did not see it happen, but it is so clear in her dreams and visions it is as if she was there.

Her mother called when she saw it on the news.

'I am so sorry about your flatmate,' she said. 'Your friend.'

Adeline had kissed her up against the dresser that morning, the morning before. One of the boboys from the Chinese bazaar had rolled underneath the futon. Small smiling cat, one paw raised in greeting, little gold bell around its neck.

'Leave it,' Adeline had said. 'We can get it back tonight.'

Sophie clung to that promise, even after she found Adeline's note, addressed to her, on the kitchen counter. Even after the police called when she was still in class and she had to listen to their message on her answering machine after she came home to an empty apartment. She called back to hear a cool voice asking what was

57

her emergency.

Leave it, Adeline had said. We can get it back tonight.

The monster is smaller, now, in the soft, warm light of evening and the glow of the painting, blood-red and bone-white. Its face is familiar. The way it tucks its hair behind both ears, a gesture Sophie recognises. Before Adeline, and after. Before, conversations over lunch breaks, glances across the workshop tables, around an easel. After, hand on Sophie's hand as she cried. After, Sophie waking with the monster in the morning, instead of Adeline.

Sophie reaches slowly towards it but the monster does not try to take her hand.

'I don't know, Sophie,' says the monster. 'If you will always see her when you look at me.'

The monster opens the apartment door, walks through, and shuts it without turning back.

*

In the morning Sophie scrapes burnt garlic from the pan into the bin. The apartment smells of oil paint and turpentine. She closes the shutters. She puts her Eastpak on her back, takes a bag of laundry in the crook of one elbow and swings the black plastic tube of rolled-up paintings onto her other shoulder. She does not change her clothes.

She passes Françoise Hammonais on the landing. She is on her way to school and she is late, but still she stops to joke to Sophie, 'I hope you didn't lock your monster in again today.'

'Monster' is not the word that Françoise uses, Sophie realises, as M. Hammonais follows his daughter out of their apartment into the small hall.

'Good morning, Sophie,' he says. 'You should really give your monster a key.'

M. Hammonais does not use the word 'monster', either.

The Hammonais greet M. Molinet before Sophie can say hello, but as she is less in a hurry than they are, she takes the old man's plastic chair out of his arms and helps him to set it up in front of the building door.

'Thank you, ma petite Sophie,' says M. Molinet.

'You're welcome, Monsieur Molinet.'

'It is hot again today, Sophie,' M. Molinet says.

'Yes.'

'Did you remember to close your shutters?'

'I did, Monsieur Molinet.'

'And where is your friend this morning, Sophie?' The word *friend* is loud in the busy street. 'She left early for work?'

'She left,' Sophie says, with difficulty. 'Early. Yes.'

'Martine has left early for work today, as well,' says M. Molinet. 'It is good not to be lonely. It is good to have somebody who will come home from work to you.'

'That's true,' Sophie whispers. 'Have a good day, Monsieur Molinet.'

'And you, too, ma petite Sophie,' says M. Molinet. He opens the cool cap of his bottle of beer.

Sophie crosses the road before the laundrette. She steps into the heat and steam. Jamel is standing behind the counter, reading a BD. He leans across the stacks of papers and receipts to kiss her twice on each cheek.

'How's the painting?' he asks her as he takes her bag of laundry.

'It's okay,' she says. Her hair sticks to the sweat at

her temples.

'And where's your meuf this morning?' he asks. 'Your woman. It's good to see her around here a bit more.'

The steam hits Sophie's face. 'I don't know,' she says. 'I think she went home.'

'Pity.' Jamel shrugs. 'Love is hard.'

'Life is hard,' Sophie says.

Jamel laughs. 'That, too. Life, love, work, and it all starts over again. Courage, Sophie. See you later.'

'See you later, Jamel,' Sophie says. 'And thanks.'

On the way to Belleville station every second face is the monster's, until Sophie comes closer and sees that it is a stranger. There is not a trace of orange blossom in the air, although the cart selling crêpes bretonnes is still set up outside the steps to the métro. Sophie reaches into her bag for her wallet and buys one for her breakfast, although she has no monster to share it with. Crêpe suzette, the sugar and butter and orange zest set to flame on the cast-iron pan, to the awe of passing tourists. The vendor makes a show of folding the galette, buckwheat and orange flower, into a paper parcel, and hands it to Sophie with a flourish and a 'Bon appétit'.

The air at the bottom of the stairs to the station is suffocating and heady. Sophie keeps the crêpe close to her face, inhaling the smell of caramelised sugar and burnt butter. Every second face in the métro station is the monster's. Every other hand severed at the fingers by the bite between train and tracks. Every second ribcage caved in. Every other skull destroyed on impact. Sophie lets herself through the ticket barrier and walks slowly to the platform, then keeps walking, through the crowd of commuters, towards the scent of orange flower. When the toes of her thin espadrilles touch the strip of bumpy pavement warning the drop to the tracks she is stopped by a hand on her back. It is not the scent of orange blossom that turns her, but something altogether less pleasant. Unwashed clothes and stale breath.

'Well, hello again there, chérie,' says the man with the crooked nose. 'Be careful you don't fall onto the tracks. Do you have the time?'

'No,' whispers Sophie. 'I don't have the time.'

'Well, if it's the time I think it is, this next train will not stop. If you end up on the tracks, you're finished.'

'I know,' Sophie whispers. 'Belleville is not the terminus.'

'Exactly,' says the old man.

A siren sounds across the station. The métro races past with a scream, tracks singing. A strong gust of stale, hot air pushes the passengers back on the crowded platform. Some sway, some stumble. The man with three teeth laughs.

'So that's the time,' he says to Sophie. 'It is time I found myself a phone. You know those phones? I see the young folks with them all the time, talking into them, pressing those little buttons. You not got one of those, chérie? You, or your girlfriend? You could talk to each other like that, like the other young people.'

'No,' says Sophie. 'I don't have one.'

'Too bad, too bad,' says the man.

A siren announces the next train into the station. Sophie hands her crêpe to the man with the crooked nose. 'Would you like it?' she asks.

'Oh, yes,' he says, and takes it. 'Absolutely. I love that fleur d'oranger.'

'Goodbye,' Sophie tells him, and she steps onto the train.

'Goodbye, chérie.'

★

Sophie stays on the métro all the way to Saint-Germain but she does not go straight to class. She waits for the monster in the square but the monster does not come. She buys a café au lait in the monster's favourite café but the monster does not come. She takes her ham and emmenthal panini to the Pond des Arts at lunchtime but the monster does not come.

In workshop that afternoon Sophie leaves her new paintings on the professor's desk. The professor rolls them out, spreads the monster's broken limbs across the scarred and paint-encrusted wood.

'Yes, Sophie,' the professor says. 'Yes. This is a series that speaks to grief. There is truth here.' She holds the paintings up for the class to see. They like to give feedback. 'And this one,' the professor says. She selects the canvas Sophie finished last, only this morning, after an entire night of painting. It is of a young woman lying peacefully on a futon beside a monster with Sophie's face.

The professor nods towards the student who has quietly slipped in to the back of the class, late, like yesterday, plastic cup of café au lait from her favourite café held in her hands.

Sophie, the monster, turns to smile at her girlfriend, who returns the smile hesitantly and comes to sit beside her, soft, smooth hand interlacing fingers with Sophie's.

'This one is my favourite.'

Such a pretty face

Louie's face itches. The kind of itch she knows would be real satisfying if she scratched. Nails up under the chin, round the back of the earlobes, along the hairline, deep. Like lifting a scab. Kinda like coming, if Louie is honest. The belly-groan of it.

Louie keeps her fingernails short, for obvious reasons, but there's just enough of a moon-crescent of white to really take some skin off. Her whole hands twitch with the wanting of it. She won't now, though. Later, maybe, when there's no one around. Right now there's the party, and the porch out to the decking in the garden, and the drinks, and someone's secondhand smoke curling around the hair at her temples (that itches, too). And Mina.

Mina's had a few good drinks, gin and something, curl of lime in the glass and ice cubes clinking. She picks one out with slick-slippery fingers and puts it in Louie's mouth, which is how Louie figures she's flirting. It's hard to tell, sometimes, with Mina.

The ice is brittle, cracks between Louie's teeth. She chews it so her mouth gets real cold, then fishes another out of Mina's drink to run along her face. Drips melt off her eyelashes.

'It's cooler outside,' Mina says. Takes Louie's hand (another point for flirting) and pulls her outside to where Tegan, Rob and Rob's boyfriend are sitting in the grass, tugs Louie's arm so they're all sitting together (point for not flirting). Louie doesn't get why they stick so close at parties when they all bloody live together in the first place. She's not used to them yet, really. She's the blow-in, the new housemate, new colleague, new in town. She should be glad to have some time to sit together in the fresh-cut grass of the garden, without the dishes or dust-balls or unplugged chargers to argue about. With so many other people around. There's friends of Mina's and co-workers of Tegan's and Rob's boyfriend's band-mates, which is a mouthful at the best of times. Louie knows nobody.

You're like the bride at the wedding with nobody on her side of the aisle, says Tegan, with a laugh. Bubbles in her prosecco glass.

Louie's face itches when she cracks a half-forced smile.

Louie's a lady of mystery, Mina says. Her legs are bare, real long, real close to Louie's. (Point for flirting or just proximity? Hard to tell.) *We don't know where she's from or where she's been.*

You know where I've been, says Louie.

Mina laughs. *Mystery woman*, she says again.

You've got a low profile, is one of the first things Mina says to Louie, six months ago now, on the night she first moves in. Louie pretends not to know what she means. *By which I mean you've got no profiles.*

And we're good at stalking potential housemates, Rob adds. He's set up Louie's coffee machine in a corner of the kitchen. It's the biggest thing she's brought with her.

Are you one of those anti-internet people? Tegan asks, where the word *people* isn't the one she would've picked if she wasn't being polite. *You think it's rotting our brains or collecting our souls or data or whatever, spying on our every move?* Tegan isn't often polite, in fairness; Louie thinks it strains her to try.

I mean, Mina says, aligning herself on Louie's side, *it is. We all know that.*

I'm just a private person, I guess. Louie smooths her hair down over one shoulder, still not used to the brown, the straight ends. *I'd rather just live my life without needing a witness.*

Tegan rolls her eyes but Mina smiles.

Can we witness? she asks. *Pull up a chair. Have a drink. Tell us where you've been.*

This is what Louie tells them: she's been on the road for months. What roads, Tegan? Well, the long way from the airport. Different countries' roads, before. Which countries? You know. The usual. Louie travels for work. She took a gap year to travel the world. A gap from what? College, post-grad, a mid-career switch. She took a couple of gap years, what can she say, rich family. She has family all over, really, ex-pat kid of ex-pat kids of military brats. What military? You know. Got some American, some British, some Indian ancestry. Irish too, obviously. Family in Australia, New Zealand, Polynesia. Can't place her accent? That's why. International schools in Tahiti, Kerala, Germany. How many languages does

65

she speak? A bunch, with varying degrees of proficiency. That doesn't answer your questions, Tegan? Too bad, too bad, really, Louie can't be more specific.

Woman of mystery, Mina says.

At the party, smell of gin-breath and weed-smoke, blacker smoke from the fire someone's started in the cement pit they use for barbecues. Louie vaguely wonders what they're burning. Belching and billows. Rob's boyfriend pulls him to his feet to join them. Mina stretches her legs – bare, white, long, blue-glitter varnish on her toenails – and her knee knocks Louie's. Louie doesn't move away.

Tegan leans into the space on the grass Rob left behind. It's his party, technically. The first of them all to turn thirty, although Louie's turned thirty a couple of times. She doesn't say this, obviously. Her birthday's supposed to be in September. Thirty next September. It's hard to keep it straight, with the gin. The smoke drifts over and the garden smells like burnt sugar, itchy.

One good scratch, deep in under the hairline, that's all she wants.

Well. That's not all she wants.

Mina tips her glass towards Louie and Louie takes a drink. Eyes locked, lashes long. Definitely flirting.

Later, more good drinks later, little lime shavings tanging their tongues, they are talking about exes. Their circle has expanded; even the ones who had been burning biscuits in the barbecue fire are sitting on the grass on cushions or the throws from the couch or just their own bare legs, dimpling a little with the chill of the dark night.

They've known each other a long time, most of them. Some since childhood, more since college. Between them, they can draw invisible strings, an incestuous spider-diagram of who has dated whom, slept with whom, kissed whom in teenage games of spin the bottle. Mina's number's highest, when they've counted the tally. Tegan right behind her.

Mina almost spits her drink when Louie tells her.

You aren't friends with any *of your exes? Not a single one?*

Not a single one.

Tegan's laugh is mean as fingernails on a blackboard. *You can't have had many exes, then.*

But Louie's count is higher even than Mina's. She keeps the real number to herself, only shrugs at Tegan and says, *I guess I'm just hard to get over, Tegan.*

Right, says Tegan, and Louie can tell she's holding back real carefully from saying something the others will chastise her for.

So tell us, Mina asks, her whole face an invitation. *Since we'll never meet them, tell us about these exes of yours.*

This is what Louie tells them: there was Preeti, in high school, brown eyes and white teeth, that perfect gap between the two front ones at the top that you could fit a fingernail in. Dark hair, bobbed under her chin. Cheeks these perfect apples, lips like something you could eat. How did it end, Mina? Well. When Louie's ma found out she was livid, put a stop to the thing at once, but they were only going to move on anyway. There was Anja, dyed blonde hair and plump lips. *Dollface*, the men called at her from building sites and bar doorways. *Hey, doll.* She tossed her honey hair. There was Julianne, first year out of secondary school, one of the gap years, Louie says. Brown curls and freckles, braces that bit when they kissed. Caustic bite to her words, too. Sharp little teeth in that lovely mouth when the braces came out. When she broke up with Louie they were all that she could see. Sharp and white and lovely.

There was Sarah and Coral and Amy. Red hair, black, dyed purple and chopped to pieces, undercut so bleached it was almost green. Pale skin, brown skin, freckles, lips, teeth. Eyes all shades of blue and brown, one pair green.

And the latest? asks Mina. *The one you left before you came here?*

Louie touches the lids of her own eyes, her cheeks, so gently. *That one*, she says, *looked a little like me.*

Sometimes at night there's this litany of names. Names Louie's called out in bed, names she's since called herself, names that then get moaned by mouths who own other names that may then one day be hers. Pink lips, red lips, lips bitten and bruised and smiling filthily or sweetly. Sometimes at night the ghosts of those names whisper in Louie's ears, lips touching her skin.

There are places in the body where skin is thinnest. Shallow cuts along the forehead, little line drawn on a wrist, small nick in the inside of nostrils, fingernails a little too sharp against that inner vaginal wall. Easy to bleed, there. Small wounds weeping so much blood.

Louie's lips crack first. All the chapstick in the world couldn't keep them supple. Each kiss a fissure. That's when Louie knows it's time.

That, or she goes and gets her heart broken again.

Hearts bleed hard from shallow cracks too.

Later still, every bottle of gin well empty, the party disperses. Mina and Tegan kiss their exes and their exes' exes, and their exes' new girlfriends who are now their friends too. Rob retires to his bedroom with his boyfriend.

Mina put some kind of dried flowery herb on the black-smoking fire a while ago and now the garden smells like a summer forest, sways like Louie's on a tyre swing between the trees. She should go to bed, get out of her clothes, turn on the shower in her en-suite and dig her nails into the skin of her face to scratch this goddamn itch but Mina's wrapped her in a soft patterned blanket and there's still a few ice cubes left in the bottom of her latest drink. Besides, Mina's still up, heavy lids on her eyes, legs all languorous so close to Louie's skin.

Tegan looks at Mina's legs stretching the length of the sheepskin rug she's dragged out of the sitting room to lie on and sighs, *See, that's why you've been with so many exes.* (Her esses are sibilant with the drink.) *With a body like that. Thin as a reed, those legs. S'no wonder.*

Mina's body's a willow, bending with the breeze. She swings a cushion at Tegan, playing. Misses by a mile. *Oh, come on*, she says to Tegan. *With that ass, anyone'd have you.*

Tegan stretches like a cat and turns her back, leans over one hip to look at the others. Tegan is a Botticelli painting. With claws.

Tegan looks at Louie, then, as if realising she hasn't been complimented yet. Louie knows her own body. It's stocky, strong, utilitarian. Louie's body is not a reed or a cat or a painting. Tegan says, with deliberate hesitation, *And Louie, you're, well, you've got* such *a pretty face.*

I do, thinks Louie, it's true. It is a pretty face.

She had screamed when Louie took it. They don't often scream; usually they stay asleep, eyelids twitching over shades of blue and brown, one pair green. Maybe their lips part when she slices the skin, maybe they breathe a little deeper as she peels it off them, sinew and bone exposed. It takes forty-three muscles to make a human expression; Louie read that somewhere once. She makes sure they're all slack, those muscles. Easier to get a knife in. The eyes come last, with a coupla good pops. Louie loves the sound. Loves how the world looks different, afterwards, through her ex's eyes.

Louie watches Mina: beautiful, laughing, tripping over the steps up to the decking, hand in Louie's hand. They tumble into a bedroom – Mina's, tangle of fairy lights around the headboard, cluttered desk overflowing with coffee cups. Mina doesn't hesitate at the threshold, which Louie thought she might. Small show of nerves, that dance of consent before clothes come off. Louie imagined Mina biting her own lip, casting her eyes down and then up again, ready to let Louie lead. She doesn't let Louie lead.

Mina pulls her down with a force Louie couldn't have expected. Mina: trust and laughter, a light touch, sweet hesitation. Or so Louie thought. Instead Louie finds there is a ferocity to her. Her long, slim limbs suddenly all muscle, her hands hard, her lips insistent. Before she can think, Louie's up against a wall, head arching back, lips busy, all but trapped. Suddenly Mina is calling the shots. Louie likes it, this unexpected outside force.

It's Louie who's thrown bodily onto the bed, not Mina. It's Mina who climbs on hands and knees over Louie, teeth at her shirt collar, hands at her belt. It's Mina who strips her, fast and fierce, barely letting Louie take a breath between kisses, clash of teeth around her bottom lip, almost hard enough to draw blood. It's Mina who leaves a trail of wet bruises along Louie's jaw, her neck, each collarbone like Mina could rip them right out of Louie's skin.

Louie's never felt this before but also she has. She's a bit drunk, maybe, she realises a little too late. She's a bit more pliable. A bit more ready to lie back and let somebody else lead for once. She ignores the itch moving like pins and needles along her hairline so that it almost feels like sweat from the warmth and the willing body above her, like the tingles when Mina fists the hair at the nape of her neck and *pulls*, meets Louie's mouth again and again before pressing her back into the mattress, hard.

Julianne was the meanest, in a way that wasn't calculated, carefully adopted, like Anja. Like Louie herself can be, if she's honest. Julianne was mean down to her bones. Blade of bite to every word she spat. Those things'd make you bleed. Tegan reminds Louie of Julianne, sometimes. Sharp toothed, sharper tongued. The things that tongue could do.

Louie'd been the one to tongue her, at the end. Break-up sex, hot and hard and humiliating. Long gasp-groans far above her, thighs both sides of Louie's pretty face. Sex makes people sloppy, loose. The drugs she had given Julianne took a while to hit and Louie'd only ever fuck her sober. Consent is vital, always.

Not so mean now, eh, Julianne, Louie'd thought, gently touching her ex's sleeping face. Each muscle slack and soft. Pliable, nowhere near the sharpness Louie'd been cutting herself on for months.

Now whose heart is broken, Julianne?

Most of the time, they never even wake up.

Lying half on Mina's pillow, half on the lean ridge of Mina's upper arm, Louie's face itches. She gives a small experimental scratch, quick and contained so it won't wake Mina, right under the back cartilage of her left ear. Shudders all through her. She stifles a groan. There's nothing like scratching an itch. Her bare legs wrap around Mina's, still wet where they meet. Almost nothing. Her eyes close, briefly, and when they're open again Mina's staring at her.

You okay? she asks.

Yeah, Louie whispers. *Never better. Just a mosquito bite or something. Go back to sleep.*

Mina happily closes her eyes again and Louie breathes easy.

Six months she's been here. Eight's the longest she's lasted and that time her face was pretty much falling off by the end. Red rash along her hairline, deep welts from scratching in under her jaw. They got infected, the scratches. Oozed yellow pus and clear liquid all over the pillow. Crusted up every evening. Hot water and a flannel to loosen the scabs.

She can feel it coming. Deep, relentless itch. Skin crawling. Heat in every pore.

Not long now.

Louie looks at Mina's face, so close her features blur. Scatter of freckles on the bridge of her nose. Eyebrows half a shade darker than her hair. Bow lips. Cheekbones to kill for.

Such a pretty face. Prettier than Louie's, even.

Louie reaches out a finger and traces the outline of Mina's face from a centimetre away. Makes a map. Soft touch of intent and air. The hollows of her temples, the curl of her fringe, the pout of her lips in sleep, the dip of her dimpled chin.

What are you doing? A whisper against Louie's knuckle. The tickle of breath makes Louie surge forwards and kiss Mina, open-mouthed and desperate, fold herself against her sleep-sated body and take Mina's face in both her hands. Her fingers press against the hinges of Mina's jaws, her hairline, the sweet soft spot in under her throat. Short, sharp nails against flesh. Mina moans into her mouth.

Right there, right here, this is where the knife goes in. Slick slice and a wet caress. Louie traps Mina underneath her, heavies her hips as weights against her, moves when Mina moves, matches her moan for moan. Still her hands won't leave the sides of Mina's face.

What are you doing? A soft groan spoken over Louie's lower lip, followed by sharp teeth, a grunt, hip-thrust. Louie doesn't answer. Grinds harder, thigh high between Mina's, rocking on her elbows, fingertips pressed against her temples, her throat, those cheekbones. Very soon Mina stops asking what she's doing and only pleads for more. Louie comes so hard it takes fifteen thuds of her heart before she can take a full breath again.

Did you do this kind of thing with all those exes of yours? Mina asks, a little later, when she's got her own breath back. *Eh, mystery woman?*

What kind of thing? Louie's breath's still quick, upper thighs still slick.

I dunno, Louie. Learn their faces by heart?

Louie barks a laugh. *Do you always take charge right off the bat?*

It's Mina's turn to laugh. *Did I surprise you?*

You did, yeah.

Mina lifts Louie's face to hers with a fingernail right up in under the pulse point of her throat. Mina's nails are longer than Louie's but Louie's not complaining. Later, there'll be a mark. Small white crescent where she swallows. *You underestimated me*, she says.

There's something to Mina's words, something to the tone of her voice. Something like a mirror, familiar. More familiar than the reflection that looks out at Louie, later, when Mina has fallen back asleep. Louie in their shared bathroom, tilting her chin to take in every bruise necklacing her throat. A love bite along the line where the knife slides in. Louie may not recognise her own face now, not fully, but she recognises that.

And so, she begins to think, does good, kind, delicate Mina.

Amy was kind, Louie remembers. Kinder even than Preeti, who'd been only barely seventeen, hesitant as Louie and just as broken-hearted in the end, not that it mattered. Amy was delicate, cried quietly when she and Louie broke up. Black liquid eyeliner running in grey rivers down her cheeks in the prettiest way, watercolour lines connecting her freckles in pretend constellations. Louie thought of those tears often, in the years that followed. Even with her pretty face, Louie never made crying look that good.

Louie cried, the first time. Preeti's closed eyes, jaw slack, every muscle at rest. Louie's hands shook. She thought a lot about the nature of things. What made a person. How she could live with herself after. Turns out she didn't have to, when she could live as somebody else.

Still, she cried when she took it, blamed her broken heart. And that evening, she cried with different eyes, red-tinged tears mingling with the smell of bleach, fingers raw from scrubbing. There was a lot of blood. She's learnt, long since, to lay down sheets.

Now, Louie loves the mess. Slick slide of the knife, spill of warm blood sudden on her hands. It's a little like sex, when Louie gets down to it. That give, two fingers lifting willing flesh from giving gore. The wet ridges of muscle over bone. Slippery sheets. Quick breaths. Sweet release.

At this point Louie needs it. And not just because of the itch threatening to overwhelm her, the skin of the edges of her face on fire, nails right in under, digging deep. Low growl of satisfaction but it's not enough. Beside her, Mina sleeps, little ring of bruises already forming along her jaw.

Mina comes up behind Louie at the sink, whispers in her left ear so low Louie can barely hear her.

You tired me out so much I didn't notice you get up.

Louie reaches around for Mina's hands, links them across her own waist. The water is sudsy, sloshing over the sink. At Mina's bare toes the bag of bottles Louie's spent the morning filling clinks.

Louie arches her neck back, grins into Mina's mouth. *You're welcome.*

Come back to bed, Mina murmurs.

What, you want me to tire you out some more?

Mina's laugh's like the tin wind chimes strung up in the garden.

Now it's my turn.

Wasn't that the first time? Louie chuckles, remembering how she'd underestimated Mina, how Mina called her on it proudly. She can feel her heart beat in every bruise.

Mina nibbles at her bottom lip. *Fair's fair, Louie. I give as good as I get.*

I'll say. Louie turns, overflowing sink forgotten, clink of bottles barely registering at her feet.

Leave the dishes, Mina whispers. *Let me help you scratch that itch.*

The problem with skin is that bodies are stupid. Bodies see anything foreign as a threat, an invasion. That's why pregnant folks get so sick in the first trimester. That's why transplant survivors have to work so hard for their bodies to accept the newly donated organ. Skin's an organ like any other. Louie's face can't take it.

She's not sure of the science but some last longer than others. This one's been quick to fall apart. Maybe it's because she screamed when Louie took it, the drugs diluted somehow so she didn't just stay asleep, breathing shallow while Louie's knife ran deep. Whatever the reason, Louie's skin is seething like there's something electric underneath, the itch like a constant shock zipping at her temples. There's a burn behind her eyelids every time she blinks. Even her gums tingle around her teeth, and those have always been hers.

Mina's noticed. Louie doesn't know how but Mina's noticed.

76

Points for flirting, Louie's thought, a handful of times a week until now. Points for friendly, points for proximity. It's only later, when Mina pushes her down on Louie's own bed, kisses the itch under her skin hard enough to burn, that she considers points for Mina being the love of her goddamn life.

Back in bed Mina traces one long nail along Louie's hairline, down around the whirl of an ear, lining her jaw with sharp white that fast fades to barely red.

Mystery woman, she whispers, and to Louie it feels like a declaration.

You're unexpected, Louie tells her, arousal loosening her tongue.

Mmm, says Mina. *Were all of those exes of yours expected?*

Louie just nods, even if it's only partly true. Then she allows herself a small smirk. *Why*, she asks. *You planning to be my next ex?*

Mina matches her smirk for smirk. *Not gonna happen.*

Then what is this? Louie motions at their bare bodies, more tangled than morning bedsheets.

This? Mina leans forwards, not the slightest trace of hesitation, and kisses Louie first firmly on the lips, then at the point under her left ear where the itch is fiercest. *This is true love.*

It's much later when Tegan and Rob and Rob's boyfriend emerge from their respective rooms to reluctantly help clean. There are stains on the couches and singe marks on the grass around the fire pit in the garden, something that looks suspiciously like the burnt remains of a shoe in amongst the sticks and the ashes.

They can tell, the others, that something's happened, even through the haze of their hangovers. It's in the way Mina orbits Louie, makes excuses to touch her, compliment her (all of those were points for flirting, Louie realises with hindsight). Rob and his boyfriend exchange a look while Tegan smirks knowingly.

Have fun last night? she asks, syrup-sweet, slightest of emphasis on the second word.

Mina glows too much for a woman who drank seven glasses of gin and something the night before. Louie lets her face crack into a smile, ignores the way her skin feels papery around the edges. Her jaw aches.

You okay? Mina asks, back against the hall door, heel of her foot kicking against the wall. *We don't have to tell them.*

Tell them what? Louie's teasing.

Mina smiles, shakes her head. What she says surprises Louie more than anything Mina did last night. *Tell them what you're about to do.*

They round the door to Louie's bedroom, Mina leading again, pressing Louie back, chest to chest and knee to knee, no room to manoeuvre.

Oh yeah? Louie asks, voice slightly muffled by Mina's bared throat, hands already roaming, voice rough around the edges. *And what is that?*

Mina reaches around Louie, clicks the door shut behind them. She untucks Louie's t-shirt and runs her hands up Louie's front, fingertips grazing her breasts. When Louie makes a low *Hmm* of pleasure Mina grabs her hips and moves her thigh high between Louie's legs. It hits just right.

Louie moans into her open mouth but Mina takes Louie's chin in one hand and holds her steady. She murmurs the words but they're clear as anything, eyes on Louie's dry, itching eyes. *You're about to take that knife in the bottom drawer of your wardrobe and slice the skin from Tegan's pretty face.*

Anja laughed a lot, called Louie's humour 'dry'. *You're killing me,* she'd say, her eyes wide blue, her doll face smiling. *Who gave you the right?*

When she found Louie's knife in a wardrobe drawer she chuckled. *Big bad,* she called Louie, pretty mouth mocking. *You don't scare me.*

Nothing scared Anja. She was the one people fled from. When she broke up with Louie it was brutal: a list of her least-desirable character traits falling off Anja's plump lips like drops of honey. All Louie could hear, though, was the sharp, awful sound of her own heart breaking. A mouth is a weapon even if it can't skin a whole face.

Anja smiled when Louie took it. Like she was in on the joke. It took hours to pull those lips off. Careful force, sharp slow tugs, and still Louie almost tore them. By the end she was sweat-soaked and panting with the effort, the deliberation. For weeks afterwards she slept like the dead.

Louie has to admit, this is easier with two. She's used to mixing a drink with sweat still on her skin, letting her kisses slow and deepen as it kicks in. She's used to knowing every inch of the body below her, to tracing the gentle marks she's made. It's different, when the still-sex-sticky body next to her is very much alert, and handing her the sharpened knife. It's different when the house isn't empty, all three housemates out cold, one lying fully clothed between them.

79

It's Mina who bends her neck to check Tegan's breath. Steady, slow. It's Mina who tilts Tegan's head back, exposing her throat. Her chest falls and rises in the silence. Louie wields the knife but it's Mina's sharp intake of breath that she hears when the tip slides in.

At any minute, Louie thinks, Mina's going to stop, scream, pass out, something. At any minute she'll realise she can't stomach this. It isn't when the knife slices clean and wet through skin. It isn't when blood spurts bright between them. It isn't when Louie, not without relish, angles both her thumbs at the same time, applying that perfect pressure at the red, wide corners of Tegan's hazel eyes, and twitches at just the right angle to pop them right out with a satisfying splat.

Louie's face itches. Deep frisson at her hairline, tingle of burn along her jaw. With Mina watching she hooks her nails right in, digs up and under, shuddering like she's coming, breaths fast and hard. Mina's pupils widen but she doesn't say a thing. Louie gives one of those belly-groans, fingers working faster, deeper in under the skin, hard bite of nail like the best fucking thing in the world.

Her whole face peels off and it's like a benediction. There's nothing that comes close to this satisfaction. Louie groans again, harsh and low. Mina's breath is quick.

When Louie pops her old eyeballs out she's in the dark for a time. It's like the biggest trust exercise she can imagine: her face, her future, in Mina's willing hands. Mina's breath stays steady as the wet rustle of her fingers.

Here, she whispers, and Louie can feel the slide of mucusy membrane easing over her empty sockets. Before they're even attached she can feel Mina's fingers pressing so carefully. A small moan curls in Louie's throat. One slippery *pop* each and they're in and *oh*, the relief. Louie groans.

Fuck, she says. *Yes.*

Louie can't blink yet so Mina's fuzzy, like dust over an old picture. Still, Louie can tell she's smiling. Smiling at Louie like she's the most beautiful woman on earth. Louie, who doesn't have a face.

Mina leans in, dust-flecked and gorgeous, and with Louie's muscle and sinew exposed, blood dripping from jaw and chin, rivulets running along her neck like sunset-streaked mountain streams, Mina kisses her ravaged lips, red on red, licking into her mouth, opening wide. When she breaks the kiss it's Mina who moans.

Over her kisses Mina presses the fresh face and the relief is immediate. The skin's pliable, smooth. The lips are moist. The eyelids soft. Louie blinks and smiles and frowns, testing her reactions. She opens her mouth wide and Mina kisses her again.

There you are, Mina says.

Only corpses stay

They walked for three weeks, hiking inland, skirting the mountains. Rifles ready, bloodshot eyes, single file along the fence. Splintered wood and hum of wire, taller than the tallest of them twice over. In the distance, snarls and screams.

The kids were wired, Heidi on high alert, but June's mind was elsewhere. Elsewhen. The path felt familiar. Old scars prickled, stretched every time she raised her arms to clear the path ahead, to signal the others, to reach into her rucksack for water. They were all scarred, even the youngest kids. Especially the youngest kids, the few of them there were, the ones who'd been dropped at the barracks fence by dying parents, half dead themselves. There hadn't been any new kids for a while.

They reached the outpost before nightfall. Reddish tinge to the setting sky. Heidi went around back to kick up the generator and June waited with the kids out front in silence until the crank and the hum broke across the barracks and the lights flickered to life. A couple of the kids cheered. Rucksacks sank from knotted shoulders, some of the tension in their faces cleared. June cracked her neck and then her knuckles.

There were tinned rations in the kitchen, ammunition and some old rifles in the training hall, piles of folded sheets in the dust of the bunk rooms. The taps ran after a few good thumps and a minute to let out the rusty gunge.

'Another quarter, another outpost,' Heidi yawned, arms stretching high over her head.

June found a limescale-crusted kettle, plugged it in, flinching at the spark. 'Home sweet home,' she said.

Keira and Pam and a third of the kids had taken the longer road, scouting the outskirts. The officers and the oldest kids had left before them to cross the mountains. All going well, they'd meet here within the week.

The kids were lively, all over each other, ready to let out their tight-wound bodies after almost a week of watchful walking. By lights-out June and Heidi had had to break up five separate fights, pulling swearing, sweat-soaked girls apart by the scruffs of their shirts, their hair, anything to stop them landing another punch. It would be a few days until they had the other bunkrooms cleared so they all slept together, snores and mutters and the moans of nightmares echoing through the night.

June's dreams were all Mara.

The first time June got gouged by one of the things she was eleven. Routine fence patrol. Stokes had let June take the lead, small hands firm around her rifle, head clear, boots steady. The officers all knew they could count on June. Mara, as always, fought to be placed right behind her, although the rest of the team voted for her to take up the rear. Stokes had sighed heavily and waved Mara to June's side. It was easier, sometimes, to give Mara what she wanted. Saved time and energy. Besides, this was just a routine patrol.

They were just past the perimeter when the thing appeared. June had never seen one up close before, didn't get much of a look before Mara's bullet hit it in the head. It roared. Charged. Laid June's belly open like it was nothing. Later, June learned that Mara sent two rounds into the thing before running to help Stokes carry June to the infirmary.

There were no medical teams to call, no hospitals to fly to, even then – not for kids like them anyway – so June drifted in a haze of pain while Mullet, who'd pulled the short straw for infirmary duty that week, administered medication, cleaned and bandaged the wound. But it was Mara June called for, enough that Mullet finally threw up her hands and let the other girl deal with June's stitches.

Most nights Mara slept beside her till morning, stiff and straight in her sleep, careful to keep her distance. Whispers threading through the space between them. Keira's sharp glare in the morning. The others all rolling their eyes.

Some of the other girls shared beds from time to time, as they grew older. June learned, like they all did, to turn away, tune out the noises, like she'd learned as a child to turn away from the sobs, the screams of nightmares. Nighttime was for noises they could never dare to make in the day.

It was never like that with Mara. They never touched at night. Only ever felt skin on skin in daylight hours, partnering up in training, sparring at rec time, or some-times in the darker, empty corridors of the south barracks, alone, fighting hard and breathless, curled fists sinking

85

into stomachs, feet bracing, arms grappling around throats, teeth drawing blood.

'Go to sleep,' Mara whispered.

June's eyes were already closing, one hand splayed across the scar puckering the skin of her lower abdomen. Silky-soft and new. '*You* go to sleep,' she muttered back, and she could feel Mara's smile, her breath against her shoulder.

'What do you two have to whisper about so much after lights out?' Keira had snarled in the morning, jealous. June had seen her eyes shine in the reflected light of the exit sign in the middle of the night, seen them watch Mara climb quietly out of her bunk and into June's, seen them narrow at the soft-muffled shared giggles.

Mara shrugged, offhand. 'None of your business.'

Keira bristled. 'It'll be my business if I report you.'

Mara took a warning step towards the older girl but June, the peacekeeper, came between them.

'Nothing, really,' June said. 'Just talking.'

Keira's hands were still fists. 'So talk at break, not at night,' she spat.

Mara laughed. 'We'll talk whenever we want,' she said, and turned her back to undress.

Her first night back from the infirmary, June heard about the fight. Mara had settled herself in her usual spot, over the thin blanket – grey, standard-issue, somewhat scratchy but warm enough – a careful hand's-width from June on the narrow bunk, and her skin was a map of bruises.

Fights weren't unusual; sometimes they were the best way to prove who was strongest, who was right, whose group someone belonged to, who was the better friend.

Sometimes they were the only way to touch, and be touched.

It was rare for the whole team to gang up, though. Fights were how they settled things, and the adults were watchful but didn't often intervene (the adults fought too, of course, for much the same reasons; even now June sometimes went to bed with split lips, Keira with bloody knuckles; old habits were hard to break). But bullying wasn't allowed, was punished fiercely. Ganging up was bullying.

They'd ganged up on Mara, the whole squad, when June wasn't there to de-escalate, to come between them, to protect her. Every kid had got a good kick in.

June closed her eyes. 'What did you say to them, to make them gang up on you like that?'

Mara gave a low laugh. 'I could've said anything. They were just waiting for an excuse.'

June opened her eyes. 'Mara —'

Mara's fingers twitched in the empty space between them. 'They've been waiting for an excuse for years,' she said. 'They just needed you out of the way.'

Sometimes months would go by when June didn't think of Mara. Months of routine checks and patrols, eating and fighting and training. Other times not an hour would go by when Mara wasn't in her thoughts.

'Where's your head at, Darcy?' Heidi asked, appearing in front of June so suddenly she started, fingers reaching for her rifle before her thoughts caught up. Heidi backed away a pace. 'Easy, tiger.'

June unclenched her fist, tried to shake another memory of Mara off. She'd been a child back then, younger than the youngest of her team. And Mara was ten years gone now. Ten years this week, or close to. 'I'm fine,' she said brusquely. 'Let's get this place cleaned out.'

Heidi nodded, let it go. 'We're all on edge,' she said, almost gently. 'But we made it.'

June watched the kids run laps around the courtyard. 'We'll have made it when the others are here, too.'

It took two days to get the outpost in a liveable condition. Rats in the store room, dust and grime in the kitchen, some kind of black mould creeping over the bunkroom walls. They beat back the vines and ivy, cleared the track to the fence, posted rotating guards who did little more than look out for the other leaders, the other kids, rifles held loosely, eyes on the horizon, waiting for a glimpse of a friend.

It was almost a week before Keira and Pam's team arrived. They were late, but the other officers, the ones who'd taken the trail further inland, were even later. They should all have been there by now. The kids on June's team converged on Keira's the moment they reached the barracks. Hands slapped backs, hugs bowled girls over, they rolled in the cracked tarmac of the front yard, laughing, although they were half-starved, exhausted.

'You made it,' June said from the door, leaning against the hard jamb of it, hands in her pockets, shoulders stiff.

Keira watched her kids, all filthy and lean, all broken and bruised, all laughing. Her face was lined, unsmiling. 'Just about,' she said.

'I can see that.'

'And the others?' Keira asked.

June let her eyes drift to the calm horizon. 'No word.'

Keira said nothing.

Pam strode up to them, face scratched, clothes torn, boots mostly mud. 'Any hour now,' she said bracingly. 'God, I hope there's hot water.'

There was hot water until the generator broke down, close to midnight. June had taken one of the empty first-floor offices as a bedroom, Keira the other, to be close to the kids if needed. From time to time the soft sound of feet crossed in front of her door, between the sleeping quarters and the bathrooms. The odd owl hooted from distant trees, barely audible over the constant hum of the generator, the groan of the pipes when somebody ran the water, the sounds of snores and soft cries from the kids' sleeping quarters.

When she couldn't take it anymore, she slipped into Keira's room. Keira was asleep, one arm flung above her head, jaw tight, brows frowning. She didn't hear the shush of the shutting door behind June, didn't feel the dip of the mattress when June lowered herself down beside her. June watched Keira breathe for a few beats, had only just decided to go back to her own room when Keira stirred, the arm above her head moving towards June, fingers pressing into the flesh of her thigh.

'June.' Keira's voice was rough with sleep.

'I thought you might be awake,' June whispered. 'I should let you rest.'

'No,' Keira said, eyes opening. 'Stay.' Her hand flattened against June's skin. 'It's good to see you.'

June let the relief she'd felt seeing Keira lead the kids up to the outpost earlier that day seep into her voice. 'It's good to see you too.'

Keira raised herself up onto one elbow and brought her other hand to cup June's face. 'Did you think,' she said softly, 'I wasn't going to make it?'

'The thought crossed my mind.'

'And?' Keira touched her lips to June's, gently.

'And it wasn't a pleasant thought. Kiss me harder.'

Keira kissed her harder. Turned and pressed her into the mattress, kissed her harder still. Swelled her lips with it. Raised blue bruises on her breasts, long red marks along her arms and thighs. Keira kissed like fighting, or maybe June did, or maybe they both did. Collision of lips and flesh, fast and breathless, tangle of limbs. Maybe fighting was the only measure they had for intimacy. Slick slide of skin, voices rasping just-barely words, low grunts, eyes shut.

Two deep shudders and a groan that shook the barracks. The exit light blinked out. In the absence of the hum of the generator, that constant background noise, low and reassuring, the night was suddenly all around them, dark and loud.

'Shit,' said Keira, gathering her clothes. 'Generator's down.'

'I'll go find the petrol.'

'Old basement offices, Pam said.' Keira pointed the torch at June, watching her dress. Beam of light stroking bare skin. She licked her lips.

'Cut it out,' June said. 'And give me the damn torch.'

Keira snorted a laugh. 'Don't be long,' she said. 'The bed'll go cold.'

June's bed was cold the week Mara left. A decade ago, in a colder season. Frost creeping in the windows of the sleeping quarters. The mud froze to their boots in the evening, left puddles by their bunks overnight. They slept fully clothed, two pairs of socks. Mara held herself stiff and careful, sleeping body a hand's-width from June's on the narrow bunk, the slats of Mara's own bed above them in the darkness. It was the end of a quarter. Another few days and they'd be on the move, trekking the coast for long, cold weeks, making camp at night, following the fence to the next outpost. They would hear the things in the night, would sleep with their rifles right under their fingers, ready to be wrenched awake by a scream, a roar, a shouted command to assemble. June hated the quarterly trek between outposts. They all did.

'I wish we could just stay here,' she whispered to Mara. Even in the crowded bunkroom, her breath formed clouds. 'At least until the end of winter.'

Mara softly said the words drilled into them from childhood, spoken by the whole team every quarter before moving out to the next outpost. 'Only corpses stay.'

June closed her eyes. 'Only corpses stay.'

They'd buried two of the junior cadets that morning. Kids, the both of them, still a couple of milk teeth in their mouths. Spade handles bending in the hard ground.

June hadn't seen it, not this time, although there had been other kids, other adults, other deaths, so many other deaths, before. The first one got picked off repairing a part of the fence that had been snapped by a fallen tree. The other died rushing out to save her. Eleven years old. June remembered a round of bullets straight in the face of the thing that gouged her. She ran her fingertips absently over the scar.

They'd been those kids' ages, her and Mara, when Mara had first whispered of running away. Six years later now and nothing had changed except that those who'd died didn't follow them from outpost to outpost. Only corpses stayed. And June and Mara could have been eleven, fifteen, eighteen years old, lying carefully side by side on the bunk under the top bed closest to a window Mara always claimed and rarely slept in, whispering softly through the night, only ever touching to check each other's hands for splinters. Bruised from a day's training, stiff from patrol, bloody from secret spars in the south barracks when they'd wound each other up so much only fists could solve it.

Outside the high windows, the wind whined. Frost forked across the roof.

'I saw a report,' Mara had whispered. 'In Jackson's office, when she wasn't looking.'

June raised her eyebrows.

'There's an outpost,' Mara said. 'Maybe a ten-day walk from here, along the coast, where no squad ever gets stationed.'

'So?'

'So?' Mara groaned, tossed her head on the other side of the pillow. 'An empty outpost? On the coast? Kept secret?'

'Mara —'

'It's our way out. I'm telling you.'

June sighed. 'There is no way out.'

Mara smirked. 'Not with that defeatist attitude.'

'So, what?' June asked, lowered her whisper, brought her face even closer to Mara's so nobody could possibly overhear. 'You want to run away? Desert? What the fuck, Mara?'

'What's the alternative?' Mara hissed. 'Stay here forever? Move between outposts every four to six months, losing half of us on every journey? Become senior officers if we survive into our twenties? Train up any new kid that gets thrown our way until we've outlived our leaders and let the cycle go on again until there are no new kids and the things pick us all off one by one so there's no one left to staff the outposts?'

June muttered the familiar words. 'Only corpses stay.'

For ten long minutes, only the storm spoke.

Mara broke the silence. 'June.' Her hand twitched even nearer. 'Is that really what you want to do with your life?'

'That's –' June felt the heat in her face, the fluster in her stomach. 'That's not –'

'What? We could just go. You and me. We could.' Mara's face was more earnest than June had ever seen it. June took a breath. Could they? Could they just go?

June shook her head. 'What if there's nothing beyond that outpost?' she whispered. 'There'd be no going back.'

'Well,' said Mara, and the lightning glowed on her grin. 'Then we die free.'

Under the snorts and snores of their bunkmates and the footfalls of the officers on night watch, under the hum of the generator and the high whine of the icy wind, June thought she could hear the sea. Six, seven years in the future and where would she be? In the smaller bunk rooms the officers slept in, or in the private quarters the commanders sometimes took. Mara sneaking into her bed after lights-out, lying a hand's-width apart, whispering about escape. Moving out every quarter. Rounds of bullets biting into the things that got through the fence as they marched. Kids dying on their watch.

June looked right into Mara's eyes and bridged the gap between them to grasp Mara's cold hand in hers. 'Okay,' she said.

93

Mara shifted, moved so close their foreheads were touching, hand still clutching hand. Suddenly, June could no longer feel the cold. They stayed like that all night, bright spots of heat where their foreheads, hands, knees touched, breath mingling, lips near, feverish rush to their whispered plans. When June fell asleep, finally, it was with Mara's arm slung heavy around her waist, hers at Mara's hips.

June passed Heidi in the hallway, torch in hand, leading a small group of kids.

'I'm taking a team,' Heidi told her. 'To check for a breach in the perimeter. You're on the generator?'

June nodded.

'Be quick.'

The small training yard outside was black without the floodlights. June crossed fast, shouldered open the basement door. Stacks of files on desks, walls of cabinets, long-defunct radios covered in dusty controls. One outpost was very much like another, but this one flicked a switch in June's memory. She shone her torch beam around each wall, found the petrol cans behind the door she'd entered from.

A long pour, a creak, a crank, and the floodlights flickered to life outside the basement window. June unclenched her jaw.

She thumbed the light on and leaned against one of the desks for a minute, took deep breaths. There was a map on the wall. Each outpost circled in faded red, outline of the fence in dusty blue. June crossed the office in a few fast steps.

There it was. Abandoned outpost, a couple weeks' walk from this one, along the coast. The fence had been pulled back around it, stood maybe fifty kilometres inland from it now, lining it out. Had for years, obviously. This outpost hadn't been staffed in who knew how long. June left a fingertip trail in the dust. From the training yard, the sound of boots hitting packed ground: Heidi's team back from their perimeter check. June would soon be missed. A part of her wanted to tear the map, rip the piece that connected the barracks to the abandoned outpost, stuff it under the tongue of her boot so even Keira couldn't see it. Ten years since she'd been here before. Ten years since Mara'd seen this map and dreamed up escape. Longing sat sharp on her tongue. Instead she gave the map one last long look, then turned off the light and climbed the stairs.

'All clear?' she asked Heidi, last of the kids trudging back into their bunkroom, yawns splitting their faces.

'All clear.' Heidi yawned herself. 'Must have been an animal, or maybe the generator needs a service. I'll have a look at it in the morning.' She looked pointedly into the room June hadn't been sleeping in. 'For now we should all get some rest.'

'Sure,' said June, still wired, a hum like electricity singing in her veins. She made for Keira's room, saw Heidi's raised eyebrows and said, in a voice that immediately reminded her of Mara's, 'What, Heidi? Are you gonna report me?'

Heidi's eyes narrowed.

'Oh, wait,' said June, and she pushed open Keira's door. 'There's no one left alive to report to. We're not kids any more, Heidi. See you in the morning.'

★

Keira said it was Heidi who'd reported Mara that day when they were teens. She didn't say what for. Girls shared beds, girls whispered after lights-out, girls spent nights alone or together gasping heavy in the dark. Nobody reported them because the adults didn't care. The adults had their own nighttime affairs.

Intimacy was not encouraged but was difficult to punish. And June was liked. Respected. By the other kids and by the adults. She was upbeat and charming, hard-working and driven. The officers said she'd run the place someday. Mara was a dark shadow, seeding doubt, holding her back.

June waited all night for Mara to return to the bunk-room but her bed stayed cold. Frost set their boots to slipping during morning training, despite the salt the officers threw over the hard ground of the yard. They ran drills, Keira beside June, sparring with her one-on-one, bigger, older, stronger. Slower. It was almost easy to duck her punches, dance around her, use Keira's own weight to overbalance her, pin her arms behind her back and kick out her legs at the knees, land hard on top of her, breathless. June pinned her to the frozen ground over and again, Keira's huffed laughter making white clouds.

'Never thought you'd get this good sparring against Mara all these years,' she said, after yielding for the third time in a row.

June held out a hand to help her up. 'You sure you're not letting me win?'

Keira brushed melted ice from her trousers with a grin and let June pull her to her feet. 'I never let anyone win.'

Keira held on to June's hand for a moment longer than necessary, eyes locked somewhere over June's left shoulder. When June turned, Mara was a shadow leaning hunched against the furthest wall, watching.

'Where were you?' June asked, coming up to Mara as Stokes blew her whistle for break.

Mara's eyes were red-ringed, her face pale. 'Punishment,' she shrugged.

June's face fell. 'Mara,' she breathed.

'It's fine.'

'No, it's not,' June hissed. 'Punished for what?'

Mara rolled her shoulders off the wall and stood, half a head shorter than June, chin jutting. 'It's not a big deal, Darcy. Happens to most of us. Not that you would know.'

'What's that supposed to mean?'

'Nothing.' Mara shouldered past her. 'Forget it.'

'Mara.' June grabbed her arm, pulled her close, muscles still twitching from sparring with Keira, ribs tender, shirt soaked with sweat. 'What about the plan?'

Mara's whole body relaxed against June's. She didn't look at her, just kept her gaze on the other side of the training yard, arm slack and still in June's grasp. Her voice was stripped of its usual bravado when she said, 'You're still . . .' and let the words trail off.

June dropped her arm, took a small step back but kept her voice low. 'I'm still in.'

Mara's face was set. 'Okay,' she said.

'Okay.'

Keira had June's clothes back off in seconds, laughed into her open mouth.

'Did you just dare Heidi to report us?' she said.

'Shut up.'

June hooked one leg around Keira's, twisted an arm tight behind the other woman's back. Keira shut up. June flung her down on the narrow bunk, climbed on top of her, chest heaving with every breath. They fought for it, bedsprings screaming, bunk legs shaking, until they fell to the floor with a muffled thump. Keira was stronger, always had been, but June had long learnt to fight dirty. She wasn't a kid any more, bright-eyed and charming, boisterous, friendly. She was helpless rage and desperation, looking for anything that would give her release. And weren't they all, at this point? Those few of them who had survived. Around her the barracks hummed and echoed. Fewer now, still.

Afterwards they lay and breathed together, slick and heavy against each other. The night was mild and loud. Footsteps shuffled in front of the door, the noises of night animals came through the narrow window, the thin whine of the electric lights in the corridor, the generator hum.

'What do you think happened to them?' June whispered. 'The others.'

Keira spoke into her hair. 'Maybe they're just delayed. Took a longer route.'

The barracks were large and empty around them. 'Or maybe we're the only ones left.'

The plan was simple. Ten years ago. They'd been hoarding rations for a week, June nicking from the kitchen because no one would suspect her, rucksack hidden deep in the empty rooms of the south barracks, where only they ever went. In three days they'd all move out, march to the next outpost. Mara had the map. Along the way, along the fence, the wind icy and the path treacherous, mountains looming between their company and the sea, June and Mara would just slip away. Let the others believe them lost. A small stumble off a steep slope was all it took; it had happened before. There were things, sometimes, that breached the fence, picked off a straggler. At night when they made camp it would be easy to just quietly get left behind. Dead, not defected. Just another couple of kids lost along the way.

They tried to sleep, but even with June banishing Mara to her own bed after hours of whispers, going over everything in voices so low they could barely hear each other, it was impossible to rest. Long before dawn Mara climbed back down from her bunk to June's, settled in her space over the blanket, a careful hand's-width apart.

In the morning when June opened her eyes Mara was already awake, standing between their bunks and Keira's. Keira was up in Mara's space, chest to chest, all aggression. June sprang out of bed, ready to break them apart, but Mara held out a warning hand.

Keira took a step forward, forcing Mara back. 'You have your own damn bunk, cadet,' she said.

Mara's look was insouciant, her chin angled high. 'You think I don't know that?'

'You think I can't get you transferred to another bunkroom if I report you?'

'You think that'll stop me?'

'That's enough.' June elbowed her way between them. 'Cut it out.'

Keira took a half-step back, fists still clenched. Mara didn't move. 'We're moving out in two days,' Keira said. 'If you two aren't rested, you're a danger to the team. Understand?'

June nodded, put a calming palm on Keira's arm. 'We understand.'

Keira glared at Mara who shrugged, leaned lazily against the bunk behind her. 'Sure,' she said. 'We understand.'

They'd fought about it, June and Mara, that exchange, alone in the south barracks after rec time, more rations snuck into their hidden bag.

'Are you trying to get Keira to report you?' June hissed. 'Because you know she will.'

Mara huffed.

June went on, dogged, shutting her rucksack with more force than was needed, catching the zip in the fabric. 'And if she does, if anything changes, the plan –'

Mara knocked June's hands away, closed the rucksack with an angry tug. 'I know, okay.'

June pulled the bag away from Mara, roughly. 'Do you?' she asked. 'Because it seems like you're doing everything you can to piss her off.'

'Like what?' Mara was standing now, feet apart, legs braced. 'Sleeping in your bunk? Talking to you at night? Being your friend?'

June dropped the bag, stood more slowly, spoke fast. 'Well, maybe if you were more friendly to Keira –'

Mara's laugh echoed around the walls of the empty room. 'Like she'd let me.'

'You don't even try –'

'And you don't get it,' Mara said. 'You never have.'

June raised her fists, instinctive. 'They're not as bad as you make them out to be,' she said.

Mara threw the first punch. June dodged it, but only just, Mara's knuckles grazing her left ear. Mara blocked

June's hit with a raised arm. When Mara went to punch again, June lunged forwards, smacking her head into Mara's, driving her back. Mara's boot connected with her shin, her fist with June's gut, winding her. June doubled over.

'So what,' Mara shouted, breathless, bending over June. 'You're just gonna stay here?' June gripped Mara's hair, smashed her elbow into Mara's knee, sank with her to the floor.

'You just gonna give up on this and just stay with them?' Mara croaked. 'Since they're *not that bad*.' She surged up, forearm to June's throat. June kicked out, connected with Mara's ribs. They fell apart.

'No,' June said, panting, pushing herself onto her hands and knees. Mara lay on her back beside her. 'I'm not gonna stay.'

Mara's laugh was more of a cough. She winced, held her ribs. 'Only corpses stay.'

June tried to steady her breathing. 'Right.' She crawled over to Mara, flopped beside her on the dusty floor. 'So please. For the love of fuck. Stop trying to get a rise out of Keira.'

For a few long minutes, they were still.

'Will you miss them?' Mara asked. June turned her head to look at her but Mara's eyes were trained on the ceiling.

'Yes.'

Still, Mara didn't look at her. 'But you're still coming?'

'Of course.' June's hand was so close to Mara's, both their knuckles bruised. 'It's like you've always said.' A millimetre and their fingers could be touching. 'This is no way to live a life.'

'And if we die out there?'

It was June's turn to laugh. 'It's the same as dying here.'

'Inevitable,' Mara whispered.

June twitched her fingers, allowed her hand to touch Mara's. 'Only corpses stay.'

Mara rolled over, right on top of June, and kissed her.

In the dim, swinging light of Keira's room, June closed her eyes. Time kept circling back. Nothing ever changed. From outpost to outpost, drills and training and lookouts. Fence patrols, shots fired into the things, retreating or being forced to retreat. Burials in soft ground and hard. Climbing into each other's bunks for a few hours' sweet reprieve. Mara's face a beacon in her dreams.

The kids in her company were the same age she was when Mara left. Sixteen, seventeen, thereabouts. Left from this same outpost. Left her behind. The loss was a weight on her chest. The betrayal. Quarter after quarter, time hardly counted and yet it just kept going. Only corpses stayed.

June couldn't get past the heat of her: Mara on the floor of the south barracks, frost glistening in the windows, condensation dripping down the walls. Kisses like kindling for small fires that could burn the icy place down. They laughed into each other's necks, breathless with possibility. And behind the door, slightly ajar, down the once-deserted corridor, another girl slunk away.

The commanders split the teams the next day, partnered June with some of the younger kids to train, sent Mara off with the older girls to patrol the fence. Mara bumped June's elbow with hers before she left.

'Don't have too much fun without me,' she said.

'Don't piss anybody off without me,' June replied.

Mara laughed, followed Keira and Heidi to the fence, rifle over her shoulder, head high. 'No promises,' she said. 'See you tonight.'

Tomorrow morning they would move out, and then June and Mara would slip away quietly in the night.

Mara didn't wait.

Her team returned after nightfall, broken and bleeding. There had been a rupture in the fence. One of their party had been dragged through by a thing on the other side. June stood at the foot of the main staircase, both hands clutching the rail for balance, as Keira spoke to the officers. As Keira spoke Mara's name.

June barrelled down the last few steps, raced to the door. It took Keira, Stokes and Mullet to hold her back from running all the way out to the fence and further, to wherever Mara was, whatever was left of her. Long, low roar coming endlessly from her throat. Hot tears on the hard ground. They were all yelling but June drowned them all, didn't stop struggling until Keira's words finally pierced through.

'June,' she shouted, then hissed hot in her ear. '*June.*' Keira spun her, tilted June's face up to look at her. She said, 'There's something you need to see.'

They crossed the training yard, June's legs unsteady, Keira shaking her head over her shoulder so the others wouldn't follow. Across to the south barracks, boots echoing on the hard ground. Down deserted corridors, dust packed tight in corners, rodents scurrying away at their approach. Keira led June into the room where she'd sparred with Mara in secret for months. Where their rucksack was stowed, filled with enough rations to last them to the abandoned outpost and beyond. Where they had held each other more softly than either had ever been touched before.

Keira lifted the crate in the corner that had hidden their bag. She had to hold June to keep her from falling. The crate was empty. The bag was gone. With Mara. She hadn't been attacked. She'd left without her.

The kids were more settled over breakfast. June took the first fence patrol with Keira while Heidi's team checked out the generator. Along the perimeter, girls stood with their eyes on the horizon, hands on their rifles. Nothing moved.

'I still feel like we're waiting for something to happen,' June said.

Keira's back was straight, muscles tense. 'We're waiting for the others.'

'Right.'

From beyond the fence June could almost make out the smell of the sea, salty as longing, too deep to fathom, too far to reach. 'It was this outpost,' she said.

'What was this outpost?'

'Ten years ago,' June said. 'When Mara left.'

Keira's hand landed soft and heavy on June's shoulder. 'I didn't think you'd recognised it,' she said. 'It was so long ago. One outpost looks so much like another.'

'Where's the break in the fence where Mara got through?'

'Not far.'

'Show me,' June said.

Keira steered her by her shoulder, fingers squeezing slightly as they reached the furthest stretch of fence.

They nodded to Michaels, up on the lookout, as they passed. The fence was unbroken, high and shining in the morning light. Weathered wooden posts spat splinters and the wire was rusted from so many rainy summers, but it held. It had to hold.

Keira looked out across the fence and June looked at Keira. When she stopped June was so close she stood on her toes.

'You okay?'

Two hands on her shoulders to steady her.

'Of course.' She shook Keira off. 'It was right here?'

Keira gave a quick nod. There was no indication the fence had ever been breached, but they were experts at repairs, the lot of them. Iron grips on pliers and hammers since they were girls. June looped two fingers around a coil of wire. It sang under her skin. Waves breaking on a distant shore, the sound of seabirds. It was supposed to be them, together.

Keira pointed. 'Heidi went after her. Three things came at us, there, there, and there. They were fast. We almost missed them.' A split-second pause. 'It was like she'd planned it.'

Beyond the fence, all was clear except a niggle in June's memory, bright like a migraine.

She spoke slowly. 'How'd you know where our ruck-sack was?'

'What?'

'The one we hid. The one Mara took.'

Keira let out a breath on the ghost of a smile. 'You know how it is now,' she said. 'Kids think they have so many secrets. But somebody always knows.'

'Right.'

'Kids think they're so careful. But we hear their whispers, see their kisses.'

June kept her eyes on the fence. 'And I'm sure they see ours.'

'Maybe. Does it matter?'

June let out a mirthless laugh. 'Not anymore.'

Keira's hand was back on her shoulder. 'They'll make it,' she said. 'The others. They will.'

June said nothing. Keira ran her hand down the length of June's arm, squeezed her wrist, turned to leave. 'I knew you'd never do it,' she said over her shoulder.

'Do what?'

'Go with her.'

'How's that?' June's voice cut, but Keira was used to it.

'You would've died out there. Just like she did.'

'You don't know that. You don't know she didn't make it.'

Keira scoffed, turned to face her. 'Oh, come on, June. Of course I know it. We all knew it from the start.' She spread her hands, spun on her heel again. She tossed the words behind her like grenades. 'Mara's death was inevitable.'

June partnered with Pam that evening, sparring heavy in front of the kids, showing them how it was done. Circling, lunging, ducking, blocking. She pushed Pam harder than normal, kept up a speed Pam wasn't used to, threw her to the ground and waited for her shouted yield.

'What's got into you?' Keira asked as the kids cheered, partnered off quickly to try for themselves, coached by Pam, red-faced and breathless.

'We need to be stronger.' June ran a sleeve along her brow. 'If we're the only ones left. You want to go a round too?'

Bright sparks of feral joy in Keira's eyes. 'I thought you'd never ask.'

Beaten, bruised and aching, they continued that night in Keira's bunk, fast and silent, full of furious desire, June only leaving when dawn started to tinge the sky. Her head was singing like the fence wire, iron and salt.

June took the dawn shift, relieved Michaels at the western lookout. Beyond the fence, all was calm. Low grey sky throwing dim light on the landscape. June jumped down to check the nearby posts, wind-splintered but still strong. The rusted wire hummed its siren song.

There it was, now. Slight seam where once there might have been a tear. It would have taken boltcutters rather than pliers to wrench it open, but June had time. Hands finding their grip, knowing just where to let the wire rip and twist. It was good work, this mending, well done. There was better work in the undoing.

The memory of Mara's voice whispered in from a decade ago with the sea breeze, still so far away but June could taste it.

Will you miss them?

Yes.

But you're still coming?

Of course.

Aloud, June whispered, 'Only corpses stay.'

Mara held her rifle tightly, walking steady behind Keira, followed by Heidi, uncomfortable with the whole situation. She was used to June leading. Five or six others in a loose line behind them. Unbidden, the memory of each pair of boots now marching on the frozen ground behind her stamping into her skin. Eleven years old, curled around her softest parts, feet landing on her back, her legs, her shoulders. She'd held her ground for longer than the others had expected, and they kicked her all the harder for it, for refusing to lay down when they told her. But Mara never did what she was told.

Every sound was loud. Keira's breath, the swish of Heidi's legs, the birds beyond the slightly singing fence. It had always reminded Mara of the sea.

Ten days and they'd see it. Her and June. The sea, and whatever lay beyond it. Mara could almost smell the salt.

Keira signalled to the two girls perched at the lookout. They signalled back, all clear, then made another, furtive gesture that Mara couldn't interpret.

'Okay,' Keira said, voice set. 'Let's do this.'

Mara forced an eyeroll, a performative yawn. 'Do what?' she said. 'Fence is fine.'

They were closer, suddenly, the others. Heidi and Keira hemming her in.

'Okay,' Mara said, backing up and hating herself for it, heart beating quickly in her throat. 'What is this?'

Keira didn't answer, instead threw the words carelessly over her shoulder, 'Cass, fetch the boltcutters.'

Mara instinctively widened her stance, found her balance, raised her fists slightly and cast around for an easy exit.

Keira chuckled, low and humourless. 'Not so easy to wiggle out of things when June isn't around to save you, is it?' she asked.

Mara's grin was flat, grim. 'You set this up.'

'Caught on, have you?'

Cass returned into Mara's line of vision with the bolt-cutters slung like a rifle over her shoulder.

'Heidi, help her,' Keira said, eyes not leaving Mara's face.

'You gonna tell me what you're doing?' Mara tossed at her. 'Since I'm obviously outnumbered. Again.'

'It's nothing personal,' said Heidi, holding a portion of the fence steady so Cass could cut it. 'You're just a bad egg, Mara. You're holding us all back.'

Mara didn't break Keira's stare. 'Holding June back,' she said softly.

Keira grinned. 'Got it in one,' she whispered.

Mara swallowed. 'So what's the plan?' Her voice barely shook, still that hard edge of bravado to her words, never ceding ground. 'Beat me up again? Put me out of action? Or are you just going to kill me this time?'

Keira and Heidi exchanged a look that intentionally excluded the others. Something passed between them and Keira gave the barest of shrugs.

'Up to you, really,' she said casually. 'We don't have to kill you.'

The slightest loosen in Mara's shoulders.

'But,' Keira went on, 'you aren't coming back.'

Cass had finished with the fence. Half-metre gap in the wire, stretched wide open like a mouth.

'Out you go,' said Keira, and Mara raised her fists higher.

Heidi took up her rifle. 'Don't make this hard on yourself, Mara,' she said.

The others closed around her in tight formation, bigger, older, stronger. Silent and watchful. Obviously hand-chosen. No one with even passing sympathy towards her. Mara was eleven years old again. It didn't matter that she was fast, that she fought dirty. It only mattered that she was outnumbered. And that June wasn't there.

'What are you going to tell her?' she asked, stalling for time, still trying to find a way to escape.

Keira watched her assess the situation, watched her understand the game was up. There was no way Mara could get out of this.

'Here's what happened,' Keira said. 'There was a rupture in the fence. You saw your chance. You'd been planning to defect for months. Years, maybe. You ran out. Slipped through the gap. A few of us tried to follow but we had to tear the fence open even more. You were so much smaller than us.' Keira grinned. 'Thin and wriggly. Little snake. But we went after you. Almost immediately, attracted by the sounds of our shouts, a thing came out of the darkness. By the time we'd killed it, you were gone.'

'We did our best,' Heidi added. 'But we heard another thing in the distance. Maybe more than one. We heard you scream. We knew you were gone.'

'So really,' said Keira, 'it didn't matter that you'd defected. That you'd abandoned your team in the heat of the action. We tried to save you anyway. You died as one of us. We are ready to mourn you as a friend.'

Mara's head was high, her hands in fists. 'Fuck you,' she spat.

'No thanks,' said Keira. She nodded to the hole in the fence. 'Better hurry, or the things will get in.'

Heidi raised her rifle.

Mara opened her mouth to scream but Keira's hand clamped on top of it.

'If you make this hard for us,' Keira breathed hot in her ear, 'I will kill you.'

Heaving chest, hard breaths, faces close together.

Mara bit down.

Keira bellowed, smacked Mara across the face with the back of her bleeding hand. She staggered, almost fell. Shook her head sharply to clear her vision. Ears ringing, Mara flew at Keira, all teeth and nails, almost fearless, out to hurt. Ring of girls around them, shouting. Voices ringing through the torn gap in the fence. Even the two up on lookout were watching.

Mara kept close, jabbed punches, carefully aimed kicks, seeking out the soft spots. Keira roared her frustration, tore Mara away from her and flung her against the fence. One arm hard on her windpipe. Mara's hands scrambled, fingernails breaking in Keira's skin. Against her skull, the fence sang like the sea.

There was a roaring in June's head. Waves crashing on rocks. In one hand, slid out from under the tongue of her boot, was a map, tightly scrolled. In the other, the tools she needed to mend the fence behind her. From far off in the wilderness, things circling, as always, coming close to the fence and then retreating, watching for a break, waiting for a mistake. The sound of them was closer already. She shifted her shoulders to feel the reassuring weight of her rifle.

She could mend the fence. Like Keira did after Mara left. The next kid wouldn't come to relieve her watch for hours yet. She had time.

So seamlessly. Keira knitting the fence wire back together after Mara, slipping into Mara's spot on June's bed, nudging the memory of Mara aside in her heart.

She left, June. She left without you.

I knew you'd never go with her.

She could mend the fence like Mara surely meant to. *It was like she'd planned it.* Keira's knowing eyes. Snarls in the distance.

June shouldered her tools and moved out, leaving the fence open, unstaffed and torn.

She reached the outpost late on the tenth day. Crested a cliff and there it was: real, although it felt like a mirage.

At first sight it was practically derelict: half the roof missing, training yard overgrown with neck-high weeds and rushes, sand blown in every crevice. The remains of where the fence once stood was marked out in rotted posts, tumbled like teeth. There were no signs of life except the gulls, screaming. Still, June shouldered her rifle before she approached.

Out past the side of the south barracks the cliff ended in a sudden drop where before there had probably been more training fields, a prefab or two long dashed onto the rocks. The sea surged, spilled over, beat itself against the base of the cliff, relentless. The landscape was unsteady, eroded more from year to year.

As in almost every outpost, the south barracks was the first to fall to ruin. The fewer new kids there were, the more adults died off, the less space they needed. June picked her way over weeds and rubble, the layout of this place as familiar as any other. Similar offices. Similar corridors. Similar now-empty bunkrooms, the wood of the beds long since broken up for fires.

Quick sweep: everything empty. There was no water in the taps but a well out back. There were no rations in the kitchen but a can and a half of petrol in the base-ment. With a bit of grease and her biceps straining, June cranked a rusty lever and the generator thrummed to life. Let the things hear her. Death was inevitable if there was nowhere beyond this outpost. Only corpses stayed.

A faded map still stuck to a wall, half crumbled. Underneath it, the dust was disturbed. June trained her eyes on the ground around her. It was scuffed and trampled. Maybe by the things, maybe by some animal. Ten years. Maybe Mara had made it.

The roaring of the sea wasn't just in her head. There was a corridor connecting the crumbling south barracks with the north building, away from the cliffs. June followed the disturbed dust through the office to what was left of the corridor beyond, along the hall and into the last room at the end, the one furthest from the sharp drop to the sea.

The room was fortified, a cell maybe, once, although it also locked from the inside. A bunker, then. An escape if the things breached the barracks. In one corner, the remains of a fire. Along another wall, shelves of rations missing from the kitchen. Barrels of water. Small stove. Utilitarian bathroom behind a shuttered screen.

And Mara. Or what was left of her.

That same defiance.

It had been ten years. And Mara had stayed.

The summoning

So say. Just for instance. Somebody. Not Katie. Had like. Summoned an interdimensional demon from some kind of hell-world. And like. Unleashed it on earth. (Definitely not Katie.) That would be. Like. Not entirely the worst thing somebody – definitely not Katie – could do.

Because. For instance. Earth as it was wasn't particularly great. Really. So maybe, in fact, this person. (Not Katie.) Would actually be doing the earth a favour. By summoning this demon.

The demon was actually. Pretty small. (Not that Katie would know, not ever having summoned an interdimensional demon from some kind of hell-world.) Like, small as Katie small. And kind of. Human shaped.

Girl shaped.

Kind of. Hot-girl shaped.

Not that Katie would know.

Or think a girl could be hot.

Even less an interdimensional demon from some kind of hell-world.

Was it getting warm in here?

It was just. There was this portal. And somebody. (Not Katie.) Might have accidentally left it open. The portal. To some kind of hell-world. So really it wasn't as if Katie had actually. Summoned. Anything. Just sort of. Left the door unlocked. So to speak. It's not like it was an invitation. Really.

(But like. Really hot-girl shaped. You have to understand.)

(This grin. Right? Like. As if that mouth was hiding fangs. The good kind. Not that Katie would be into that. But like. Cocky-ass grin. Sharp teeth. And hair? Like, billows of it. Layers. Real silky. Like. Run-your-hands-through-it-and-sigh silky. Not that Katie ever thought of running her hands through girls' silky hair and sighing. Because. Like. Ew. Gay.)

Anyway this demon. Not the worst thing to happen to the earth by a long shot. With her silky hair and her sharp grin and her. Uh. Real tight clothes. Just stepping out of the portal like it was a dressing room door and the world was a stage.

It took a while for Katie to close her mouth. Because. Like. Tight clothes. Shiny hair.

In her defence! Matt was also staring. But possibly. Like. Because of the interdimensional demon from some kind of hell-world. Thing. Which was true! Like. Very demon! Very interdimensional portal! Very fire-and-brimstone behind her, puffing smoke all around the drama society's black-box theatre under lecture hall C. It was. Very impressive. Katie has to admit. Very scary.

And then out walked this girl.

Demon.

Interdimensional demon from some kind of hell-world.

Tight clothes.

Shiny hair.

That smile.

Not Katie's kind of thing. Because. Obviously. But if it had been. Hoo boy.

When she opened her mouth. The interdimensional demon from some kind of hell-world. Her voice was. Well. Deep and growly. But like. Also feminine? Like. Girl demon. Growly voice. It was all very overwhelming.

The demon said, WHO HAS SUMMONED ME.

And Matt. (Katie was going to kill Matt.) Said. 'Katie, it was Katie, here, look, this is my friend Katie she opened the portal and summoned you I'm just going to. Like. Go now, okay?'

And Matt just. Disappeared. Up the lower ground floor fire exit staircase underneath lecture hall C. Leaving Katie totally alone with the demon she'd just summoned.

Katie said, 'He–ey?'

The interdimensional demon from some kind of hell-world cocked her head. (Shiny hair fell over one bare shoulder and Katie. Like. Didn't even notice.) She said, HEY.

Katie played it. Very cool. Very suave. Super smooth. The most confident. She said, 'Uhhhhh.'

Which. You really can't go blaming her for. Because. Like. Demon! Literal interdimensional demon from some kind of hell-world! You try forming coherent sentences when faced with that shiny hair. That is to say. Fire and brimstone. Very intimidating. Very scary. Took Katie's whole entire breath away.

The sound of Matt's footsteps echoed down the fire exit staircase.

The demon said, WHAT DIMENSION IS THIS and Katie felt the demon's voice go all the way to her. Uh. Toes.

'Uh,' Katie said. 'Like. Earth?' In a not-at-all-squeaky, totally normal voice.

The demon looked around the drama society's black-box theatre under lecture hall C with a very unimpressed expression. Which like. Okay. Point noted. If you were going to summon an interdimensional demon from some kind of hell-world. (Which Katie totally. Absolutely didn't do.) Probably you shouldn't summon them into the drama society's black-box theatre under lecture hall C if you wanted to impress them. Which Katie absolutely didn't. Want to impress. This interdimensional demon from some kind of hell-world. With the very shiny hair. Very tight clothes. Sharp smile. Growly voice.

Did Katie mention the hair?

OKAY, said the demon. NOT EXACTLY WHAT I WAS EXPECTING.

Her voice vibrated.

Like.

Vibrated.

Anyway.

'Uh,' said Katie. Still sort of. Processing. The vibrations. 'Uhh.'

USUALLY, said the demon, THERE'S A CEREMONY.

'Oh,' said Katie. 'Uh.'

LIKE. WITH ROBES, said the demon. AND CHANTING.

'I can. Uh. Chant,' said Katie. 'If you want.'

(Which. No Katie couldn't. Fucking. Chant. She wouldn't know a chant if it bit her in the ass. She barely even remembered her prayers from school. Katie? Was a dumbass. There was no way she could follow through on this. She knew this. Why did she fucking say it? Who the fuck knows.)

(Katie knows. It was because of the hair.)

The demon shrugged. THAT'S OKAY, she said. I WAS NEVER REALLY INTO THE CHANTING.

She stepped out of the chalk circle.

Katie blinked. The demon wasn't supposed to be able to step out of the chalk circle. Shit. Shitshitshit. Katie had screwed up.

'Uh,' she said. 'How did you. I mean. How can you. Do that?'

DO WHAT, asked the demon.

(*Vibrated*. The demon. Katie just. She just. Had to take a minute.)

'Uh,' said Katie. 'Uhhh. How did you step out of the circle?'

The demon glanced down at her long, long legs in the very tight clothes and looked confused. I MEAN, she said, WITH MY LEGS? DO YOU NOT WALK WITH LEGS IN THIS DIMENSION?

'No sure,' said Katie. 'Sure. Totally. We do. Absolutely. With our.' She looked down the length of the demon to her long, long legs in the very tight clothes and back up, with difficulty. 'Uh. Legs. Uhhh. But like. You weren't? Supposed? To be able to step out of the chalk circle?'

The demon looked back at the scuff of blackboard chalk on the floor behind her. OH THAT, she said. YEAH. SORRY. YOUR CONTAINMENT SPELL WASN'T VERY GOOD.

'Oh,' said Katie. Shitshitshit.

The demon looked apologetic. I MEAN, she said, I CAN TEACH YOU, IF YOU LIKE. TO CAST A BETTER ONE, I MEAN. IT'S ALL IN THE WRISTS.

Okay.

All in the.

Okay.

Katie took a breath.

'Sure,' she squeaked.

IT JUST TAKES A BIT OF PRACTICE, said the demon encouragingly. WAS THIS YOUR FIRST TIME?

Katie took. Another breath. Quick breath. More of a gasp really. Not quite in the region of a splutter. This was fine.

'Noooo,' Katie said. 'No. Nope. Totally not. I like. Have summoned. So many demons. Dozens of demons. Scores.' Which was more, dozens or scores? Fuck. Didn't matter. 'I'm just out here,' Katie said. 'Summoning demons three times a week. Sometimes four.'

The demon laughed. The laughter vibrated even more than her voice.

Katie just.

She just.

Uhhhh.

Anyway.

The demon said, YOU'RE FUNNY. I LIKE THAT. And she took two steps closer to Katie. MAYBE THIS PLACE ISN'T SO BAD AFTER ALL.

Katie. Was absolutely fine. With this proximity. Absolutely.

TO BE HONEST, the demon went on, IT'S KINDA NICE TO BE OUT OF THE HELL-WORLD FOR A BIT.

'Sure,' said Katie. Her voice was. So steady. So suave. 'I can imagine.'

(Well, actually. Katie couldn't imagine wanting to be out of some kind of hell-world because any hell-world was better than. You know. This one.)

SO, said the interdimensional demon from some kind of hell-world. WHAT DO YOU DO FOR FUN AROUND HERE.

'Fun,' Katie said. Katie had fun. Katie was a very fun person. Super fun. She was fun and also cool and knew where all the. Cool. Fun. Things to do were around campus. 'Uh. Yeah. I guess. There's. The sports bar? And, uh. The student bar? They do cans? You can sometimes. Sit outside? If that's your kind of thing?'

HMM, said the demon.

(Vibrations. So many vibrations.)

SURE, said the demon. OR. And here her smile got fucking *wicked*. (Katie's knees went weak.) WE COULD TAKE OVER THE CAMPUS AND BEND ITS INHABITANTS TO OUR WILL.

If this were a cartoon, Katie's eyes would have been hearts. 'Oh,' she said. 'Yeah. I'm into it if you are.'

★

So say. Just for instance. Somebody. Not Katie. Had like. Agreed to take over the campus of one of the leading Irish universities with an interdimensional demon from some kind of hell-world. And like. Bend its inhabitants to their will. (Definitely not Katie.) That would be. Like. Maybe not even in the top five worst things somebody definitely not Katie could do.

Because. For instance. A lot of the inhabitants of this particular university were like. Pretty awful. Like. Actually really awful. (Katie could tell you. Katie has stories.) And like. If the bending of the inhabitants of the campus to their will thing was going to happen. (And Katie's not saying it was her who made it happen.) Half past eleven on a Wednesday night was probably the best possible time for it. Because like. All the sound heads had already gone home. Except Katie. And she guesses Matt. And the interdimensional demon from some kind of hell-world, who, it turns out? Pretty sound! Probably a lot sounder than. Like. Seventy-five per cent of the people currently on campus! So actually? No harm done!

The demon took Katie's hand. (Hand in hand. This was normal. This was fine.) And pulled her towards the lower-ground-floor fire exit staircase underneath lecture hall C. When Katie turned back the portal had disappeared, the drama society's black-box theatre just smoking slightly. Katie allowed herself a small smile. She would've been fine if the whole thing'd just burned to the ground.

SO, said the interdimensional demon from some kind of hell-world. WHERE DO YOU WANT TO START?

Her hand was. Right in Katie's hand. Like. Right in there. Palm to palm like something Shakespearean. Katie fought the urge to interlace their fingers.

'Me?' Katie said. (Not squeaked. She totally had the squeaking under control by now.)

YES, said the demon, clearly amused. YOU.

The *vibrations*.

'Me,' Katie breathed. The demon's hand was hot in hers. It was particularly difficult to concentrate with the demon's hand hot in hers.

YOU'RE THE ONE WHO SUMMONED ME, offered the demon.

Which like. Point: Katie did not actually. Summon. The –

So. Fuck it. Okay.

Maybe Katie did. Slightly. Summon the interdimensional demon from some kind of hell-world. But in her defence! She never actually thought it would work! Also! What lonely nerd hasn't tried to open a portal in her university basement! Right? I mean. There's a reason it's a stereo-type! It's practically standard!

(Not that Katie was lonely. Or a nerd! And not that there was anything wrong with being a nerd! Or! Or lonely! There was nothing wrong at all! With Katie!)

(Despite what the rest of the drama society! (Except Matt.) Kept fucking saying!)

(And like. Writing on the toilet stall walls. And on the class forums. And in emails to the two (2) girls in the drama society Katie had seriously thought about kissing and then made the mistake of admitting to seriously thinking about kissing during a rather inebriated game of truth or dare last Freshers' Week. Which. Okay. Katie shouldn't have done. (See above point: Katie is a dumbass.) And like. They said was a joke and Katie gets jokes so she sort of laughed it off and then locked herself in one of the science block toilet stalls with only minimal graffiti about. Like. How to cheat on your college exams without getting caught. And ugly cried for like. Fifty minutes.)

(Afterwards even Matt said she was being too sensitive.)

Katie pressed her palm harder against the demon's. She said, 'I know where I want to start.'

*

So say. Just for instance. Somebody. Maybe Katie. Had led an interdimensional demon from some kind of hell-world to the student bar where the least sound heads of the drama society of a leading Irish university drank on weekday nights because they survived on pure superiority complexes and not. Like. Sleep. Or a working liver. Or a passing grade. Or whatever. And that interdimensional demon from some kind of hell-world then just. Stood in the threshold of the student bar for a few moments and just. Looked around at them with something very like disgust. Still holding Katie's hand in hers. That would be. Like. The next logical thing to do.

Because. For instance. It wasn't exactly. Like. Good practice. To keep a demon waiting. Katie didn't know a whole lot about demons but she could figure that much out by herself. (Especially not when said demon was so. Uh. Intimidating. With her growly voice and her shiny hair and her tight, tight clothes.)

The least sound heads of the drama society were drinking steadily and talking loudly on three couches and a grotty armchair around a low table. One of them was Matt.

Katie saw red.

Fucking Matt. Traitor. Brutus. Judas fucking Iscariot. Who does that? Who just. Helps to summon an inter-dimensional demon from some kind of hell-world? To like. Unleash it on earth? And then just. Abandons? Their co-summoner? For the fucking least sound heads of the drama society in the grotty old student bar at half past eleven on a Wednesday night?

Matt, that's who.

WHAT'S THE MATTER, asked the interdimensional demon from some kind of hell-world, noticing the change in Katie's expression.

'Ugh,' Katie said. 'You see that guy? The one in the red jacket? With the kind of. Dumb floppy hair?'

YES, growled the interdimensional demon from some kind of hell-world, immediately glaring daggers at Matt's dumb floppy hair. I SEE THAT GUY.

It was. A very low growl.

Did Katie.

Did Katie mention.

The effect. That voice. Had on her?

Katie. Uh. Refocused. With considerable effort. 'He, uh. He's supposed to be my friend. He helped me summon you. And then just. Like. Fled,' she said. She looked at Matt and the other unsound drama heads and her eyes narrowed. 'You asked where to start?' Katie said to the demon. 'I say we start right here.'

EXCELLENT. The demon took Katie's chin in the hand not holding Katie's hand. And she just.

She just.

Lowered her lips to Katie's.

And kissed her.

Just.

Like.

Fucking.

Kissed her.

In the doorway to the student bar.

Right in.

Right in front of.

Right in front of at least one-third of the active (and least sound) members of the drama society.

There were. Lips and. Hot breath. And. Was that her tongue? And. Hot hand in Katie's honestly right now pretty much equally hot hand that was getting kind of clammy actually was it hot in here? It was so. So hot in here.

The demon pulled away too quickly.

Katie swayed. The demon's hand still holding her chin. The taste of the demon's lips still on Katie's mouth.

The demon smiled her wickedest fucking smile yet.

Katie couldn't.

She just.

She couldn't.

From the table around which the least sound heads of the drama society (and Matt) were clustered there came an incredulous. *Look at that.* Kind of noise. Which Katie mostly ignored, because. Like. Demon. Kissing. Hot lips. Hot hands. Shiny. Shiny hair. Wicked fucking smile.

When Katie's one remaining brain cell finally started firing up again she noticed Matt's dumbstruck look. He wasn't the only one. More than a few non-sound jaws hit the floor.

Katie didn't puff up like those spherical fucking fish in cartoons. Not Katie. Katie was. Very chill. Very cool. With the incredibly hot interdimensional demon from some kind of hell-world on her arm. Katie totally. Acted like this happened every day. Just going around. Kissing girls in student bar doorways. Just. Holding hands like it was nothing. Like it was like: What? Oh *this* interdimensional demon from some kind of hell-world? This one here? Yeah? Totally here with Katie.

'Yo, Katie,' called the least sound of the least sound heads of the drama society from his ragged student bar armchair throne. 'Who's your friend?'

'Yeah, Katie,' chimed in the fourth-least sound head from her perch on the least sound head's armchair arm. 'Who's the *girl*?'

'That's right, Katie,' said the second-least sound head, his voice dripping with something better left on the sole of a shoe. 'Come introduce us. We won't bite.'

'Much,' muttered the third-least sound head from the inside of her half-empty pint glass.

The interdimensional demon from some kind of hell-world raised a delicate, perfect eyebrow and tossed her shiny hair over her bare, perfect shoulder. Katie only slightly melted. Barely visibly melted. Her hand had totally not crossed the line from clammy to sweaty. (Katie is not going to tell you what was happening in her underwear.)

WOW, said the demon. THESE GUYS ARE PRICKS.

'Right?' said Katie, after swallowing. Several times. 'Bending them to our will would honestly be the best thing to happen to this shitty place.'

AGREED, said the demon, and she squeezed Katie's (totally not sweaty) hand. SO COME ON, KATIE. INTRODUCE US.

So Katie just. Walked up to the drama heads. Hand in hand with a hot-girl-shaped demon. Just. Totally cool. Very casual. Very about to take over the student bar and bend the least sound heads of the drama society to her will. Which she had. Like. Totally not been dreaming about since the like fourth time they had lied to her about when to come help paint the newest sets since she'd obviously never get a part in any play and she arrived several hours later than everyone else who'd already formed airtight cliques and she kind of just laughed it off because nobody likes a paranoid, oversensitive nerd right?

(That's what Matt said, anyway, and Matt was the one who was actually her friend. And like. He kept getting cast in background parts. And was told the right time to show up to help with the sets. And tagged along to house parties sometimes too, recently. So like. He clearly knew what he was talking about.)

The least sound heads of the drama society stared at Katie and the demon's approach because the demon. (Katie could attest to this.) Was even hotter up close. (Katie had been up close to the demon. So close. The closest. Katie had kissed the demon, has she mentioned? Right there in front of everyone. They were still totally holding hands.)

Matt, however, wouldn't meet Katie's eyes. He kind of just picked at the edges of a soggy beer mat.

'Hey, Matt,' Katie said, and her voice was hard.

Matt muttered something that might have been *Hey, Katie.*

The interdimensional demon from some kind of hell-world watched this interaction and her eyes were small flames. She interlaced her fingers with Katie's. Totally not sweat-slippery. Fingers. And pulled her over to the couch where Matt sat. The least sound heads of the drama society were talking at the demon but the demon was staring daggers at Matt and ignored the rest of them. She pushed Katie down onto the couch and just. Sat down. On Katie's lap. Just. Sat her. Uh. Tight, tight clothed. Uhhh. Ass. Right on Katie's legs. Katie nearly choked on her own spit.

Now Matt looked at her.

SO, said the interdimensional demon from some kind of hell-world, stroking Katie's hair with her hot, hot hand. (Katie. Uh. Might have slightly lost conscious thought at this point.) The demon's voice was dangerous. YOU'RE KATIE'S . . . FRIEND.

'I –' Matt said. 'Yeah?'

For some reason the rest of the unsound heads of the drama society snickered a bit at this. The demon narrowed her eyes.

REALLY, she said.

'Uh,' said Matt. (Maybe he was also feeling the vibrations.)

IS THIS WHAT PASSES FOR FRIENDSHIP IN THIS DIMENSION, the demon said to the world at large (and the student bar at small). She looked into Katie's eyes and Katie just. Couldn't breathe.

Katie's voice was strangled. 'Told you this was a shitty dimension,' she whispered.

The demon raised one eyebrow and smiled just for Katie. I UNDERSTAND WHY YOU SUMMONED ME NOW, she said.

And then the demon just. Like. Reached out from where she was sitting on Katie's lap, which was a completely cool and normal thing for Katie and she was not already running detailed unprompted fantasies in the back of her mind that included lap-sitting and demon-voice vibrations and how those tight, tight clothes actually came off. And snapped Matt's neck with one hand.

There was a.

Crunch.

And Matt fell back against the grotty student bar couch beside them, eyes wide open.

Nobody screamed. They didn't believe it. At that point. They probably like. Thought it was some kind of. Performance art. Audition. Or some shit.

Nobody moved for a minute. (Katie couldn't have moved if she'd tried and there was no way she was going to try when the demon's shiny, shiny hair was flowing over Katie's own shoulder and Katie's not at all sweaty hands were around the demon's sleek hips in those tight, tight clothes.)

But when the interdimensional demon from some kind of hell-world turned to the rest of the least sound heads of the drama society and said. (In her deep. Growly. But yet feminine. Vibrating voice.) RIGHT SO. WHO'S NEXT. That's when the screaming started.

Look.

Okay.

Katie's not saying she didn't feel remorse. She did. Of course she did. Katie's not a monster.

But you have to understand.

Katie never expected any of this to happen!

The hand-holding! The kissing! The lap-sitting! Did Katie mention the kissing!

The hot-girl-shaped interdimensional demon from some kind of hell-world with the shiny, shiny hair and the tight, tight clothes and the. Uh. The uh. Tongue in Katie's mouth back there for a second Katie swears.

So like. The murder was kind of. Secondary? Then? Kind of? In the gamut of new experiences Katie was having that night?

And like. In her defence! Matt had also summoned an interdimensional demon from some kind of hell-world to unleash it on earth! Matt was entirely complicit in the summoning! It wasn't Katie's fault he'd run off when the portal opened! That was very bad demon-summoning etiquette! Katie didn't know much about demons. (Except like. How to kiss them. Because Katie had kissed the demon, did Katie mention? The demon was still. Totally sitting on Katie's lap.) But she knew that much.

The demon got up from Katie's lap and clicked her fingers and the doors to the student bar shut by themselves. The locks clicked with the same crack Matt's neck had made.

There was. Panic. Total fucking pandemonium.

The demon's wicked grin was fucking *delighted*.

Then there were.

More screams.

Flames.

And blood.

Some. Like. Katie guesses. Disembowelment?

And a lot more screams.

And exposed bones from torn-off limbs.

Still more screaming.

And every few minutes the demon would just. Slink on over to Katie on the couch. All covered in blood and bits of brain. And kiss her full on the mouth. And Katie would grin and the demon would go right back to taking over the student bar and bending its occupants to her will and Katie's grin was just. So wide. So pleased. Because this demon? This limb-tearing. Disembowelling. Neck-breaking. Jugular-tearing. Head-smashing. Interdimensional demon from some kind of hell-world? Was here with her. With Katie. And they were taking over campus together. Hand in hot, hot hand.

It was like.

So great.

Just so so great.

★

So say. Just for instance. Somebody. (Katie.) Had intentionally summoned an interdimensional demon from some kind of hell-world. And like. Unleashed it on earth. (Still Katie.) That would be. Like. Actually a pretty understandable thing for Katie to do.

Because. For instance. Taking over campus and bending its inhabitants to the demon's will. (And Katie's.) Was a completely reasonable response to the absolute shit Katie had to deal with. On a daily basis. The demon agreed! So. You know. That definitely counted for something.

When the interdimensional demon from some kind of hell-world was done taking over the student bar and bending its occupants to its will she was. Understandably tired. That much murder will really take it out of a demon.

She lay across Katie's lap on the gore-splattered couch of the trashed and bloodied student bar and kissed Katie's lips and then her neck and then her. Ohgod. So. Like. There was this one spot just in under Katie's jaw and uh. Ohgodohgod. Katie absolutely did not make some kind of high whining noise because like. That would be embarrassing. And Katie was. So smooth. So experienced. So totally a natural at

137

pulling on the interdimensional demon from some kind of hell-world's shiny, shiny hair so she'd press her teeth to that. Exact. Spot. Again. And pull her hips so close to Katie's Katie thought she might spontaneously combust.

WELL, said the demon when she finally pulled back from Katie's red-marked neck and (let's be real here) even redder face. DISEMBOWELLING ALWAYS GIVES ME AN APPETITE.

'Uh,' Katie just about got out. Not moaned. No moaning here nope no way. 'Uhhh. Okay. Yeah. Uh. We could. Uh. Get some pizza? Or. Or something?'

The demon grinned fondly at Katie. NOT THE KIND OF APPETITE I HAD IN MIND.

Katie's brain just. Like. Fucking short-circuited.

The demon kissed her lips again.

THIS WAS FUN AND ALL, the demon said. AND I KNOW WE SAID WE'D TAKE OVER THE WHOLE CAMPUS. BUT DO YOU WANT TO COME BACK TO MY PLACE FIRST?

'Uh,' said Katie. 'Uhhh. Sure?'

I CAN JUST KILL THE REST OF THEM AS WE GO, offered the demon. OR WE CAN CONTROL THEM FOR THE REST OF ETERNITY AND RULE AS THEIR QUEENS.

'Cool,' Katie choked out. 'That uh. That second one sounds good.'

OKAY, said the demon. JUST GIVE ME A MINUTE. She kissed Katie's lips quick again. DON'T GO ANYWHERE.

Without you? Katie thought. But didn't say. Because hello. Needy much? *Never.*

The demon was gone for barely half an hour. Campus was awfully quiet on the way back to the drama society's black-box theatre under lecture hall C. On the walls of the lower-ground floor the photos of the drama society committee members had been shuffled around and replaced. Some just about covered bloodstains. In the lecture halls and corridors there were posters of Katie and the demon. They were. Very flattering. Not entirely realistic. Of Katie, at least. The demon was true to hot-girl-shaped life. On the noticeboards Katie caught a glimpse of the new curriculum. She smiled to herself, then at the demon. The demon smiled right back.

★

So say. Just for instance. Somebody. Like for example Katie. Had like. Summoned an interdimensional demon from some kind of hell-world and unleashed her on earth. And then had like. Kissed her for like. Several amazing hours. (This was Katie this happened to Katie this whole thing involved Katie and a very hot-girl-shaped demon and it was just. So so good. So good. I don't know that

139

Katie's explained enough how good it was.) That would be. Like. Quite possibly the best fucking thing Katie could ever do.

Because. For instance. It turns out? When Katie visited her demon's hell-world? She discovered that. That hell-world? So much less hellish than earth was. Like. So. So much less. And the demons that lived in that hell-world? (One of those demons anyway. The only one that matters. Katie's demon. Katie's interdimensional demon from some kind of hell-world.) Actually really enjoyed kissing Katie? And not like. Making her feel weird about wanting to kiss her?

And the other inhabitants of the demon's hell-world all just. Seemed to like Katie too? (Not in a kissing way, don't be weird, Katie totally has a girlfriend now, did Katie mention she has a demon girlfriend whom she frequently kisses and also has sex with? Oh yeah. Damn right. You heard Katie. Katie has sex. With her girlfriend. Sex with her interdimensional demon girlfriend from some kind of hell-world.)

Anyway.

Those other demons also like. Didn't judge Katie for wanting to kiss a hot-girl-shaped demon even though she is also a girl?

(Although Katie's not. Like. Hot. Or a demon. Although her demon girlfriend begs to differ. On like. Both counts. Since Katie's really taken to disembowelling lately. She's actually getting. Pretty good at it. If she does say so herself.)

(Her demon girlfriend is like. So proud of her.)

So actually.

Really.

Not only was summoning an interdimensional demon from some kind of hell-world and unleashing her on earth and then taking over the campus of one of the leading Irish universities and bending its inhabitants to their will and then becoming the demon's girlfriend and joining her in living between her kind of hell-world that is pretty fucking heavenly compared to how earth used to be and earth itself where they both rule campus as queens and get cast as leads in every play and decide what time the sets get painted and also are invited to all the house parties and if anyone pisses them off they disembowel them the best thing Katie has ever done in her whole entire life. It was also better for all the sound heads on campus! You know? Having the least-sound heads gone? And for the earth in general! Because like. It's honestly so much better now! Don't you think? Katie agrees. Katie thinks so too. Katie and her interdimensional demon girlfriend from some kind of hell-world both think so.

And if you want to keep your bowels inside your body so do you.

Rath

In the beginning, there was the rath. Round mound of earth built on the bones of buildings filled with a million stones, left to settle into history. Fire and ashes, the captured scream of the sacrifice buried inside. That wasn't me. Don't you go thinking I died like that.

After I died they buried me standing. Wouldn't anybody dare to take a torch to me.

They cut off my breasts to form the peaks of mountains. When I pissed it made rivers. My cries have killed a hundred men. You do not know my hunger.

What do you think it will take to wake me?

★

It is summer and Elly's cardigan is falling off one freckled shoulder, hand in Trina's hand, running through the gaps in the bushes that tug at their clothes, small white scratches on summer-pinked skin, and this is how it starts.

In the beginning there is the rath, soft long grass of a hilltop sheltered from view by a ring of trees, a wide ditch; somewhere to the west, the road.

They say from the top of the rath you can see five counties, but unless you count the nipple-tips of far-off mountains that may be part of another county's range it's two, max, by Elly's reckoning.

Trina, honestly, could not care less.

Dermot's sister's boyfriend has sold them a little pebble of hash, hard nub wrapped in chewing-gum paper, and they are thirteen years old, haven't a notion how to roll it. But Elly pulls Trina up the rath, grass past knee-height and whispering around the frayed hems of their jeans as they trample across to the space between the two bent trees, which was once the entrance to the processional. The girls don't know this, of course. All they know is the summer evening chill on their skin, the sleeves of Elly's cardigan touching their joined palms, the cushion of grass in the spot they pick carefully so as to avoid the thistles that only grow around the edges, sharp in the ring ditch, never on the mound.

Elly pulls a half pack of cigarettes from a trouser pocket and Trina slips her penknife out of her bra, noting with satisfaction the impressed fluster on her best friend's face, the anticipation of which is exactly why she put it there in the first place. She has more than enough pockets, but there's something to having a blade that close to the breast.

They perform cigarette surgery, shave some of the hash off with Trina's penknife and roll it all back in again, faces focused, the picture of concentration if there was anyone else to see them. It is coming on to ten at night and there's barely a car goes by every hour here, even on the main road to the west. The sun hasn't yet set. It won't for another good while; tonight's the solstice, the longest day and the shortest night and Trina and Elly are going to spend it here, together, on the rath, and not go home till morning.

Scratch spark of a lighter coming to life.

'My mam's going to kill me,' Elly says, as though her mam's the murderous one.

Trina brushes it off with a thumb-flick, tobacco dust falling to her crossed knees. 'Your mam'll never know.'

'She'll smell it on me.'

'Stop being a baby.' Trina's inhale's sharp as a penknife and in the shadow of her cupped hand the cigarette tip glows.

'Stop pretending like you're so mature.'

Comfortable point of contention between them; they've worn these words into the dust already and it's barely been a year. Trina's kissed three boys, Elly none. Not for lack of wanting, or so she says, but Elly's got her fiddle lessons on Saturdays, speech and drama after school and ballet three times a week so when's she going to find time to kiss boys? Trina's got Dermot's GAA mates who'll give her a clumsy grope over her clothes for a fiver so sometimes she kisses them and she loves how hard it makes her sound to say it. Nub of shame under a white pulse of pride.

'Whining about your mam isn't doing you any favours here, princess,' Trina says lazily.

Elly'd love to have kissed some boys, let them feel her through a t-shirt and a bra stuffed carefully with the insides of an old teddy bear to make it look fuller. Elly's never liked being the good girl in this duo but there's no other role available so she sits back and takes it. Still, whenever she can she'll give her best friend a little dig, take her down a couple of pegs. Theirs is, in their experience, a completely standard relationship. All best friends carry around hard seeds of resentment. All best friends bicker until they figure out the exact words that'll cause real wounds, bring them out on special occasions and see at the end of the massacre who comes out on top.

'That tough-guy act doesn't work on me,' Elly throws back, but she knows that Trina's won. The side-eye she gives Elly over the cigarette, the carefree way she sprawls back on the grass, legs still crossed, arm outstretched to hand over the cigarette: a peace offering, a truce, an acknowledgement of Elly's defeat.

Elly's breath is fire when she inhales and after the first burning breath she finds she likes it. She imagines herself a dragon on this mound of a mountain, skin becoming scales. She imagines what it would be like to kiss with a mouth as hot as this.

When the cigarette is ashes and they are cutting apart the next one to roll again, Trina looks over at the far side of the rath and says, 'You know this place is haunted, right?'

Elly scoffs. 'Of course.'

'That kid from Dermot's sister's class died up here. And he wasn't the first.'

'My nana says it's a sacrifice. That the queen of the rath asks for one every year.'

'It's not every year.'

'It is.'

'How would you know anyway? Your nana's full of shit.'

And the shadow at the far end of the rath doesn't fade into the familiar shape of a deer or a person or a tree, but the two girls find themselves laughing so hard they can barely breathe, and as the shadow watches they let the hash and the laughter and the small spark of fear on the shortest night become a cover under which they can roll together in breathless mirth on the soft grass, elbows in sides and cheeks hitting hair and hands grazing breasts accidentally on purpose and when their lips finally meet they both know this is not one of the things they will ever bring up in a fight against the other because they are both implicated and already they foolishly think they will never speak of it again.

★

Haunted? I do not haunt this place. This place was built for me, by the hands of men who would have put their hands on me but instead were beaten by mine. I chained them together and brought them here to break their backs over the building. I do not haunt this mound, nor the long-rotten beams of the rock-stuffed structure beneath it. I do not haunt the rocks, or the long grass. I do not haunt the skulls of those buried beneath me.

I am so much more than a haunting.

★

It is summer and Elly sits on the mound of the rath by the ditch between thistles and waits for Trina, who is late. Ten at night already and the sky still light; longest day again. At half past Elly rolls a joint with the weed Gráinne's boyfriend sold her a few weeks ago. Thin lick of the skins, flick of the wrist to seal it. She lights up alone.

Three years they've been doing this: sneaking up to the rath for the shortest night, just the two of them: a small secret in the grand scheme of things. Couple of joints, bag of cans, two girls against the scant hours of darkness.

This year Dermot wanted to come too, jealousy paling his cheeks when Trina mentioned it, but Dermot's nana doesn't know where the rath is and Elly won't tell. She half-expects Trina to turn up with him anyway, just to spite her, but when a small figure approaches from the clutch of trees closest to the road she is alone.

'You're late,' Elly says when Trina's close enough to hear her. (Other things are close enough to hear her too but she only really knows this in the same way as she is aware of the dust motes on her glasses: something so common she can see right through them as if they weren't there.)

'As if you have anywhere else to be,' Trina answers.

'Did it really take that long to shake Dermot off?'

Trina drops to the grass beside her, plucks the joint out of Elly's fingers. 'It's over with Dermot,' she says.

'Since when? You were all over each other at lunch yesterday.'

They were constantly all over each other, and if it wasn't Dermot it was some other boy, he and Trina the centre of concentric circling friends, Elly always on the periphery.

Friendship with Trina had got harder, recently.

Short inhale, exhale so deep Elly wonders where Trina was hiding her breath all this time. 'Since an hour ago,' she says.

Elly takes the joint back and Trina busies herself with the cans. 'You're late because you were breaking up with Dermot again.'

Trina waves a can in her direction. 'Last time this time, though.'

'Huh.'

'He's such a lame-ass.'

'That hasn't changed. And you're a lame-ass for getting with him over and over.' Elly affects a yawn. Everything about Trina's new crowd is relentlessly boring. Rumours and drama and shitty house parties that always end in tears and vomit.

'And your ass is the lamest because you've never even *had* a boyfriend.'

Elly rolls her eyes. 'That shit doesn't work on me anymore, Trina.'

Trina shoves one shoulder into Elly's. 'Like hell it doesn't.'

Elly shoves her shoulder back so they're practically chest to chest, hearts aligned, as if their hearts'd ever be in line.

'Give me one of those.' Can of something cheap in one hand to balance the joint in the other. Slowly, the sky darkens and the shadows crowd around the trees that ring the rath.

It's always warmer, here. Latent heat of the day held in the long grass. Under the hill, a dragon, Elly thinks, although she doesn't mean it. This isn't a land of dragons. The more she smokes the more she thinks of that time, some months ago now, when she got bigger for a few minutes. Thinking of dragons under mountains and mouths of fire, Dermot and Trina making out across the yard, all tongues, and Trina's other friends egging them on. Elly'd felt so small, mouselike, the leftover sidekick from a kids' cartoon when everyone has outgrown it. She'd thought of the rath, then. Every summer solstice up on the hill and how she never really remembers coming home. Walking through the fields after school that day she saw her shadow lengthen. Broaden. Felt her bones groan. Felt the urge to run. Not away, little mouse that she was, but towards. Across the fields faster than a horse could. Over hedges like she was made of muscle. For maybe two miles she was majestic: legs easily leaping over thick stone walls, top of her head touching the high branches of trees, fingertips stretching to bird nests. For maybe two miles she was eight foot tall and built for movement and it was warm like the rath, familiar, a thrumming in her bones. Lift of the latch of her house, though, and she shrank on the threshold. Barely five foot one and scrawny again. Enough to make her think she'd dreamed up the whole thing. She thinks she did. Knows it, even. But up on the rath that knowledge is shifting.

She smokes some more. Trina drinks. They talk of other, safer things.

It takes a few hours, but eventually Trina's tongue loosens. 'You hate my friends.' She says it staring out at the growing shadows of the trees on the far side of the hill. The one that looks like antlers, like horns.

'Duh.' Elly blows smoke and thinks again of dragons.

'You hate me.'

Elly's surprised enough to look at her best friend. Or. At the girl who was her best friend three years ago, and maybe two, but who is probably just a friend, now. A friend she has increasingly little in common with.

'I don't hate you.' Elly gestures at the flattened grasses around them, at the cans and the skins and the little bag of weed she bought off of Gráinne's boyfriend and felt like such a fucking hard-ass about. 'I just hate your dumb friends.'

'Yeah, well.' Trina chucks a can into the ditch behind her. 'They hate you too.'

'Like I give a fuck.'

Trina squints at her friend. 'When did you get so . . .'

Elly smirks. 'Cool?'

'Fuck no.' Trina snorts. 'Just. I dunno. You're different, lately.'

Eyes that don't dare meet yet, eyes that look out over the rath and the gentle pinking of the summer sky.

'So are you.'

Here the unspoken: they wait until the sun sets to kiss. Neither acts like they expect it but for this one evening the ghost of the last kiss lives before the new first falls. And it does feel like falling. Right through the grassy mound of the rath into the pit underneath. Elly's read about how they were made. Thousands of hours of manpower to build huge round structures. Wooden beams and thatched roofs set around a wheel-spoke pattern, more sophisticated than the pebble-dashed houses the girls live in now. Maybe those halls were lived in. Maybe ancient kings and queens drank and fought and fucked under those spiral roofs. Elly wonders if that's what makes the ground so warm. That, or what happened to the building after.

There's fire here. Suck of ashes at the end of the joint, loose warmth of drink pooling in her belly. Easy to blame it on the alcohol. Easy to blame it on the darkening sky of the longest day.

There is a shadow, again. Between the two trees that might once have marked the entrance. They couldn't have; no trees are that ancient. Their descendants, perhaps. Elly thinks too much about these things. This is why she's the quiet one and Trina's the wildfire. Trina never seems to think at all. She's all action.

The shadow has horns.

When the sun sinks over the mound of the rath Elly takes Trina's face in her hands and the kiss is the small space of soft grass between thistles. Move too far to either side and you're sure to get hurt.

★

My rath is the space between wars. The holding place. Always was. Companies came and companies went, my husband at the helm of each and I stayed, although I'd shed more blood than he and his men combined.

It was never his rath, but mine.

In our room, the skins of deer stretched across the floor. He wasn't the one who'd speared them.

In our room – the company moved out again, all the king's horses and all the king's men – a fire burned in the pit. Smell of charred meat enough to make a mouth water.

In our room, her hair long over both shoulders, her fingers untangling the twists like a child's weaving game. Over, under, in front, behind.

In our room, her fingers.

★

It's summer again. It's never summer for long enough, not in Trina's opinion. Tanned legs and cropped t-shirts, wide expanse of freckled skin she slicks enough lotion on every morning to keep smooth and white and not burn.

She's at the rath and Elly's late and she's antsy. Leg

152

tap-tapping against the soggy ground. Rain-soaked seat of her jeans and hair frizzing with it but she didn't think to bring an umbrella.

There's something about this place. Not just the fact that it's the only place – the only time, the only night, few dark hours before the dawn – where she and Elly kiss. Make out. Whatever. It's been five years of midsummers. Trina worries this'll be the last.

She knows she fucked up. It was inevitable; there was no way Trina wouldn't fuck up. She's sure Elly expects it at this stage. Maybe Elly's new friends didn't but Trina figures people should know who she is. Bit of a wrecking ball, really.

And maybe going crazy, a little bit. Not that that's an excuse. Trina wouldn't try that.

Her ma's new fella brought them camping. Weird thing to do, Trina thought, with her ma and her flawless acrylics, Trina and her acerbic remarks, but the fella persisted, she has to give it to him. Persisted through fields and trees, put up the tents himself, her phone losing signal halfway up whatever mountain and her iPod out of battery by nightfall. Two tents and a small stove, her ma letting her have a few cans by the fire. Marshmallows. In the night Trina got up to pee in the bushes (she pretended she hated it but there was something about it: pants around her ankles on a prickly hillside, piss making rivers on the moss; she's been thinking about it since) and the moon was so bright she clicked off her torch and walked further than she would have with her ma and her fella, complaining all the while, earphones in and music blaring loud enough for them to hear the tinny squall. Wound up at a cliffside with claw marks on rocks and she lay down and became a river. Body collapsing into water, drenching the rock she lay on and lower, droplets sinking into the ground and staying there, muddying. The rest of her wound around stones and over grasses, flowed down the side of the mountain, leaping on the overpasses and crashing over the steep sides to the valley below.

All night she was a river, gushing. In the morning she was so sore she could barely move, but the good kind, the kind after hours of sex, where you're light-headed from heavy breathing, mind blissed out, muscles sore and still wanting. Some wet dream. Every time she thinks of it she squirms, which means – another can, then, and another – she needs to stop thinking about it right about now, here on this wet, warm hillside, waiting for her ex-best friend.

She's well buzzed by the time Elly shows up. She's glowing. Elly. Big fuckin' glow off of her. Like she just got laid or landed her dream course or something. Could be either. Lighting up her insides. Everything else is shadow.

Her hair's grown out and she must be wearing contact lenses because Trina can see the sharp upflick of black liner on Elly's eyes instead of rain speckles on wire-framed glasses. It's like missing the bottom step and the ground shudders all though your foot.

'You're late.' Trina's mouth is hard around the words.

Truth is, Trina wasn't sure Elly would even show up. Five years of midsummers and each one this precarious thing. They've barely spoken in months. Pressure of exams, sure, end of school, sure, but mostly it's that they aren't friends. Haven't been for years. They're just two girls who know each other, sort of, who were best friends when they were kids. They have nothing in common, not any more. Nothing except the rath.

When Elly's close enough to speak without shouting she says, 'I didn't think you'd be here,' calm as anything, like she's talking about the weather, like it barely even matters that Trina went and fucked up and is fairly sure Elly hates her, even though she's here, now. Late, and wearing eyeliner.

'Yeah, well, I am.' Trina crumples a can between her palms and cracks open another. Elly falls heavy to the damp ground beside her and plucks the can from Trina's hand.

Elly downs the can in a minute flat, reaches for another. Speeding through the introduction, the part where they smoke and chat, drink at a leisurely pace like they're lying to themselves about where the night is going. Whispers about that antler tree and the ancient queen who eats the souls of the rath's sacrifices. Every summer the same ritual: this is their processional. And Elly's taking this year's at a run.

Trina has it in her head she'll apologise. Say to Elly what she's been meaning to for months, since Gráinne's eighteenth. She rehearses it in her head, the words a little fuzzy. *I'm sorry for getting shitfaced and insulting your new friends.* (The words that'll obviously go unsaid: *I was jealous.*) *I'm sorry for starting a very public fight with you where I dragged out every low blow I could think of.* (The words that'll obviously go unsaid: *I'm not your friend and it's my fault. I don't know any other way to be than to push you away.*) *I'm sorry for outing you, loudly, even though you laughed and didn't care because your friends all knew already.* (The words that'll obviously go unsaid: *You never told me in words. I was only making assumptions but your new friends*

155

know you better than I do.)

'We're climbing the rath,' Elly announces, and she pulls Trina to her feet and they leg it up the hill, wet grass slapping the backs of their bare knees, beer sloshing over the lips of their cans, laughter like bells. On the crest of the mound they drop to the ground and while Trina's catching her breath on her back Elly rolls over on top of her. Hands either side of her head, knees hugging her hips.

'Here's how they built this place,' Elly says, and her voice is low. 'They hauled rocks from miles around, huge limestone and quartz, four men to a stone. They felled trees and lugged their trunks to the highest place in the land. They built a huge building, pillars and thatched roof, and in it they had a feast and held ceremony.'

Elly's face barely inches from Trina's and it's like they've never even kissed before her mouth's so dry. Sharp dark liner over sharp dark eyes.

'Afterwards, a sacrifice was left behind. Right here.' Her palms pressing into the earth on either side of Trina's flushed face.

Who is this girl? Trina thinks, just barely. *I don't think I know her at all.*

'They filled the building with stones and earth and people alive inside it. They covered the building with stones and earth so the mound was higher. They built this hill, Trina. Thousands of years ago. They made this place and underneath us there are the bones of the people buried alive inside it.'

Trina's clothes are soaked through, back pressed down into the grass of the rath, and she shivers.

Elly moves lower. Trina watches her lips.

'After that, they held ceremony on the rath. Right here. They came through the gap between the horned trees and their processional led them in a spiral to the tip of the mound, the high place. We don't know what that looked like. We don't know if these things are true. But you can feel them, can't you?'

Trina's not going to get into what she can feel right now, not with Elly and not with herself, so she just chokes out, 'You're such a fucking nerd.'

Flash of fire in her best friend's eyes. She blinks and is Elly again. 'Nice try, Trina.'

'How do you even know all this?'

Elly tilts her head. 'Don't you?'

And through the shiver up her spine soaked from the long, soft grass on the top of the rath Trina feels it: this knowledge is warm and right there, close as a thistle with a flower like a pretty purple bulb that she could reach out to touch and not feel the sting of the green leaves below. The whole mound is a hearth and she can feel it glowing.

'Not buried,' she says, as Elly closes her eyes and lowers her lips slowly towards hers.

'Hmm?'

'Not buried alive. Burnt.'

When they kiss Trina thinks of dragons. When their hips buck together she forgets to think at all. In the misting rain on top of the warm rath they unbutton each other's shorts and come in gasping bursts, hands working together under layers of fabric and denim and if the rath heats warmer than before they don't notice. They are fire enough as it is.

*

We were the two wives of the god of battle but she was mine more than she was his. And I was hers.

In the early years we fought. He tried to pit us against each other: this wife is the prettiest, this wife is the strongest, are you not jealous, both? Which wife will I favour today?

We were not jealous. Not of his attentions. We had no desire to win his favour; the rath was mine, and so, then, was he.

She took longer for me to conquer.

*

Summer. Hotter than it should be. Hotter than Melbourne, at least at the moment, Penny emailing Elly pictures of their dog in his little coat on the windswept beach. Elly's home for a flying visit – couple of weeks, just enough to get over the jetlag before it's time to leave again. It's always this way, now. Her mam wringing her hands. But it's only the two of them left and Elly can't take the empty house, the quiet hovering. There's no one else around. Everyone her age left straight out of college when they realised there weren't any jobs going. Nothing left for them here but the recession and their mas' houses filled with photos of their younger selves.

Elly got lucky. Walked into a job that came with a visa and an office opposite the university where a pretty brunette lectured on ancient civilisations. Chance encounter at the coffee shop on the corner and Penny, hearing the accent, talked Elly's ear off for an hour about pre-Christian Ireland and that was it for her. Three years later and they share a sunny unit in Richmond and an ugly pug named Setanta.

Penny always wants to talk about the rath. 'Right on your doorstep,' she sighs, often. 'No visitor centre, no protections except a gate, one lonely signpost.'

'It's really not that romantic,' Elly has to tell her. 'It's a place where teens go to smoke a few joints, drink some cans, make out. It's high, surrounded by trees. Secluded.'

She takes Penny's rant about disrespecting ancient sites in her stride, keeping to herself that she was, for years, one of those teens, only counters occasionally to say that ancient teens probably did the exact same thing.

'They're weaving patterns,' she protests while Penny huffs. 'Honouring those who came before. Eating, fighting, drinking, fucking. Nothing changes over thousands of years.'

Nothing changes over thousands of years and very little has changed in the last twelve. Midsummer evening, sun hot up over the rath. Elly sits between thistles and a warm breeze flattens the long grass, rustles up her skirt.

Beside her, a six pack of cans and a plastic lighter. In her pocket, a small stack of skinny joints, neatly rolled with Gráinne's weed. One of the few who stayed, Gráinne's still home, surrounded by baby photos, caring for her parents (both much older than Elly's). In her spare time she's taken over her brother's crop in their old lambing barn. It's good stuff. Smooth and easy. Elly sparks one up while she waits.

She doesn't doubt Trina will show. Not anymore. They're barely friends, never speak, don't even have each other's numbers or new addresses, only occasionally comment on some big news on Facebook. And still there is this strange compulsion to meet here, every midsummer for twelve years, now. Through the worst of their fights, through university in different cities, through the grief and joy of losing various family members and finding various partners and jobs, through them both emigrating only to time their return holidays coincidentally to align with the solstice every damn year.

Few cans of something cheap and a couple of joints up on the rath to mark the shortest night.

Dark shadow by the cluster of trees on the other side of the rath and for a minute Elly sits straighter, thinking Trina's come from a different path than usual, but it isn't Trina. The shadow unfurls into a murder of crows. Bigger than crows. Ravens, maybe. Giant fuckers, beaks the length of Elly's fingers it looks like. Five of them, all feathers.

And Elly remembers. Early morning last week, jetlag waking her with the sunrise before five. She'd almost forgotten how bright it got here. Moth holes in the blackout curtains sending laser beams of yellow light. She'd dreamed of the rath, woken with low fire curling between her legs. She considered calling Penny on the house phone – her ma'd got a card with long-distance minutes, cheap as chips – but just rubbed one out instead, quiet against the pillow, goose down prickling her cheeks through the thin pillowcase. She must have fallen asleep again, after, because she dreamed waking, dreamed dragging her limbs, yawning, to the mirror, rubbing the sleep from her eyes. Dreamed noticing five black specks along her jaw, absent-mindedly grabbing tweezers to pluck the offending hairs. Pinch of metal, hard around the little dot that lengthened as she pulled. And pulled. Tweezer tip gripped around the base of a black feather that whispered with a sharp slide out of the skin of the side of her face. Dreamed the horror, the caught breath. Dreamed taking the tweezers to another, and another, soft black feathers pulling out from underneath her skin.

Elly takes a can from the pack beside her and throws, knowing she won't reach the birds but hoping to scare them away with the noise of the beer can flying fast through the air, thudding heavy to the ground.

A loud laugh sounds out across the rath and the birds flutter up into a tree, glaring, but less large already between the branches.

Trina's voice reaches Elly before she does. 'Good to see you too, Elly.' She picks up the can and hoists it in her hand like a ball for a dog.

Elly has to shade her eyes against the low sun. 'I was aiming for the birds.'

Trina throws the can from palm to palm. 'You have shit aim.'

'Eh, you try from this distance. I just wanted to scare them away.'

Trina reaches her arm back like she's about to throw, gives Elly a look over her shoulder. 'And here I was thinking it was me you were trying to scare off.' She lets the can fly. It goes further than Elly could have got it, lands on the top of the mound and explodes, soaking the ground.

Elly gives her – what? Childhood friend? – a long, slow clap, says, 'That one was yours,' then laughs when Trina produces another six pack from the bag on her back.

''Mon and let's get shitfaced,' Trina says and Elly can't stop the grin that slides over her mouth.

No catching up, this year. Trina doesn't ask about Penny, the dog, the apartment, and Elly doesn't ask about California, about − Dave, was it? She's seen pictures. Big, strapping Cork lad Trina met in a backpacker hostel in San Diego. They have a room in a house on the beach, or did this time last year. Maybe there's no Dave any more. Elly doesn't ask. Instead, she lights a joint and they share it and they drink, and instead, they talk about the rath.

Some years it's easier than others. Slip into a known rhythm. As though they aren't essentially strangers. One short night where they're friends again. Just two women up on a hill overlooking five counties of the place they left behind. Some midsummers they talk all night, relive the year between this and the last, like they know each other. They get drunk and the words are easy until one of them strays too close to the reasons they aren't friends, the reasons they don't actually like each other, past fights morphing into a new one where each secret one knows about the other is ammunition in the game to see who can land a killing hit. Some years they don't even kiss. Denim catching on hips, bruised thighs, nothing but harsh breaths and the rath matching them: the mound under the grass rising and falling, heating like their faces, humming under their cut-off cries.

This year, though, they wander to the top of the hill and sit cross-legged, making short work of the beers, hands running through the long grasses like they're stroking its hair. It. The rath. Murder still side-eyeing them from the branches.

'You remember when we thought this place was haunted?' Trina asks at one point.

Elly gives her a look. 'I've always thought this place was haunted. I mean. Have you seen the state of those birds?' She glowers over at the crows, tries hard not to think of feathers.

'Creepy fuckers,' Trina agrees.

'Do you ever . . .' Elly trails off, lies back, puffs smoke at the sky. Feels Trina watching her blink up at the clouds, sun already sunk beyond the horizon, pink streaks across her vision like fresh stretch marks.

Trina waits. 'Finish my sentences?' she supplies.

'Hmm?' Elly's still watching the sky.

'Do I ever what?'

'Do you ever have . . . weird things . . . happen? When you think of the rath? Dream of it?'

Trina's laugh is maybe a little bit forced. 'You are so high right now,' she says.

'Maybe.' Elly is undeterred. 'But still. Sometimes it feels like something follows. Some weird warmth. I don't know. Every time I come back here it feels stronger.'

'Maybe you're just going crazy, ever think of that?'

Elly giggles. 'All the time.' Because she knows there's something kind of fucked about this, the draw of this place, the way when they are here they're outside of time, entirely themselves but also something other. And she knows there's something extremely fucked about how easy it is, as the sky finally shifts to navy, to pull Trina on top of her and press their mouths together, open already, ready since this time last year, it feels, press their bodies together, take their clothes off, sky still darkening and yet the heat keeps rising.

A fire burned in the pit and her words were sharpened into spear points, made to wound. I could have been pierced by a thousand of them and come back wanting.

Our husband laughed, thinking we were rivals, revelling in the power he believed he held over us. But she and I knew this was our processional: long march to the mound, feet beaten bloody, hearts pounding in anticipation of ceremony.

We: warrior queens. Not peaceful women, by nature.

Before I was a wife it was I who led the charge to battle. I outran the army's horses. My body prickled into crow feathers and flew across counties. I forced another man's men to build my rath and into it he strode: the god of war with his horses and his hounds and his heifers thick for milking. A match of status, of calculated economics. What better wives for the god of battle than two warrior queens? Good fighting stock: a homegrown army.

We raised our young to become soldiers. Sometimes we forgot which child was whose. Some slithered out of our bodies with crooked claws at the ends of their toes. Some had black feathers for hair. Some grew to twice the size of their father, could crush a skull in their fist. Our milk ran thick.

Our husband took our children to war as soon as they were able and we stayed and led the hunt. Sword and spear and blood making rivers in the ground. It was at a river they found us: my cousin's company come far from their province. They had crossed our husband some days ago, had joined his fight against some other king's men. Had seen our children in battle. Teeth and feathers and claws.

The bodies of five deer lay on a rock, still warm. The river whispered through pine trees and fell in a rush to the valley below. We washed the blood and the dirt of the hunt from our skin, pressed kisses over and under the running water, long breaths in the heat. A noise from the shore: branch-snap and soft rustle. I rose naked from the river and raised my bow. The meat was ours and the hour was late and we had a family to feed on our return. String drawn, I approached the trees and did not look behind me.

Behind me: rain of hands on her mouth before she could call out, arms trapping her fighting limbs, hush of the waterfall hiding the splash of a dozen men pulling her away.

*

Summer again. Here is the rath. Fat hump of earth covered in whispery grass. Soft enough to walk barefoot. Trina keeps her shoes on.

The sky's low today. Roll and rumble of cloudy grey. It's late. So late the dark is starting.

No sign of Elly.

Her phone's pinged fifteen times in the last hour and if she sees Luke's name come up on the screen one more time she's going to scream but she can't turn it off because what if the baby needs her and Luke can't reach her? He has no clue she's up on the rath close to her ma's old house with a six pack of cheap cider and a block of bad hash, just like old times. He has no clue what the old times are. He doesn't have many clues, does Luke. Easier that way. She doesn't tell him much and he knows that, just takes the baby when she needs it, knows to heat the bottles gently in warm water, knows how many turns the mobile over the cot needs to sing the baby to sleep without starting at a frantic pace that'll wake her before she even drifts off.

It chokes her sometimes: the rules, the danger. Soft spot on a baby's head where the skull hasn't fused together yet. Tiny limbs, squalling mouth. So breakable. The effort of it, every waking minute and a good many sleeping minutes too, the care she has to take with everything. Her friends tell her it gets better but Trina knows girlhood, knows how breakable baby bodies are wrapped around breakable little-girl hearts. How does any woman survive?

Trina rolls a joint, badly. Hands shake. Low rumble of thunder from far off. Elly used to say you could see five counties from the top of the mound but when Trina makes her way up there, smoke trailing lazy behind her, all she can see is cloud. Cloud, and shadow. Something big and doglike down amongst the weeds and rubbish and brambles of the stinging ditch.

Lately every time Trina makes dinner the food shifts under her fingers, changes before she can get it on the plates. Every time it's the same. Spaghetti or burgers or fish or rice or spuds. Between the pot or the pan on the stove and the table, the meal is turned to dogflesh. Thick soupy stew of it, brittle with gristle, bits of rusty fur still sticking to the edges of bone. When she's eaten the lot Trina licks the bowl.

She thinks of shouting out, scaring the dog off, but she turns her back to the shadow and watches the road for a car.

It's been twenty-three years of midsummers on the rath. Can of something cheap and a few joints lighting up the short wait till morning. Her and Elly at thirteen, sixteen, eighteen. At twenty-five and thirty-six. Home from Australia and America and Spain and Scotland. Married, both, now. Three babies between them. Trina's pretty sure she heard Elly's settled in Dublin. Maybe even not far from her own two-up-two-down on the north side. Never expected to buy a house back home but here she is, less than an hour's drive from where her fragile baby body grew up around her fragile little-girl heart. Less than an hour's drive from the rath.

Twenty-three years and Elly's never not shown up. Even when she lived in Melbourne. Even when her da died. Even when her Australian girlfriend broke her heart and she ran away to Spain and took up with an artist. Even when she met her wife, started planning a wedding that wouldn't be recognised if she ever decided to move back to Ireland. Even when her wife was pregnant. Even when Elly finally got pregnant herself.

And even after everything Trina has ever said to try to break her. Twenty-three years' worth of ammunition that can only be used once a year. Even after every fucking fight. Even after three hundred and sixty-four days of silence a year, they always meet back here.

The sun sets and Trina is alone.

She lies on her back at the top of the mound and lets the stormy warmth soak into her bones from below, lets the summer rain fall on her face. She thinks, *Come to me*. She thinks it deep into the mound, through long grass and earth, through rock and stone, through the rotted remains of the building far below, to the bones and the skulls and the bodies and the fire that still exists in there somewhere, she knows it. She thinks, *Come to me*, and she means Elly but somebody else comes to her instead and she is hardly surprised. Maybe this is what she meant all along. Somebody large and ancient, seven feet or taller, hair in two long ropes out of her head, built like a bull. This is who stands under the mound and Trina is only afraid for a moment because soon the woman is standing above her, then kneeling over her, then pressing against her, slow and heavy and Trina's breath catches in a moan. The woman – *queen*, Trina knows, the queen who haunts the rath, who requires yearly sacrifice, the one Elly's nana used to believe in but Trina never did – has a mouth hot as flame, has hands heavy as the rocks that were hauled to form the base of this hill they lie on.

And it is her but it is also somehow Elly, and her hands are small and nimble, and her tongue is quick, and all Trina can do is lie there and take it, fists filled with grass, until the queen's face between her thighs cracks into black feathers and underneath it Elly is gasping, soaked slick and glistening.

Trina tastes herself on Elly's lips.

She says, 'Is it you?' because she isn't sure, and Elly replies, a little breathless, 'Who else would it be?'

Trina pushes herself up on her elbows, looks as best she can around the rath, cloud-cloaked, midnight-shrouded, silent. 'No one,' she says. 'No one.'

Elly wipes her mouth with the inside of her right wrist and says, 'Sorry I'm late.'

Trina shivers through the warmth in her bones. 'You're here now,' she says, and behind it there is an echo that whispers, 'I missed you.'

'I'm glad you came,' she says, and behind her words the echo whispers, 'I waited so long.'

'Let's not talk, this time,' Elly murmurs into her mouth.

They don't speak another word until sunrise.

★

I outran the army's horses. My body prickled into crow feathers and flew across counties and I could not find her.

When I pissed it made rivers that washed their raths away. Every meal they made turned to dogflesh. Their children were sick from it. Their wives rarely carried a baby to birth. Still I could not find her.

I grew to twice my size, sprouted fur so wild and wiry it ripped trees to ribbons as I ran by. My teeth tore through their throats. I burnt their towns to the ground and still I could not find her.

I opened my mouth to scream and blood came out of the ears and eyes of the few that remained. My cries have killed a hundred men. You do not know my hunger.

Even the god of war could never best me in battle. He knew better than to try.

My wrath was a thing of legend. Across the land I burnt and I tore and I flooded and killed and still I could not find her. Eventually, the druids told my husband to tame me. There wouldn't be a province left populated at the rate I was going, they said. They believed, and he let them, that I was doing this for him. As revenge for the taking of his second wife. My sister, they said, my rival. His wife, not mine. They wondered was she worth it.

I killed the druids in their sleep and returned to my slaughter.

When they caught me it was my husband who swung the sword. A warrior queen was suddenly no longer the best wife for the god of war.

After I died they buried me standing. Wouldn't anybody dare to take a torch to me.

So I stood, straight as a torch and a thousand times as strong as the fire, and I waited, hot and hungry, for somebody to wake me.

★

It is summer and they climb the rath together, two cars pulled in off the road at almost the same time. They laugh when they see each other through the windshields, even though last time they parted it was with insults and tears. It's funny what a year's rain will wash away. It's funny the things that remain. Thirty years tonight they've been doing this and you'd think they'd be used to it but every time it's like the first: few cans of something cheap and a couple of joints up on the rath to mark the shortest night.

They sit between thistles on the treeline by the ditch and the pink heads nod along with the sway of the long, soft grass of the mound. Bad cider from the local Lidl and good weed grown by one of Gráinne's boys in the old lambing barn. Elly's eyeliner's sharp as a blade, Trina's hair half shaved up the side, tattooed nettle sneaking behind her ear. *Midlife crisis*, her ma spat at her when she saw it, *couldn't you just buy a sports car like every other middle-aged divorcée?*

But Trina didn't want a sports car, only wanted to see the shape of her skull.

Becky keeps running her little fingers over the stubble, asking when she can have her hair the same. Sends Luke into a rage every time, texting Trina how she's a bad influence and it's on her if their kid turns out queer. *Like mother like daughter*, muttered with a curled lip, low enough that if she asked him to repeat it he'd be able to answer, *What? I didn't say anything.*

Trina often thinks of Elly at eighteen, surrounded by new, kinder friends, dancing with a wine cooler in her hand at Gráinne's birthday party. Often thinks of the words she screeched in panic, in jealousy, not that that was an excuse, that started every fight they've ever had. Words she's always, somehow, known she could use on her own damn self. Words she thought belonged at the rath on the shortest night of the year, that stayed and sank into the mound like stones. Words she hoped she'd never have to bring home.

Beside her, Elly's stretched out, eyes on the sky, smoke curling from the sides of her lips like her mouth is smouldering. There's barely a cloud. It's early, not yet nine, still a couple good hours of daylight left. The boys are with Cliona and her new missus, who Elly hates just out of principle but who is honestly good with the boys. If Cliona marries this one – *when*, Elly thinks bitterly – she'll be the boys' stepmum. *Too many mothers*, Cliona likes to laugh, and Elly laughs along because they're *friends* now, because *it's been five years, Elly, come on*, because *we're all adults here*, because *let's not perpetuate harmful divorce stereotypes in front of the boys, shall we?*

Elly groans. 'D'you know what's shit?' She's maybe already a bit buzzed, edge of the high gentling her vision, bad cider sloshing in an empty stomach.

'What?' Trina asks.

'Adulthood.'

Trina laughs. 'You're only figuring this out now?'

Elly keeps looking at the sky. 'There's a lot that takes a few decades to figure out.'

The silence seems sudden, like nobody is breathing but the rath.

'Yeah,' Trina says finally.

More silence, stretching like the long sunset, hours away yet but if they kept their eyes on the horizon they'd be able to see the slow progress of the sun making tall, skinny shadows of everything. Enormous crows in the crooked trees, a horned something at the entrance to the processional, a dog-shaped blur climbing out of the opposite ditch. The mound of the rath itself rising and falling slowly like a chest. Every blade of long grass multiplied by its longer, darker shadow.

'Still don't think this place is haunted?' Elly asks, although Trina's admitted to it many times now. They've gone over the weird things that keep happening, usually wasted, watching the sky wide-eyed, words all whisper. This is a space for wildness. Madness. Secrets. Nobody has ever known about these midsummers but each other. And the queen under the mound of the rath, who rises year on year through rock and packed earth, through the structures that once were, through the bones of the sacrifices and the fire that still burns deep. They buried her standing and slowly she reaches for air.

They know this, now, Elly and Trina. They've figured it out. It's been thirty years, after all, and although some years they only fight and some years they only fuck, they aren't stupid. They've given up on disbelief. They understand they're haunted. They just aren't quite ready for the final piece.

Slow stumble to the top of the rath. Few cans of something cheap and a couple of joints. Soon the sun will set and the shortest night will start and they will understand that the last thirty years have been the processional. Long march to the mound, feet beaten bloody, hearts pounding in anticipation. Thirty years' spiral and tonight they hold ceremony. Two women weaving patterns, honouring those who came before.

We were the wives of the god of war but she was mine more than she was his. And I was hers. Echoes calling like for like. I screamed from my standing grave for years and still I could not find her. Thousands of years of children climbing my rath. Eating, fighting, drinking, fucking. Thousands of years of echoes until these two kissed between thistles and I recognised them. And, little by little, I rose.

Fingertips ghosting the underside of the mound beneath them. They buried me standing so now I can reach. What do you think it will take to wake me?

After the processional, we hold ceremony. And after ceremony, the battle.

My rath is the space between wars. The holding place. The pause in my slaughter. They should have taken a torch to me. Instead, I'll burn their whole world down to find her.

Interval:
Sad Straight Sex at the End of the World

A small hotel bedroom, lit by one
fluorescent bulb which buzzes quietly.
The room is clean but sparse,
utilitarian, furnished only by a double
bed, a chair and two nightstands. At
the back of stage left there is a door,
ajar, leading to a tiny bathroom. A sink
and mirror can be seen through the door.
The two characters have just entered the
room. They stand awkwardly, avoiding eye
contact. They are both wearing white-
collar office clothes and speak more to
the audience than to each other. One
only looks at the other when the other
is preoccupied with what they are doing.

MAN:
Last night in the world and we're
going to have sex. Just got off
work. My tie won't come off. Need
your help to loosen it. My fingers
fumble.

WOMAN:

Last night in the world. We
decided without saying much that
we should spend it this way.
Together. Your tie is too tight
and you don't seem to know how to
untie it. I pick at the knot with
my fingers. Pink nails. I painted
them this morning. I knew tonight
had to be something special.

MAN:

Pink nails. You look pretty. Your
hair all back, those stocking
things that probably stop
halfway up your thigh. My dick's
getting hard. Tie's gone. Shoes
next. Don't want to dirty the
bedsheets.

WOMAN:

You tie your laces so tightly,
like your tie. All knotted.
Double knots, like kids make. We
learned it this way, as children.
Two loops, butterfly wings. Tie
them together. Ta-dah. What a
pretty bow.

MAN:

End up pulling the damn things
off. Who cares if the laces break
anyway. They snap. Fuck. Want to
kick the shoes across the room.
Should be able to, last night
in the world and all. Lose my

inhibitions. I put them neatly by
the door instead. Fuck.

WOMAN:

You don't even notice my shirt's
off. Too busy staring at your
shoes. Kind of old-fashioned for
your age. Really shiny though.
WOMAN unties her hair. Maybe
we're trying too hard.

MAN:

Turn around and your shirt's off.
Bra all lacy like those underwear
teens on the internet. I'd stay
late at work and jack off on the
screen. Your hair's all loose
on your shoulders and you have
a spot, just there, a blackhead
beside your left breast. I wonder
what you taste like.

WOMAN:

Licks her lips anxiously.
Shouldn't have worn lipstick.
It'll get everywhere if we kiss —
when. When we kiss. It'll get all
over. Oh God, I hope he doesn't
want a blowjob.

MAN:

Licking your lips like that. This
was a great idea, fucking great.
Got to spend it right. Last night
in the world. You and me beside a
bed. No music. Should've thought

of that. Maybe silence is better.
But then there's those noises
— slurping and slapping. Maybe
the bed'll squeak loud enough
to drown them out. *MAN pauses.*
I wonder if she'll give me a
blowjob first.

                    WOMAN:
Skirt off, shirt off, shoes off.
It's like a checklist. It's like
when you board a plane. I think I
look kind of like an air hostess
in these clothes. Air steward.
Usher. And here we are ushering
in the end of the world. *WOMAN
pauses.* I didn't think this would
feel so lonely.

                    MAN:
Great. This is great. *MAN takes off
his trousers, folds them neatly
along the crease in the leg.* Not
what I imagined, but great.

                    WOMAN:
You have your trousers off.
Unbuttoning your shirt so
carefully. I wonder if a part of
you wishes you could tear it off.

                    MAN:
Who invented buttons this tiny?
I'm afraid she'll think I'm
nervous.

WOMAN:

Getting nervous. Wish I wasn't.
Only my bra and knickers on now.
The floor's scratchy. Sticky spot
under my right heel. I hope the
bed's clean. I hope that's an old
stain. Can't imagine getting into
it. You look eager. Last night in
the world. I guess all I have to
do is lie there and wait for it
to be over. I wanted so much for
this to be something special.

MAN:

Imagined this different. Like the
way it was with my ex sometimes.
Candles and wine. Why didn't I
think of wine? Haven't had sex
in years. Not since her. Hope I
don't finish too quickly, fuck it
up. I never was good at getting
women off. Better if she just
finishes herself off after. Back
arching into the pillows, hand
between her legs. I can watch. I
like to watch.

WOMAN:

Oh God, what am I doing? That
gormless expression. Like one of
those goggle-eyed cartoons. One
look at a woman and their jaw's
on the floor. I hate this.

MAN:

She's not even looking at me.

                    WOMAN:
I wish he'd stop looking at me.

                     MAN:
What the fuck is the point of
this if she won't look at me?

                    WOMAN:
What was the point of this?

                     MAN:
Maybe I should turn off the
lights.

                    WOMAN:
You make a move to the switch by
the door and for a second I think
you're leaving and I feel such
relief. But no: you just want to
turn off the light. You hesitate,
though. You're second-guessing
everything too. Tight tie,
double-knotted shoes. Cartoon
eyes half out of their sockets.
Small frown twisting your brows.
You look like someone who doesn't
know how to lose control. *WOMAN
laughs to herself, humourlessly.*
I suppose I could say the same
for me. Maybe this is right.
Maybe we're made for each other.

                     MAN:
What's she laughing at? Fuck.
What's there to laugh about?

WOMAN:

You look angry. Suddenly I'm
scared. Last night in the world
and it's only now I'm scared.
This was a mistake.

MAN:

Maybe this was a mistake. There's
something fearful to the way
you're looking at me now. Like a
kid who's realised they've done
something they shouldn't.

WOMAN:

I shouldn't have done this.

MAN:

Last night in the world. How
many hours do we have left now?
It's almost over. We agreed. She
agreed. She wants it.

WOMAN:

It'll be over soon.

MAN moves deliberately closer to WOMAN,
who is in her own world and doesn't
notice. They are maybe two metres apart
now: he could reach out his hand and
touch her. They face each other but
still don't look at each other. Suddenly
there is a loud sound. A bomb blast,
maybe. The lights go out. The stage is
lit only by the exit lights and a low
glow close to the audience, who can
just about see MAN's and WOMAN's faces.

Offstage, the sound of sirens, gunshots, screams. MAN and WOMAN don't move. In this intimate darkness, they finally start to speak directly to each other.

                    WOMAN:
    Do you think this is it?

                    MAN:
    Probably.

The stage lights close to the audience flicker.

                    MAN:
    Do you think it'll hurt?

                    WOMAN:
    Probably.

The sounds grow louder. MAN and WOMAN flinch but do not touch each other or move closer together.

                    MAN:
    This isn't how I was expecting it
    to go.

                    WOMAN:
    Me neither.

The sounds grow louder still, then fade somewhat, as though something has passed by the hotel and is moving away.

MAN:
Do you want to sit down?

WOMAN:
I don't think so.

MAN:
Yeah. Yeah. Better to face death
standing.

WOMAN:
I'm not sure I'm ready to face
death at all.

*The sounds from outside grow fainter
still. MAN and WOMAN still stand two
metres apart, half undressed.*

WOMAN:
Do you have anybody, at home?

MAN, *surprised by the question*:
I had a dog. A collie. Sandy, her
name was. Gorgeous girl. After my
marriage — well — after I moved
away, she's all I had. Slept on
my bed. Gave me a reason to wake
up in the morning. *MAN speaks
faster, lower, more to himself.*
She needed me. Needed me to feed
her. Walk her. Pick up her shit
in those little baggies. I needed
her. Had to get out of the house
every day. Put her lead on, bring
her to the park. People talk to
you, when you have a dog. Ask

her name, her age. Kids come up
to you, ask if they can pet her.
You can have conversations. What
kind of treats are her favourite.
What was she like as a puppy. How
is she coping with the storms,
the bombs. They don't ask how
you're coping, but that's part of
the question. *MAN pauses, as if
realising where he is.* Sandy died
six weeks ago.

                WOMAN:
I'm sorry.

                MAN:
Yeah.

                WOMAN:
I didn't even know you had a dog.

          MAN, *heated now*:
That's what I'm saying. Nobody
talks in the office. No water-
cooler chit-chat. Just the
odd *good morning.* A couple of
closing *see you tomorrow*s. As if
we're all certain there'll be a
tomorrow. Everyone's wrapped up
in their own end of the world.
That's why I thought — that's why
we agreed —

                WOMAN:
This would be a good idea.

MAN, *a little desperately*:
It is, isn't it? A good idea?

WOMAN, *after a pause*:
My parents are dead years now,
but I have sisters. Two of them.
One married, three kids. They
live in the same town. Small
town, everyone in everyone
else's business. It's where we
grew up. They left, travelled
the world, then came back.
Settled down. You don't need
marriage and children to settle
down. My youngest sister's
single but she's settled.
Started a business, has friends,
ran for council. Involved in
the community. I could have been
like that. Didn't want to, when
I was younger, and now it's too
late. I'll never see them again.
I tried to get back but the
airports —

MAN:
No one got to go home.

WOMAN:
So this. *WOMAN gestures around
the sad, dark room.* This was the
best I could do.

MAN *looks around*:
It's shit.

WOMAN, *surprised at his frankness, laughs*:
It's so shit.

                    MAN:
So. If this is it. If this is the
end and as good as it gets. *MAN
moves further into WOMAN's space,
his intent clear.* How about we
make it count?

*From outside the sound of another few
faraway blasts. They are dull and
distant but MAN and WOMAN flinch anyway.
They turn away from each other again,
face the audience.*

                  WOMAN:
He leans in to kiss me and I
startle back. I thought we were
talking. Connecting. Why is he
still insisting? I know how
this goes. In, out, in, out and
it's done. I'll be lucky if he
even tries to make me come. My
sister's best friend's a lesbian.
The way she looked at her wife.
I've heard they just keep going.
Both of them. Until they're
all pleasured out. Climax after
climax. Someone has to call it,
I've heard. Otherwise they'd both
just give and receive, give and
receive and just keep looking
at each other that way forever.
Pause. I bet they'll die happy.

MAN:
What's she moving away for?

WOMAN:
I'm starting to think I would
have been better off alone. Run
a bath, light some candles. Put
on a record. Something soothing.
I could have left the bathroom
door open and the music could
have drifted into the steam,
made me forget the world is
ending.

MAN:
The motherfucking world is ending,
what more reason does she need?

WOMAN:
Maybe I could have taken a couple
of pills. Drank a whole bottle
of wine. Staining my lips and
teeth red, pinking the bath water
with it. Bubbles. I could have
got bubbles. Even just soap suds
would do. Washing-up liquid.
Anything to get that shimmer.
They'd pop on my eyelashes and
I'd laugh, alone. Maybe the music
and my laughter would drown out
the noise from outside.

*The noise from outside gets louder for
a moment. MAN and WOMAN don't seem to
notice.*

                    WOMAN:
I should have done that. Ended it
like that. Not been so afraid of
being alone.

                    MAN:
Being this close to death does
things to people. Makes them
want. Desire.

                    WOMAN:
I'd almost stopped wanting. Now
I can't stop thinking about that
bath. Candlelight flickering as
the bombs fall. Just me in my
apartment waiting for the end.

                    MAN:
I couldn't be alone tonight.
That's why we agreed. Sex,
before all that death. You said
we'd have sex.

                    WOMAN:
I should have been alone tonight.

                    MAN:
We agreed.

*There comes another rumbling explosion.
It is closer this time. The hotel
room's scant furniture shakes. MAN and
WOMAN look back towards the closed door,
the windows. At the next blast they
stumble; the whole room shakes. MAN
covers his ears. WOMAN shuts her eyes.*

*They are braced, ready. But the last
blast doesn't come.*

MAN *slowly lowers his hands. He speaks directly to WOMAN.*
Come here. Come to the bed.

WOMAN, *as if in a dream:*
My legs are like jelly. Like a
foal who hasn't learnt to walk.

*MAN sits heavily on the bed. He bends
forwards and rubs his bare legs. WOMAN
perches gingerly, a metre or so away.
It's not a big bed. They are close,
suddenly. WOMAN wraps her arms around
her bare sides, curls into herself. They
speak directly to each other but do not
face each other or meet each other's
eyes; instead both stare into the
distance, into memory.*

MAN:
Growing up, my folks raised
sheep. Big field right beside the
house. Every spring me and my
brothers would be called out to
help with the lambing. My da'd
have to put his whole arm into
the odd ewe sometimes, untangle
umbilical cords, shove a shoulder
in the right direction. He'd be
up to the elbow in sheep vagina,
blood and shit everywhere. You
can imagine.

WOMAN:

I don't have to. My grandparents
were dairy farmers. My sisters
and I would —

MAN:

The thing about lambs is that
the littlest don't survive.
The ones with the shaky legs,
like foals, like what you just
said. I was listening. They're
too shaky. Can't find their
feet. Can't suck their mothers'
milk. Tiny bandy-legged things,
bleating pathetically. Mewling.
You'd have to put them out of
their misery.

WOMAN:

That's nature.

MAN:

That's life.

WOMAN:

Survival of the fittest. *WOMAN
laughs humourlessly*. Guess that
means we're not the fittest.

MAN:

We could help some of them. The
lambs. Sometimes they'd pull
through. My mam'd take them in
the house, put them in a basket
like a dog. Cosy by the fire.
Covered in blankets. At night

she'd check on them, make sure
they were still breathing. Me and
my brothers would feed the runt
— that means the smallest, the
weakest, the one who shouldn't
have survived. Baby's bottle
filled with milk and semolina.
Get their weight up. Some of
them found their feet. Like you
said. I was listening. They'd
be shaky but then they'd get
strong. A couple of weeks and
they'd be out in the fields with
the others. Me and my brothers
wanted to make pets out of them
but they forgot us the minute
they left. They were strong,
then. They were sheep. Not
shaky-legged lambs. They didn't
need us. They were the runts that
became the fittest. They survived
with the help of man.

*Another rumble breaks WOMAN and MAN out
of their remembering. They look around
the room — anywhere but at each other —
and go back to talking to the audience.*

WOMAN, *wearily*:
What does it matter? Last
night in the world. By tomorrow
there'll be nothing. No you, no
me, no shitty hotel room. What
does it matter that I spend my
last night listening to you go
on? Side by side on this stained

and springy bed. No love, no
chemistry. No bath, no music, no
candles. Just this. Survival of
the shittest.

                    MAN:
That smirk on your face again.
Like you're laughing at me. Fuck.
We're not going to have sex at
all, are we? Not going to get any
closer than sitting side by side
on this crappy bed. I think she
hates me.

                   WOMAN:
You keep trying to sneak your
hand closer to me across the
bedspread. Even from here I can
tell your palms are sweaty. Why
can't you take the hint? *A short
pause.* Oh God. I think I hate
him.

*A sudden blast sounds out, louder than
any before. The distant sirens that
have been in the background since MAN
and WOMAN entered the room cut off
completely. The stage seems to rumble.
MAN and WOMAN are jostled on the bed.
They stand, quickly. They take two steps
towards the door, still maintaining their
two-metre distance. Another loud bang.*

*WOMAN almost falls to the floor, which is
shaking. MAN reaches for her but another
loud crash stops him. WOMAN stands.*

MAN:
This is it, isn't it?

WOMAN:
This is it.

There is a sudden, blinding light. It drenches the stage, obscures MAN and WOMAN from the audience and from each other. When it fades to a still-harsh white, the hotel room is mostly rubble. The bed has collapsed, the nightstands lying on their sides. The door to the small bathroom is off its hinges and the mirror still visible inside is smashed. Behind the faded net curtains, outside, everything is a brilliant, empty white.

MAN and WOMAN move slowly towards the back of the stage. The frame of the hotel room door shudders and the door falls forwards onto the stage. Beyond it everything is white. The wind whistles into the hotel room from outside, bringing dust and ashes.

MAN and WOMAN look at each other in horror. They understand simultaneously but do not speak: the world has ended, as expected, but they are still alive. They are the last two people left.

The curtains close on their stricken faces, the smell of burning lingering long after the applause has faded.

The carrier

You said, *Is it in there?*

Hand on the extra flesh of me.

Is it there?

Here, I said. *I think. A little lower.*

You adjusted your hand.

Here?

Maybe? I was unsure. So much space between the outside of my navel and the mysterious watery depths. Never before had my body seemed this unfathomable.

Like, you said. *Can you feel it?*

I tried to listen. The yoga midwife had said to. *Listen to your body, feel with your insides.*

A small rumble. Maybe gas.

Yes, I said. Discreetly passed air. The rumble subsided. *Yes, I feel it.*

I held grocery bags in both arms. Bent my knees and engaged my core to lift them. Bottles of vitamins and bottles of water and bottles of vodka and bottles of bleach and lye.

You feared germs and toxoplasmosis, carried the cats to your mother's house in their plastic carriers, car boot pregnant with furry cushions and scratching posts and litter trays, pouches of beef in gravy, squeaky mouse toys.

When I brushed my teeth my gums bled.

Do you think, you said one night, much like any other, *that it can hear us?*

You'd installed the apps, knew each week the size of it, relative to a certain fruit. There is something uncanny about growth, I thought, like stop-motion videos of flowers blooming. There is something discomfiting to the inevitability of something existing.

No, I said, although I did not know. *Not yet.*

We were speaking in hushed whispers, as though it could hear us.

The midwife said to sing, you murmured, and before I could speak you started humming a song. I plugged my ears with cotton wool to drown out the sound.

It could hear us.

One night I awoke and the words you'd gasped into my ear hours before sleeping were spelled out in raised welts across the skin of my belly. I slathered rash cream over the taut outsides, curled my fingers so my nails clawed.

Stop that, I told it. *Stop that or she'll know.*

The marks faded. I felt it contrite.

Okay, I whispered to my belly. *It's okay. I won't tell her.*

A low grumble. It was not displeased.

I craved blue steak and pineapple, the green-red skins of mangoes tough on my tongue, stringy down my gullet. Blood pudding, pretzel sticks studded with salt.

You binned tinned tuna, gave our good whiskey to friends, said we'd buy more eventually. I eyed the empty shelves, cranked open another can of pineapple, waited to hear the whine of the cats thinking the tin opener was calling them but there wasn't so much as a rolling hairball in the draught from the open door. Floors bleached to shining, the smell disguised with scented candles that turned my stomach.

When a cat infects its prey with toxoplasmosis, the rodent loses its fear of felines. Mice and rats nudging closer to the murderous beasts, forgetting for as long as the parasite lives in their small bodies that this creature is their enemy. When the cat eats the rodent, the toxoplasmosis returns to the cat's gut, multiplies, ready to infect again.

You said, *I can't see it.*

Turning your head to see me in a different light, positioning me just so beside the lamp.

Is it doing it now?

Right there, I said. My fingers hovered just over the lump under my skin. *Can't you see?*

You looked like you might cry. *I can't see.*

I took your hand and guided it, crested the small bulge. A press against it, enough for my skin to become a drum before slacking again. You pulled your hand away like you'd been burnt.

You looked away. You said, *I just wanted to see.*

Soon, you saw. One lump became five, all at the same time, as though a giant hand with insistent fingers was pressing against my insides, ready to claw its way out.

You took pictures, crouched on the floor for the angle, said, *You're like an inverted bowling ball*, but a bowling ball has three small dents in it, and there were more swellings across the ball of me than a person has limbs.

I needed heat.

You rolled away from me in the bed, called me a furnace. I took your side of the blanket, folded it on top of mine, made myself a cocoon. The touch of your cold feet was enough to wake me screaming.

In the steam of the bathroom I stood under the shower, shivering. Turned the knob closer and closer to red. When you came in to brush your teeth you gasped, stopped the spray of the water, pulled me out then dropped my wrists in horror. My skin was blistered by the hot tap yet still I shivered.

You caught me up to my forearms in the kettle, swaddled my hands in cream and gauze. I wore my clothes straight from the dryer. The air of the house became brittle with the heat of the radiators groaning. You opened the windows in the spare room and sometimes slept in there. In our shared bed I layered my pyjamas and you lay naked on top of the sheets.

One evening my feet were so cold nothing I could do would warm them. When you came home you found me with my legs stretched into the fireplace, feet crackling black in the flames, face grinning all the while.

It's called nesting, the yoga midwife said. *Preparing the house, the bedroom, folding little clothes.*

You liked this. You liked lining drawers with patterned paper, hanging prints of hot-air balloons on the walls.

I made a bigger fort of my blankets, poured road salt on the sheets of my side of the bed, slept in a nest of coarse pebbles. I filled my pillowcase with broken glass and rested easy, each small slice on my face soothing the grumbling inside my belly.

What do you need? you whispered daily. *More steak? Some salt?* You massaged my lower back with sugar scrub, kneaded at the pulse points of my hands, gently pinched the skin between each finger. I dreamed of rats caught on cat claws.

There is a carrier wasp, I told you, soft and slow, *in Costa Rica.*

A what? You turned to face me in the bed, gently touched the nest of my blankets, felt the heat of me under all those layers.

A wasp.

Okay. Your eyelids dropping, your lips slack. *Like as in an insect?*

That's right.

I rolled out of my blankets, curled around you, legs over legs.

Okay, you said, sleepy. *A carrier wasp. Go on.*

My palm traced the sides of you, two doors. *This wasp*, I said, *lays its eggs on a spider's back.*

Oh?

Yeah. Palm, stroke, deeper breaths. *Safest place*, I said, *for wasp babies.*

Your eyelids fluttered open, your mouth in gentle disbelief. *On a spider?* you said. *Come on.*

It lays its eggs, I said, *on the spider's back. And when the wasp leaves, before the eggs hatch, they latch on to the spider's genetic code and change it.*

How? you said, mostly laughing.

I explained. *The baby wasps release a toxin*, I told you, *that sings a sort of lullaby.*

Mmm. Your eyes closing, your breathing progressively deep.

A lullaby, I said, *that says to the spider that it needs to spin a web.*

That's what spiders do, you breathed.

That's what spiders do, I murmured. *But this spider is listening to the recently hatched young of another species. And there are some things this spider's body knows. It knows that gravity exists* (here my belly convulsed a little – Braxton Hicks, the yoga midwife told me), *it knows that if it falls hard it will get hurt. It knows who it distrusts and who it loves.*

Who does it love? you asked, and I was surprised you were even still awake.

Who does it love? I said. *Well. It loves the young whose DNA is blending with it. The newly hatched eggs on its back. They tell the spider that the wasps on its back couldn't possibly be prey. That what the spider really wants is to spin itself a web. Pull the web close and tight, so tight it can't move, can't spin any longer. The wasp babies' lullabies sing in the spider's body, through its brain and blood. The spider dances to it, trapping itself in its own wet web, happy to die in this sacrificed suicide.*

One day, my fingers blackened from holding them to the iron instead of my shirt, I heard a voice coming from somewhere below my navel. Unintelligible words, an underwater gargle. I understood, though. Already I understood. Already I knew we spoke the same language.

I took a bite out of my arm to see how it would taste. My blood was hot as the shower, studded with coarse salt.

Good, I thought, the words in my mind coming from deep inside the core of me. *I'm almost ready.*

You wrote lists, read over them every morning in front of your coffee, my raspberry leaf tea left to cool on the counter; you wouldn't have me drink it too hot, although I asked.

In the car, a small seat, empty.

Yes, you said to the phone, to the neighbours, to your parents when they came to call with a care package of homemade meals to put in the freezer. *We're as ready as we're going to be.*

It came out of me like a ball of dough, unformed. Easy enough to slither out with the blood and the shit and the fluids all slopping onto the floor. Everything slick and glistening, gruesome.

The midwife put it on my bare chest and it gurgled, choked; no airways.

You came and forced two fingers into its mouth and down its throat, breaking thin membranes so it could take shaky breaths.

It never cried.

I held my hands either side of my hips, fingers in the puddles. Your fingers reached for the thing on my chest, pinched and pulled until two arms formed out of the soft lump of it. You kneaded a pair of legs, toes, fingers. Each joint creaked wetly.

You put your face to my breast and breathed into its eye sockets. Breaths and blinks: it lived.

It had been living for longer than I cared to know.

I had no milk.

It'll come, you said. *Try not to stress. The milk will come out sour if you stress.*

You baked cookies, ordered a half-pint of Guinness down the local and carried it home. Formula-measuring spoons clogged the counters but it wouldn't take a bottle. In the middle of the night, its cries tinning my ears, I took a barbecue skewer from the back kitchen drawer and drove it through each nipple in turn. The milk came out salty and thick.

It grew.

Doubled in size the first two weeks, fed ferocious. When it had drained me of milk it took chunks out of my breasts. I grinned through the pain, bit my own wrist to stop from crying out and waking it. Into its sleeping maw I slipped those bits of myself, pre-chewed so it wouldn't choke. Its stomach grumbled.

If it squalled you let it suck on your finger but when I put my thumb in its mouth it chewed it off. I ripped off the flesh of the other with my teeth to feed to it.

In its sleep it was a blank slate, eyes sunken back into its doughy face. In its sleep I rested. My arms were the holding room. My body the host. It knew it was you brought it into being. Moulding the wax of its body in your image. Your wasp eggs hatching inside of me.

When it woke it was you it cried to for comfort. In your arms it cooed and smiled. In mine, awake, it hungered. Smelled the salt of me and wanted. I chopped off each toe by turn before the last of my fingers. I fed them to it bones and all. The crunches were glorious.

Big round ball of light
and the water

Once there was no sun, he says, here at the edge of the world. Only the flat slope of the far side of the island and the ocean running on forever. I can picture it real easy. The way the water gets at night. The foam of the waves glow. Sometimes there's specks of blue light along the surf. I can picture that forever before we got here.

What lit the day? Poppy always asks, and Marguerite goes to shush her but he only nods fondly every time and says: *The stars. The moon for most the month. Rest of the time*, he says, *darkness*.

And then, I say in me head.

And then, he says like he's heard me.

And then, Poppy'll always sigh, waiting for the next bit.

And then Da on his boat came to the island and me just a bab in his hands and the first mothers followed.

They swam, Daisy joins in.

Like selkies, he'll always finish. *Like seal women they swam. Strong breast stroke against the current.* (The babs flinch or giggle at the word.) *They came to shore sleek and dripping.* (The babs' mouths wide.)

And then. The word on a breath, doesn't matter whose. *And then the sun rose.*

At night there's no sun. It's hiding, see, down under the water. Rises sleek and dripping but you have to call it. Sing to it like the mothers. My voice isn't much but Marguerite – Maggie, though only to me – Maggie's is magic. Rest of us on the cliff in our dresses, feet bare on the moss and rock and her song in our ears. It isn't for us – isn't for me – but it's okay to listen. Just while the sun listens. While she leads the call. It's okay to just for a wee while be pulled outta darkness by Maggie's voice. Pull the sun up into the sky.

And if her song stays in my head the rest of the day then who's gonna know?

He'll know, Poppy'd say, but there's more in my head than he knows.

I hope.

Dead morning, moon black. Shush of the ocean out the window. We keep them open, the windows; good for the lungs, or was it the bones. Salt crusts on our lashes.

Poppy's the earliest, because of the babs. Squirm of one in her tummy now. Every once in a while a wee fist makes a lump under the skin of her. She rises like the sun in the night, tries hard to sink again below the waves but for the water in her.

Some nights it's light from the moon all fat but tonight's a cavern. No blue sprinkle inside this surf. We're not allowed candles. Only our feet bare in the darkness feeling our way. Poppy at the door, whispering though the babs are sleeping in the other part of the house. Daisy just behind her, white shadow, dress stained green at the knees, like us all, from so much kneeling. Our feet hardly make a sound, soft creak of wooded floors and the moves and moans of the babs over past the kitchen. Latch of the front door and suddenly the cold.

Violet's holding a bunch of shawls in her arms against the frost. Our feet'll be blue by the time we reach the cliffs but our arms'll be covered. Fog breath in front of us. Swirl of salt in the air. The ocean's quiet mostly when we reach it. Dark heave below us. Look too hard and your head could lead you in. We lost Lily that way. Suddenly her body was hitting the rocks below and she'd only taken a turn, the others said. Face to her knees, then her knees gave way and she tumbled. I didn't see it. Lagging late with Maggie, we barely made it to sing in the dawn. It was a strangled song, stain of Lily along the cliff, dark spill of her in the water. But still the sun must rise. If we didn't sing it where'd the world be. Cold press of darkness and a mess made of the tides. The crops and animals. All the people over the world we've never seen or met, counting on us for the dawn. Maybe they know when the rising's a mourning song.

He mourned so hard after Lily he left for weeks, out off the island on Da's boat. Came back with another boat of wives, Poppy the newest.

These ones didn't swim.

Poppy leads now, sure of feet, eyes keen. Mine aren't. Unless up close the world's a blur. Maggie says I'm lucky I didn't see it clearly. Lily's body broken on the rocks. Even the smear of red and white being pulled into the water was too much for me. I couldn't have made anything else out even if my eyes were good as Poppy's.

Maggie's hand next to mine, there if I stumble. My feet are pale wee shadows, frosty grass like blades between toes. Stubbed heel, small rock of a wobble. Maggie's palm suddenly against mine. I spare a look back in the darkness as if I'd be able to make out a blur of a face in a window. Only the night and the smell of the ocean and the sounds of early birds.

Poppy gets to the cliff first, arms around the round of her. She sways. Daisy holds her hips and draws her away from the cliff edge. Poppy blinks as if she didn't realise how close she'd got. It happens. Depth is different in darkness and we're tired, all. We're cold. Toes numb in the biting wind. It comes up from the ocean, guarding the sun. We've to sing all the harder, mornings like these, to drag the dawn from the water. The wind a current that won't want to let go.

Maggie leads the song. We all hold hands now, it's allowed. We line in our white dresses and our blue feet and the shawls on our shoulders and one by one we open our mouths to sing. Same song each morning, only song that'll call up the dawn. It's work, each note coaxed from sore cold throats. The harmonies, the high bits. Wee wobble on the fifty-third round but it's a solid hundred before the sun comes up. Pushes out of the ocean all wet and glistening. Spreads light around the world. It's bright white, today. Some days warm yellow, some mornings blaring red. There's a cold to this white blinding. Eyes crinkling shut around the last of the singing. After, most of us can't speak for hours. A good thing, he says. Mornings should be quiet. Our breath spent on making the day.

When the sun comes up we kneel. Green stain on the knees. Sometimes it bleeds through white cotton to the skin underneath. Like the scabs on the babs, green knees we won't scrub clean 'cause it reminds us of the kneeling. Of the push of the sun into the world again. Reminds us our voices are strong enough to call it. For today again, at least.

Sun high, now, some warmth off it. Feet in socks and boots out the pasture. Frost turned to mud trampled by animals. Hay and silage. Heaty meaty smell. Daisy tripping over the grass, laughing, the goats doing their wee dance, following. From the house, the babs calling.

Maggie off with the horses, hair bobbing behind her like she's singing. She isn't, she's not allowed, nor any of us, unless it's morning. But her voice is in me head, making rounds, notes banging off the inside of my skull like I'm the instrument her voice is playing.

I collect eggs, make skillets of omelettes with spring onion and spuds pulled out the ground. *So many mouths*, he always says, proud. *So many mouths to feed*. Extra for Poppy who's eating for two, although last time, with Daisy, there were twins in her. Only one lived, though they were both girls. She shoulda been eating for three. He brought a doc along to the island for Poppy then, to count the babs inside her. We'd to stay out by the cliffs but me and Maggie crept back around the side of the barns. Feet bare so we wouldn't leave prints. Poppy talked about it for days: the doc with his hands on her belly, pressing. Listening to heartbeats through a cold-bottomed stethoscope. We only saw the back of the doc's head, me and Maggie, thinning hair blacker than his. Puffy jacket against the cold walking back with him to the boat. The whole hour it took him to take the doc to the mainland and come back none of us worked, only touched Peggy's belly and gossiped about the doc. He knew but let it be. *Bitta gossip is good for women*, he says sometimes. That's okay. Sometimes it's good for men too. Sometimes we like giving him summat to gossip about.

He's in the cow shed when I come in for the pails of milk after the babs' suppers.

You hiding in here? I ask him. He doesn't mind me being cheeky, long as it's not around the babs, long as it's only occasional.

One hand on a heifer, one in his hair. *Only a bit*, he says. *D'you not think it gets loud out there in the house sometimes?*

Seven wives, five babs, the sheepdog's litter still learning to sleep outside, three cats to catch the rats.

Sometimes, I tell him.

You aren't a quiet one, he says.

Not me.

Poppy all right? he asks. *With the sleeping?*

He's sleeping with Iris these days, Violet sometimes. The rest of us in the other room, across the house from him and the babs.

More or less. Snores like a storm though.

He laughs. It's a rumbly sound, not unpleasant. Makes me give a lil smile too.

She'll be away with the babs soon enough.

True, that. Only a month left, by our reckoning. Doc seemed to think she'd go early but the rest of us know better. We know how birthing works on the island. Both the sun and the daughters. Same process. We sing them slick and dripping out into the world.

I've the milk in pails again he calls to me, hand still on the heifer though the other's left his hair. *You'll send Marguerite in to me tonight, will you?*

Marguerite?

Aye, he says. *Iris has her time. She'll bed with you for the week.*

And Violet? I say although I shouldn't.

Lil squint to the look in his eye.

Aye, I say quick. *I'll tell her.*

Good girl.

Milk slops over the pail handle, over my wrist.

The sun sets by itself. Doesn't need a song. No barefoot lullaby. Just sinks down back into the ocean with a sigh and a smile, day's end. Must be comfy down there, for all the effort it takes to rise it. Easier to sink into sleep than out of it, I always think. We've some in common, me and the sun.

Maggie's voice calls us. The sun mornings, me in dreams. Wouldn't dare repeat it, not even to her, but sometimes I fear I'll be heard humming her words in my sleep. Her voice out my mouth like she'd reached right in and slipped down my gullet. Some nights I dream I swallow her whole.

We're of an age, me and Maggie. Bit old for him now. Came over on the same boat near a decade ago fresh-faced and ready to pray. He'd leaflets in the local church but followed no god only the sun. Seven sisters, he said. Seven sisters to call up the sun. I'd only brothers, knew football and fistfights but wanted softness and magic. White dresses and bare feet on the cliff at the edge of the world.

I got it, didn't I?

Got Maggie too, in a way. It's okay. This isn't a bad life, everything around the work of sun rising. And this work, it's bigger than Maggie. Bigger than me. Bigger than him with his boats full of wives. Seven sisters, he said, not seven wives. Yet here we are. It's part of the magic. The island asks for us.

Men can't sing up the sun, we known that since Sage. The island can only handle one man at a time, bar the doc or the occasional worker. And don't we stare. And don't they. Seven wives on the island, litter of babs in white. Hard not to wonder. Let them wonder, he says. Gossip's good for mainlanders. Once they don't look too close. Once they don't disturb the island's trust.

That happens, and the sun won't be coaxed to rise. And then where would we be but in an endless darkness.

Black night, no stars but clouds leaking splatters every time the wind blows. Poppy snores on her back, belly too round to roll over. Most the others sleep with cotton in their ears.

The bed beside me empty.

The island needs daughters, needs sisters, needs wives. He gives the sun his daughters. Gives his sons to the ocean but we don't speak of that. We come to him willing, we know this. Maggie knows this. I do. Long corridor between our bedroom and his. Violet woulda taken Maggie's bed but she's in with the babs, one of them teething, another washed over with night terrors, wetting the bed. Bit old for that, I think, but once she's over it she'll be grown. Might replace the next of the seven of us to go.

Counting the ones I've known under the black ceiling, the black sky. Lily, Sage and Rue. Seven's the number most minds can remember. A series, a spell. There are seven days in a week, seven sacraments, seven deadly sins. Not that we believe in sinners. Pythagoras believed seven was a spiritual number, I remember that from school. Seven seals, seven meals. Seven selkies come in on the surf, scintillating blue phosphorescence freckling their bodies. Sleek and slippery. Not of this earth but of the water. That's what he tells us but we know it best of all.

My feet touch floor, swung sideways off the bed. My hands grope along the whitewashed wall all oily with cold condensation, fingertips slipping. I know the contours of the room, can avoid each bed with my toes though my eyes see so little. Only fuzzy dark shapes in the greyness. I can tell by the breathing which wife's bed I'm passing. From the window, Poppy's snores.

The hall's colder, no bodies breathing the same soupy air. Summers we open the window to the mosquitoes but winter it's sealed shut. Wouldn't want to catch a chill, not when we've to walk barefoot to the edge of the world, not when our throats can't ever be voiceless.

Soon as I've thought it there's an itch in my larynx. Blame that on how my toes thud softly past the door to the outside. Well past, past the kitchen that still smells summat of rinsed-off egg. Past the half-cracked door of the babs' room, candlelight flickering from within. His room's at the far end of the house, ours on the other, facing themselves along the hall. Inside, silence. I'd know Maggie's breathing better than me own but there's only his soft huffs when I press my ear to the keyhole. I should turn. Should return to bed. Let myself be lulled by Poppy's snores until she wakes us before dawn. But it's hours of black night left.

The doors are never locked. The animals can't lift latches and there's always someone with the babs and where would the rest of us go but the ocean? Suddenly a swim sounds like a cure. A cure I need for an affliction I can't put a name to.

Outside's colder than the cold of the house. Bitta bite to the wind, not quite ice but not far from it. Wakes me right up, sets my senses straight. Creeping through the house, listening at keyholes. That's no way for a wife to behave.

My feet don't follow familiar paths. Instead turn away from the edge of the known world and inland, not that there's much land in. The old stone structure's maybe a half-hour walk away, another half-hour to the other side of the island. Clear days you can see the mainland but that's to the south. I go north. Go up. Rise into the world like the sun.

Top of the island's the burial ground. Little enough, if you know where to look. Small smooth stones in a circle, scratch of names and the flowers. Like a bab's clapping game, turn holding hands in a circle, stop where you drop. The boys aren't here but their names are, all secret. Iris is the artist. Nail and chisel marking flowers in stone. He knows, but pretends he doesn't, that we gave the boys names. Alongside them the two bigger stones are Lily and Rue, the smaller Sage although he isn't buried here either. His body's back on the mainland, breathing, most likely. Moving and eating and crying and speaking of us, sometimes, lick of drink in him, faraway look to his eye.

Came over as a wife, did Sage, on the first boat after me and Maggie. Says the island knew before he did. He stayed, almost two years after the other three wives went back. We don't all stay. Those three didn't get their names so off they went back to their lives with hushed tales of the island at the edge of the world, all reverence. Sage less reverent maybe.

The sun was rising later each day, see, taking longer to come up out the ocean. He knew something was wrong. Seven sisters to stand barefoot and sing the dawn out the water but for a time it was only six of us and Sage. It got harder. After our voices were so sore we'd not be able to speak until next morning. The frailest of us coughed blood. He figured out what it was eventually. There wasn't seven sisters singing up the dawn. There was a man among us, for all he looked like what we thought a woman should be. The island knew before he did. When he left and Lily took up his place from out the babs' room the sun all but shot up into the sky.

Bab wives work for the water but not men born looking like girls, that's what he says and we believe him because every morning our voices make the sun rise. And if they didn't where would we be?

There's a dark shape by the graves. Top of one, looks like. Blur of a figure folded over Lily's rock, the date of her death. Takes me a while to make out it's Maggie. Shawls on her shoulders, boots on her feet. Seems to be sleeping, back slowly rising and falling with breath. I want to fold myself over her, be the blanket against the cold, Lily the mattress beneath her.

Barely past babhood, was Lily. Just out the room with the others and into ours. Wide-eyed, quiet, excited. First time she came to sing with us already knew all the words. Voice high and bright.

I touch Maggie's shoulder real soft instead.

How long? she says, waking. Stirs into my arms.

How long you been here? I ask.

Aye.

Dunno. When you leave his room?

Her hand gentles across my shoulder.

Midnight, maybe.

I give the sky a look. *Not long till dawn now I reckon.*

Oh. A pause. *We should get back.*

Aye. I'm up in half a second, legs jittering. Pull her up by both arms and she staggers into me. Been lying in the same cold place too long, takes time to get the blood moving. I give her sides a rub, reach around to her back. Her breath's a cloud.

Doc's coming back, she says into my hair.

Ey?

For Poppy. He says he's worried.

She's grand though.

That's what I thought, but he says she isn't. Him, and the doc.

Not far, the ocean chops the rocks. The wind's a long-held note.

She's grand, I say again, follow her bootsteps home.

When we sing the sun rises red and watery from the depths of the ocean and we seven on the long cliff at the edge of the world but I amn't looking out on the big round ball of light and the water, and I amn't looking at Maggie's throat moving around the high notes, I'm looking at Poppy. The round of her, the light of her, the water of her. She looks grand by me but I amn't a doc. How she holds herself, the sweat of her top lip, I've seen it before with the others. She eats for two and sleeps sounder'n the rest of us. But yet he called another man to the island again. The sun rises dripping and angry.

Dew-damp walk back up the house, throats raw, eyes gritty. The doc's there already. He musta gone out in the boat soon as we left. Only the oldest babs to watch the littlest. She's pink-cheeked at the window already, the bed-wetter, the eldest. It comes to me the thought that if Poppy dies birthing, this bab'll take her place.

We whisper round the house and out, milk the cows, feed the pigs, send the babs out for eggs. Rose's turn to cook, Iris changing nappies. We've a quiet dance around each other most days, change partners, don't bump into another between the kitchen and the chores, two by two in the fields. It's a choreography we know as well as the words we sing to the water but into it today there's a lil new flash of something white and crinkled, passing hand to hand. Doc to Poppy to Iris checking in. Iris to Violet to Rose pounding meat with a mallet for tea. Rose to Daisy coming in for a mop. Daisy to Maggie in the hallway. Maggie following me out to the sheep.

You didn't see? she says to me.

Been waiting my turn, I tell her. We're all so used to the rhythm of our days we notice anything different. Been watching the folded paper making its way from hand to hand to hand. *What is it?*

The letter crinkles from her fingers to my palm, seven times read. At the bottom, first thing I see, is the signature.

With love, it says, *from Nate (Sage).*

A letter, I say, reading.

A letter from Sage.

What's he say? I say, still reading.

See for yourself, she laughs, small touch of her elbow to the side of my arm. It's enough to disturb my balance for days but my eyes are on the paper, on Sage's handwriting, his *hope you are okay*, his *how much better things are on the mainland*, his *maybe you've forgotten but*, his *should one day join me*, his *before like Lily it is too late.*

What is this? I say, finished, looking up from the paper as if surfacing from the sea. The air's thicker up here.

What do you think? she says.

What do the others think? I answer.

They're wondering.

Wondering what?

Wondering if maybe he's right.

Right about the mainland? Right about Lily? Right about – I cast around, checking. *Right about leaving?*

Maggie says nothing.

I whisper, *What about the sunrise?*

She gives a lil look back down at the paper, at the things that Sage said about that. *I know*, she tells me. *But still. Some of the others are wondering.*

The others wonder through the whole day. The letter makes its rounds again, paper softened by seven pairs of hands, words traced over by enough fingers they go inky grey. I don't have to wonder. I came here for a reason, good decade ago now, clutching the sides of his da's boat. Every morning for well on ten years I join the others and we sing up the sunrise. This is what we are here for. All else is just the crinkled noise of fading paper.

And Maggie. First moment I met her, church pew suddenly pitching under my thighs, her hand so close to mine. *Going to an island*, she said, *become one of those who raise the sun.*

Did you know, she said, *that once there was no sun?*

But since, he added, suddenly right behind us, hands on the backs of the pew between us, *the task of bringing the world the day comes from my very island.*

Edge of the world, she said reverently.

Edge of the world, he nodded. *Only way to raise the sun out the ocean. Make the day.*

We need you, he told me. *We need your help.*

It's Maggie I looked at when I said yes.

He's here now, walking up behind me as I hang clean sheets, breeze colding the linen. Two moths beating their wings on the clothes pegs. I leave them at it.

It's Daisy making dinner today, I tell him. He's surprised I heard him come up, I can tell, but he recovers quick.

I need your help, he says.

I'm listening.

You're close, he says. *With Marguerite.*

I am with all my sisters.

He shakes that away like moths off a clothes peg. They swirl around each other in the sky. He says, *She wants to leave.*

Leave?

Leave the island, he says. *Leave the sun to rot under the water, never rise again.*

She wouldn't, I lie.

She told me. His voice is a boy's, small and high and strained. *Says if her bab's not a girl she's leaving.*

Her bab.

I'll talk to her, I tell him.

Nail-clip moon morning, Maggie in his room again, my eyes through my open door to his closed one. Awake even before Poppy first stirs. Outside frost along the ground like a carpet, cold crunch to our bare feet. Maggie holds out her hand for me as always, the blur of my eyes greyer than the frost. Her palm warm and five freezing fingers.

The walk to the edge of the world is long. Again Poppy leads. Over rock and hill and tussock, field and drier dune. Here the wind's insistent, whips hair and shawl, drives chill to the bones. There's some light to the sky, sprinkle of stars and that crescent moon above us. Again I glance back to the house when it'd be almost out of sight for better eyes than mine and in the window instead of a shadow that could be him or one of the babs there's Lily. Hair loose and face all bashed by rock. Eyes wide and staring.

I stumble. Maggie's hand tightens in mine and her other reaches around to link my hip. Balance is tricky on ground like this. Lily's eyes shine off of every pebble. The sound of the wind is the crying of just-born boys. No one follows, it's not allowed. Only the seven of us up on the cliff at world's end, in the cold and the darkness. Usually we don't speak till the song starts so to save our voices but today there's low murmurs from beyond me and Maggie lagging in the rear.

They're whispering about the letter. I worry they wish to leave. We reach the long stretch of cliff edge together and other hands join besides ours. Breaths cloudy, feet turning blue. The whispers die out this close to the water, this soon to the dawn. We breathe as one and Maggie starts the song. With seven singing high together the sun rises slick and quick and sudden, bright yellow like the light of an old bruise.

By the time we've returned up the house there is a plan. I listen like a moth at the window but when night falls again and Maggie turns from the kitchen to his room I'm as decided as the rest of them.

Moon washed out behind wisp of cloud, frost a fog across the ocean. Couple hours to dawn and the island's silent.

Boat choppy on the water, Poppy at the helm. Between her in front and me and Maggie out back the small sleepy squalls of the babs huddled under shawls, boots on feet, as many socks as were in the airing cupboard. Maggie's hand icy in mine, grip tight. Up and down over the waves. Under us the sun warms the sea, waits for our song but won't hear it. The knowing twists my gut but Maggie's laced her fingers between mine and that's enough to hold me to the boat.

I've made this journey once before only, full of love and trepidation and this time's no different. Cold dark above and the heaving below. All around, our bodies. And back on the island the man who brought us there, alone with the animals and the edge of the world.

It's a quick voyage for all we're shivering. Poppy steers us ashore on the mainland and there is the town clustered around the mouth of the river, us on the dock feeling larger than the world around us. The town is small, by most standards, but we've been on the island most a decade, some of us. Maggie doesn't let go my hand. The others pull their babs to their breasts.

In the trees and on telephone wires, birds. They sing their morning song to the dark that looks a lot like night. Is it the sun decides the morning or is it the birds? Do days still exist if there isn't any dawn? I s'pose we'll soon enough know.

The town's sleepy. Few cars on the roads, the odd bike. Babs in dark colours headed off to class. I remember classes. Hard plastic seats that restless squeaked. Down further the train station's the braces that line the teeth of the bay. That's where Poppy leads us, address in her head. Rest of us wouldn't even start to know where to go so we follow. Clutch of sisters and a handful of babs, all in white and those wellies and shawls. We're a sight. But few enough folks are looking. All checking their watches, checking their phones, sneaking looks up the sky as if the sun'll catch them and get shy.

No sun, though.

At the station, Poppy talks to someone who talks to someone else, buys us all sandwiches out a vending machine, packets of crisps for the babs who've never seen the like. Half them cry within ten minutes. The street-lights click off one by one but still in the sky there's no sun. Only a wan moon slice behind moving cloud, few snatches of stars. Our faces washed out by the electric lights. The older babs, that should know better, stare around like they've never been told there was a world beyond the island. Always has been, but that's never been important. Only the work.

Where's the sun? Maggie whispers so low only I can hear, although I amn't sure it's meant for me.

What you mean? I answer anyway.

Thought it'd be up by now, she says, sense of vague in her voice.

222

Our hands are stiff when they come apart.

What did you come to the island for? I want to ask her. *If you never truly believed we called up the sun?*

Know what I want her to say of course, but those lil words *I stayed for you* never come out her throat.

Giz a song, I say instead, as the train screeches by, as the babs cover their ears and laugh and laugh and the person Poppy knows returns with money we haven't seen in ten-odd years. *Giz a couple notes of a melody.*

The hum of her smile right by my ear and the barest whisper. Somewhere east, edge of the world, we all feel – or me at least – the pull of the big round ball of light and the water. Maggie's lips touch my hair as her song stops and I think fuck the sunrise.

Next train that screeches up, we're on it. Nothing but the dresses and the shawls, the boots and the babs, the voices that won't work this far in away from the edge of the world and the water.

The sun doesn't rise. Days and then weeks and months. There's a world in which we leave the house we share with Sage and his wife out past the next town over, rooming together, barefoot or in boots, but the next babs born are boys left living and Poppy and Maggie both cry with the joy of keeping them. They are given names. None of us cross the hall in the long dark to his room and eventually Maggie and I get our own room, big bed and cradle for our son.

The sun doesn't rise. Electricity buzzing through the day and on the news the terror. It's all anyone out the town will talk of but we in our lil house with our small fields and our chickens speak of anything but. There's a world in which we do, in which we whisper that this darkness is traded off for our freedom. But in this world, not far from the edge of it, we and the only boat out the island still our seven voices and never sing again.

Saying its name breaks it

Here's a riddle for you: when I'm young I'm tall and when I'm old I'm short. What am I?

That one's easy. Everybody knows it.

I was always tall. In school they called me Spider, all legs. Spider sitting spindly in her web, waiting. There was a list of the photographs inside at the back of the dictionary, although you think it'd be only words, but sometimes words require illustration. Here, a diagram: eight legs, many eyes, fur that you stroke the wrong way like shag carpet pile. Spider. Do you know a riddle for a spider?

About, I mean. About a spider.

I don't.

I had a friend who was a mirror. Hold a candle up to her and you'd see the light reflected. Tall and white and straight. I had a friend who was a candle, started tall and ended up a wax splat on the floor, spent. I had a friend when the power went and because she was lit we didn't need a torch.

It left in flickers. The power. Isn't that the way they always say? You think you've all the power and it's stripped inch by bright inch until you realise you've been in darkness for days. I don't know. Maybe we never had power. Maybe we were being lit by someone else's torches all along.

The first day the power went there were giggles. Like that time everybody can remember when a dog wandered into the school. Everyone has a school dog story. Now everyone's stories are about the power. How it went, why, who had it longest, does anybody have it still.

If you line a room with mirrors one light looks like a hundred.

There were twelve of us in the Long Room, giggling. The students had left already and there were no tourists any more, following us around the Old Library with their Book of Kells tote bags. It was already only us, and the books. Someone flicked the switches, rapid click-click, to test them. Phones lit like stars blinking to life in a muddy sky. If you'd clambered to the ceiling you could have made constellations. On the ceiling: shadows. No phone-light star-watchers. On the floor: the giggles of grown women and men. The tables strewn with books and papers. The dust settling on the stacks. In the carefully pressurised room beyond, the old collection breathed in the dark.

You like riddles? Here's another. The more of this there is, the less you see – what is it?

I'll tell you if you like. It's not difficult.

It's darkness.

Jack be nimble Jack be quick Jack stuck his fingers in the socket to see if it'd spark enough to hurt. Or, wait. Is that not how that one goes? My friend – we'll call her Alice, the candle, the light, the looking-glass – held him as he cried. That was later, though. Not the first time the power went. Not quite the last but almost. Jack cried. The rest of us didn't. There were ten of us in the Long Room, shuffling. Maybe Jack'd been the one most used to power. Flick a switch and everything's illuminated, all the knowledge of the world in your back pocket. Hard to imagine now, isn't it? In all this dark and quiet.

Alice held him as he cried and the rest of us shuffled around the Long Room, awkward.

It'll be okay, we could hear Alice whisper. Leaf-swirl hush of an echo to the tall beams of the ceilings. *Don't worry. It'll be okay. It'll come back.*

What can you break, even if you never pick it up or touch it?

You know that one too, I'm sure. You know it's a promise.

Oh, but there I go again, telling things how they were and not the way they are. No way to tell a tale at all. Only way to tell a tall tale.

My tale's mid-sized, really, five eight or thereabouts, bang of a riddle to it. What can fill a room but takes up no space? That's a good one. I'll let you think on that one a while.

Alice was smaller. Not like she'd drank a potion but like she'd been grown in the dark. Slight and pale. Not mid-sized, our Alice, no. Little sweet thing, five foot nothing. Side by side we were comical. Tweedle-small and Tweedle-tall. Other than that folks said we looked alike. Me and Alice, a woman and her warped reflection.

When she left it should have made barely a ripple. Tiny person-shaped hole in the world where a friend used to be. Here's another riddle for you: what gets bigger when more is taken away?

Here's a hint: it wasn't Alice.

The power flickered for months. Little moments like held-in laughter. Then the guffaws of blackouts from when the lights just couldn't hold it in. Videos that wouldn't upload. Kettles barely boiled. Slippery pools around the freezer. It'd spark back eventually and everyone would sigh, until it took longer and longer and the sighs were less relief and more another held breath. Getting it back only to know it'd go again.

We were used to silence. There were eight of us in the Long Room, breathing. No pens, no phones, only pencil nibs tracing sharp scratches on sensitive paper. Low sighs, soft inhales. It's what we were accustomed to. In the holding room, air regulated to perfect temperature, we barely drew breath. Alice's hands turning ancient paper, encased in latex.

Does the act of reading in secret change the meaning of the text? The way you read this now informs the story. Pages splayed under blankets or spine bent in public so the cover's turned over. Who reads these words over your shoulder?

Things are quiet. Without the humming and the buzzing and the pinging and the ringing and the drumming of soft fingers on hard plastic keys. It's easy to forget how loud things were when now we speak in whispers.

In the dark the books breathe. They always did, you know that, don't you Alice? Didn't you? Didn't you hear the whispers of each page settling against the other in the night, softly, so the neighbouring books wouldn't hear them? So the books in the shelves below wouldn't look over to their sleeping bags and see the hands slipping under the covers. Darkness hides a million sins, doesn't it, Alice?

Anyway. Alice isn't here.

Here's a riddle she asked me once; you might appreciate it too. What is always in front of you but can't be seen?

Here's a hint: it doesn't exist anymore.

In the future we saw hope and it was blown out like a flame.

Outside the Long Room, Jack had a beanstalk. Well. Small line of skinny vines with peas in long pods. We split them open with our thumbnails, spilled the little balls out. They were so sweet between our teeth. He planted the seeds the first spring in Library Square. In autumn still we were untangling the tendrils one from the other, pinching the pods away from where they climbed the base of the Campanile. There were six of us in the Long Room, eating.

We'll sow again in March, he said. *Plant potatoes, carrots.*

He kept the roots of each in the holding room, temperature regulated for the keeping of old books, not vegetables.

You can't eat books, Jack said, but in the end we didn't eat the carrots either.

When it became clear that the power would go for good eventually, we began collecting rainwater in giant vats on the roof of the Ussher Library. Daily we scaled the access stairs, unpeeled the mesh from the barrels. Still, a film of dust and birdshit remained.

By then most of us had left. There were four of us in the Long Room.

Don't you have a home to go to? Gwen said. She didn't, we knew that. You should know that too.

You should know that none of us who stayed had anywhere left to go.

It became very cold. Power warms. Those without power shiver in their sleep sacks, drag mattresses across the floor, huddle together with no thought for privacy. There was enough of that during the day. We each at our desks as if the world wasn't ending, turning pages, taking notes. Alice with her smoke sponge, her soft brushes. Books shushed from their plastic sleep sacks, inspected, whispered right back in.

Jack's bags propped his head as a pillow although we had pillows to spare. Long before, he and Alice had dated. Held hands in Stephen's Green behind the fountain, kissed at the bus stop, the taste of two-for-one cocktails on their tongues, Alice's lipstick leaving the slightest stain on the side of Jack's mouth.

Who has the power when the power is all around you? Slipping lamppost to lamppost, tall sliver of darkness making a pool in the light. I blocked out the yellow gleam with the height of me, hid to not be seen, but they were looking at nobody but each other. Jack and Alice: giant-killer and a mirror, hand in gloved hand, fog streaking the city.

What part of you can touch the water but never gets wet?

I followed them, three times weekly, across the Liffey. One bridge over but I had good eyesight despite years of squinting at the rare book collection, spyglass in hand. There were special lamps back then that lit each page to near transparency. I traced the letters, the drawings, by hand, ready to be digitised. It was easy to be a shadow back then. Lamp-lit centre of Dublin City, the headlights of cars and shop signs bright in unshuttered windows. Power all around turned so high nobody could tell where it was coming from.

Have you solved it yet? The part of you that can touch water without getting wet?

I was their shadow in the river and when they kissed I watched and when they climbed the bus steps together, cards beeping by the driver seat, sheer drill fuzz of the overhead lights and the little constant buzz of mobile phones, I followed.

Who reads these words over your shoulder? That's not a riddle but still I have an answer.

I do. I, who wrote the words.

If you drop me I'm sure to crack, but give me a smile and I'll always smile back. What am I?

Alice stood in front of the ladies' room mirror in the Old Library the day the power went, wax-splattered sink under the palms of her hands, flicker of flame reflected in the glass. That morning, Jack had cried.

How long do you think we have? Alice asked. I was the only other soul in the room.

You told Jack it would come back, I whispered. Nobody had spoken at full volume in weeks.

Alice turned from the mirror and the sink and the

shadows of the water. She took my face in her soft hands. She had told Jack a lot of things but she hadn't told him this.

Her lips were a hush in the silence, a light amongst the candle flames.

That night we traded riddles to keep the dark at bay. Every once in a while the static of Gwen's wind-up radio paused for a moment and formed words, brittle, sharp, indented like fragments in the oldest texts of the collection. Papyrus. We couldn't make them out.

When I'm young I'm tall and when I'm old I'm short, Gwen said. *What am I?*

Jack held his palm above a flame and said, *That one's easy.*

A candle, I said quickly.

A candle, Gwen repeated.

Outside, suddenly, the sound of hoofbeats. We'd grown able to tell how far the riders were depending on the cadence of their horses. Iron shoes on the cobblestones of Front Square or the grass of College Park or the black empty roads outside our walls. We were well barricaded by bookshelves but yet we stilled, silent as the pages. Only the occasional dry spark of fire like the smacking of lips. The hooves moved on.

Alice spoke into the space left behind. *What can fill a room but takes up no space?*

I'm sensing a theme, Gwen smiled thinly.

Jack opened his mouth to answer the riddle but my voice was faster.

It's light, I said. *Isn't it?*

Alice held my gaze. *It is,* she said.

Jack said, *Okay, my turn. Um. Let's see. Okay. I've got one. If you drop me I'm sure to crack, but give me a smile and I'll always smile back. What am I?*

I answered first again. *That one's easy*, I said. *A mirror.*

Do you have one? asked Jack, his hand next to Alice's in the space between mattresses.

I said, *I have one. Tell me if you know it. If you've got me, you want to share me; if you share me, you haven't kept me. What am I?*

Alice whispered, *A secret.*

It's been months but I haven't got out of the habit of thinking up riddles to pass the time. Time passes, even without power. There may be no future but the present carries on.

That's what I mean by telling things the way they are. Right after you notice the moment, it's gone.

Here's a riddle, I know you like riddles. This one makes sense in context. What can you keep even after giving it to someone?

Go on. You know you know this one.

After flickering for weeks the power went and didn't come back. We read over each other's shoulders until the computers lost the last of their charge, our phones not far behind. There was nothing left to light us but fire. Just like it used to be. The books in the holding room loved it, secretly. They were created by hand and candlelight, like the books I write today. Only the soft press of pencil against the page. Once, words were the only power. This is the present but that hasn't changed.

I haven't heard hoofbeats in days.

★

One day Gwen walked into the city for supplies and never came back. We waited three weeks before mourning her as though she'd died. Alice asked me to dig her a grave out in Library Square with the others.

One of the last of us to fall, she said, as though Gwen had taken a bad trip on a cobblestone, or had fainted.

There was only me and she and Jack, then, alone in the Long Room, muck under my fingernails for days.

It was then, I think, that Alice began to shrink.

Do you remember when I asked you what gets bigger when more is taken away? If you didn't get it then you might get it now.

I dug a hole six feet across and six feet deep and into it I tossed Gwen's work because she didn't have a body to bury.

There was still so much space in the grave.

There were three of us in the Long Room, sharing mattresses and rainwater, checking the hard ground for carrots. Across the square our whispers carried, repeated against the walls of the other empty buildings.

Alice, tiny Alice, smudge in the mirror of my giant reflection. We hid behind the Campanile as if we'd nowhere else to not be seen. It was so quiet, then, in the city without power, that each touch of our lips reverberated over and over and over.

When we came back to the Long Room Jack called from his desk louder than we'd heard a soul call in more than a year.

I thought of a new riddle, he said, his chest puffed where Alice's was a hollow. Maybe he took the power from her and put it into himself. Maybe we both did.

Oh yeah? Her voice was strained. We'd been through every riddle in the book. In every book.

Yeah, he said. He looked at me and asked us, *What can't talk but will reply when spoken to?*

I knew it immediately but Alice tilted her head to one side and waited for her mind to catch up.

We'd all lost them a little at that point, our minds. Hard to find them again in all that silence.

Well? Jack said. *Do you give up?*

Yeah, Alice said wearily. *I'm sorry. I give up. I'm too tired.*

Alice had shrunk to half her size. I, who had always towered over her, was like a giant when I stepped between them.

I don't give up, I told him. *I know the answer.*

Okay then, said Jack. *What is it? What can't talk but will reply when spoken to?*

I said, *An echo.* And all around the square was the sound of two pairs of lips kissing.

The thing about silence is that when one is completely accustomed to it, its absence is a smack. Unlike the power, which left in spurts and stages, when silence is broken it's sharp as a mirror fragment. Alice didn't get it but there isn't a lick of dust on me. That night he pulled his sleeping bag between us and for days our roles inverted and he was our shadow. The whole world empty and we couldn't be alone together. Even in the ladies' room his legs would lock around the door like a spider's. Do you have a riddle for a spider? Did I ask you that before? Never mind. I'm the only spider here now besides those spinning their webs too high across the ceiling for my broom to reach.

There is another riddle we didn't think of back then. I've only remembered it now, but then my memory isn't what it used to be.

Here it is – listen carefully now because my voice is weak, I'm sorry, I may have to repeat myself. Here it is: I'm light as a feather, yet the strongest person can't hold me for five minutes. What am I?

Jack's breath was heavy but I held it so hard it flew away. There was still six feet of good grave left unburied so into it he tumbled, quick and nimble.

This isn't a tall tale, bang of a riddle about it. Six feet's hardly tall when you're surrounded by the city.

Alice asked and asked me. Where did he go, when did he leave, why did you cover Gwen's grave when we may yet find her body. With each question she shrank down to the bones of her. With each scratch of her throat she settled into silence.

There were two of us in the Long Room, kissing. I thought, now we can share the power. There wasn't near enough of it to go around before. But now, I thought, we can light up the end of the darkness together. I had a friend who was a mirror. Hold a candle up to her and you'd see the light reflected. I suppose I was the candle: tall and white and straight. I had a friend who was a candle, started tall and ended up a wax splat on the floor, spent. I had a friend when the power went but when she left it made barely a ripple. Tiny person-shaped hole in the world where a friend used to be.

★

For weeks I've been singing so long my throat is raw each evening when I lie on my mattress alone in the cold. By morning my voice scratches but I stretch my neck and keep on singing every song I know.

When I pause for breath there is nothing. No sound. I have never known such silence. Not even the books speak to me. Not even the ghost of Alice who watches me like a shadow in each mirror, in every black window on the endless empty streets when I leave the Long Room of the Old Library to breathe in the outside air.

What is so fragile that saying its name breaks it?

It isn't friendship, not even close. It isn't love, although that too breaks easily. It's not the world but it may as well be. It isn't a mind, a heart, or a voice, even if mine breaks daily here alone. Still I keep singing. I keep singing singing singing. I keep singing alone against the fragile silence.

Won't you please come and sing here with me.

A different beat

The ghost of Stephen Gately appeared to Jenny three days after her twelfth birthday, which was curious, as Stephen Gately had thirteen years left of his life when Jenny turned twelve. Curiouser still that Jenny recognised the spectral adult man as the baby-faced twenty-year-old on her bedroom posters.

Jenny had fifty-eight of them: Boyzone posters torn from the middles of magazines. In each, five shiny young men with varying degrees of floppy hair, dressed to match. Their teeth were ghost-white, their chins smooth, their eyes lively. They were fresh from Wembley Arena or *The Late Late Show* or *Top of the Pops*. They looked like they were having a great time.

I bet he'd be a good kisser, Cate said.

Jenny stared at the ghost of Stephen Gately. He was browsing the sandwich aisle, head to one side.

Huh? Jenny asked.

I bet he'd be a good kisser, Cate repeated. She picked up a can of Coke, a packet of Skips. Want some?

Jenny watched the ghost of Stephen Gately read the ingredients on the back of a ham and cheese sandwich. Um, she said. No. Thanks.

Cate shrugged, popped a handful of pick 'n' mix in her mouth when she thought no one was looking. Have you got this one already? she asked.

The ghost of Stephen Gately put the sandwich back on the shelf and looked up at Jenny. His eyes were blue as the ones on her posters.

Jenny, said Cate.

Jenny blinked and the ghost of Stephen Gately was gone.

Jenny, Cate said again.

Yeah? Jenny's heart did a little thud.

Do you have this one?

In her hand, a magazine, the title printed in big pink letters. On the cover, the real Stephen Gately, his hair floppy, parted in the middle, his cheeks untouched by stubble.

Oh. Jenny's heart did another few thuds. Yes. Yeah. I have that one.

Cool. Cate flicked her wrist and sent the magazine spinning back onto the rack. Anyway, she said, unsticking a piece of sweet from her braces with her tongue. I bet he'd be a good kisser.

Jenny's dad was painting the kitchen.

Will you do my room next? Michelle asked him.

Fuck, shit, ow, said Jenny's dad, rubbing the back of his head from where he'd banged it on the corner of the press.

Dad, Michelle said.

Jenny's dad's eyes were closed, palm pressed to his scalp, right where the hair was starting to thin.

The ghost of Stephen Gately's hair had been lighter there too.

Dad, Michelle said again.

Yeah, said Jenny's dad. No. No, I'm just doing the kitchen.

Jenny's mam came in to make a cup of tea. You're doing a base coat, she said. Right, Paddy?

I am in me hole, Jenny's dad said.

Ah, Paddy, said Jenny's mam.

Michelle fell about laughing. 'Mon, Jen, she said. Let's go before the fumes go to our heads too.

In Michelle's room the tape deck was already playing 'Wannabe'. On Michelle's bedroom posters, five young women with distinctive hair, dressed in bright colours with long bare legs, grimaced and grinned and posed with hands on slim bare hips.

They looked like Michelle's old Barbies propped up on her windowsill: waxy and smooth, with breasts like the letter V pointing out at the world. That was a lot of skin, Jenny privately thought. A lot of smooth skin on display. A lot of upper arms pushed in to squeeze cleavage. A lot of palms cupping buttocks. A lot of pursed out, pouted lips.

The Spice Girls made Jenny nervous.

Cate's comment about Stephen Gately came back to Jenny. I bet he'd be a good kisser.

Still, even Stephen Gately's lips didn't pout like theirs.

Jenny averted her eyes, stared at the poster of the cat dangling from a branch over Michelle's homework desk, the same as was stuck up over Jenny's own bed. Hang in there, it said.

Michelle had bubblegum in her mouth; she hid it in packets around her room because their mam said if she swallowed it she'd never shit it out and it'd stay stuck

241

between her ribs forever. Michelle chewed her clump of plasticky pink, blew a little bubble. Smack, smack, pop.

On one of the posters, Baby Spice's mouth made a perfect O behind a bright, shiny bubble.

Cate's dog Max loped ahead, lifted his leg and pissed against the goalposts at the far end of the field. The lead dropped from Cate's fist, dragging along the muddy ground. Up on the path, criss-crossed by bicycles and buggies, the ghost of Stephen Gately stood under a half-bare tree, his spectral hunch sheltered from the drizzle. His hands were in his pockets. His hair was short.

Jenny blinked droplets from her eyelashes.

Would you kiss Tim McCarthy? Cate said.

Huh?

Tim, Cate said. McCarthy. He wants to kiss me.

Congratulations, Jenny said.

Cate stuck out her tongue. Well? Would you kiss him? If you were me.

If I was you? Jenny considered her best friend. Side scrunchie in her fluffy red hair, white bright lines of her Adidas tracksuit, half a plastic heart on a fake-silver chain that connected to Jenny's.

No, said Jenny. I don't think so.

Would you kiss any boy? Cate asked, some curious quirk to the side of her mouth.

That one was easy. Stephen Gately, Jenny said. I'd kiss him.

Cate made a pssht noise. He wouldn't kiss you, she said.

The mud stuck to the sides of their runners, collected dead leaves and tiny twigs as they walked.

Well, duh, said Jenny. I'm twelve.

And he's gay, Cate said.

242

And he's what?

The ghost of Stephen Gately was looking up at the last remaining leaves of the tree he stood under. On a high branch, a robin hopped, the red of its breast like a blush.

Cate kicked a deflated football out of her path and the dog bounded over, took the ball in his teeth so the last of the air in it whistled out. The ghost of Stephen Gately looked up and caught sight of Jenny. Hesitantly, and with a great amount of self-consciousness, she raised a hand in greeting. The ghost of Stephen Gately gave her a smile that was the exact same as the ones the real Stephen Gately gave in magazine interviews.

Give that here, Cate said.

What? Jenny asked, still looking at the ghost of Stephen Gately looking at her.

What? Cate said. Not you. Max, give it here.

The dog didn't listen to Cate. The ghost of Stephen Gately crouched down on his hunkers and Max lolloped over, long strings of slobber behind him, and deposited the flat ball at the dead man's phantom feet.

The leaves were mush under Jenny's feet. Beside her, Cate sang her current favourite Boyzone song and her breath made clouds. Jenny's bag was heavy on her shoulders. The cold air touched the half inch of bare skin between her knee socks and school skirt with every step.

Tell me if you see Tim, Cate said. The boys' school was close; bike tyres bumped onto the footpath to cross it.

Why, you gonna say yes? asked Jenny.

Cate's gum cracked between her teeth when she grinned. Maybe, she said. Haven't decided yet. Might play hard to get.

Jenny nodded. She also spoke the language of the magazines, had learnt the theory of attracting boys by heart. Before passing by the boys' school gates she, like Cate, licked and bit her lips to pink them. The winter air stuck to the spit like dead leaves to the soles of her shoes.

Further on, down another road, a man stood against a garden wall.

Morning girls, he said.

The girls lowered their heads. Morning, they muttered. They weren't late, but this road was empty.

The man said, Want a drink, girls? He took his penis out of his trousers. It lay like a deflated balloon in the palm of his hand.

They looked at it, then at each other, then hurried on. Their eyes were wide and they stared straight ahead. Cate risked a glance behind her and when she saw he wasn't following she dissolved into giggles. They held each other's elbows and laughed into each other's hair.

Lookit, Cate said wisely. Better to get used to the sight. Once we're adults, that's our future.

They arrived at school breathless, arms still linked, hands clasped, cheeks close.

The ghost of Stephen Gately nodded politely to the lollipop lady, who pinked slightly and rose a hand to touch her hair.

Cate said, I don't get it.

Jenny looked up from her magazine. Cate's bare toe touched one of the paint tins in the living room. There was a small speck of Palladian White on the bubblegum pink of one toenail.

Don't get what?

Why Stephen wouldn't already be dating Emma, Cate said. They're perfect for each other. I don't get it.

The Boyzone album whirred in the tape player.

Do you know this song is actually about a rat? Jenny said.

What, said Cate. 'Ben'?

Stephen sang that one, although he wasn't lead singer. It was the only one he sang alone, voice sounding like it came straight from the dimples in his cheeks, deep syrup. Ben, he sang, we both found what we were looking for.

Yeah, Jenny said, pleased to have knowledge Cate didn't possess. I read it in an interview. It's a song about a rat.

Cate shrugged, hair bouncing on her shoulders. Well, she said. It still sounds pretty gay to me.

In Jenny's magazine, the Boyzone boys were being matched with their perfect Spice Girl. Each grinned out with bright white teeth.

I told you you needed a base coat, Jenny's mam shouted from the kitchen. Didn't I say it, you useless dope, do you ever fucking listen.

I'd fucking listen to you if you ever said anything worth listening to, you old bag. Jenny's dad matched Jenny's mam's tone.

Later, Jenny knew, the headboard of their bed would bang rhythmically against the wall and Michelle would turn the volume on her tape deck up so Jenny's little radio would be drowned out twice.

Michelle was doing a jigsaw. On the board on the sitting room floor, a gauche landscape rendered into a thousand broken pieces lay, giant holes through the heart of it. Jenny could see the straight edge of a corner piece in amongst the dustballs under the couch.

You want a bar and a pack of crisps? Michelle said. Her hand landed softly on Jenny's shoulder.

Okay, Jenny said.

Okay, Michelle said. Let's go to the shop.

Max strained on his lead. It was looped around the leg of the trolley bay and the metal clasp clinked against the first trolley in the line. A fat robin hopped across the path not far from him. Inside the shop window, Cate browsed the magazines as though she didn't already have all of them spread across her bedroom floor.

There was paint on the soles of Michelle's shoes. Jenny thought she might have some on hers too; one of the tins had left rings of off-white on the sitting room floor and both girls had walked through it. Jenny imagined softly fading footprints leading from her house to the shop, patchy maybe, becoming less white and more the colour of the ground the further they got from home. White paint coming off on soggy fallen leaves, marking them as having been trodden on.

How do you know, Jenny asked her sister, if you are going crazy?

Michelle pocketed a stick of gum at the same time as she placed another one on the counter beside the till. The cashier beeped the gum through, then two packets of Tayto, a can of Coke and one of Club Orange, a Mars bar and a Snickers. Michelle paid for the lot.

I don't think you do, Michelle said. I think that's part of being crazy.

Jenny ripped the crisp packet open with her teeth. Do you believe in ghosts? she asked.

Michelle looked surprised. Course, she said. Don't you?

Jenny hadn't seen the ghost of Stephen Gately in a few months. In the magazines and on the television, the real Stephen Gately was as floppy-haired and youthful as always.

How do you know, she said, following Michelle who crossed the road without looking, if you are gay?

On the grass verge between driveways, a man stood with his back to a lamppost.

Don't listen to Cate, Michelle said with a wave of her hand. Stephen Gately isn't gay.

Oh, said Jenny. No. Of course he isn't.

The man stepped in front of Jenny and Michelle. His coat was long but it was open. So was the zip of his trousers. Want a drink? the man asked. His penis was in his hands, pinched between fingers.

Michelle grabbed Jenny's hand and with the other squeezed her can of Coke so hard it splashed the man across the chest. Pervert, she said to him. She walked on, pulling Jenny behind her.

Oh, they could hear the man saying. Oh.

Jenny's dad was feeding the robin in the garden. Here, boy, he said. Here, here. Howya, girls. Want some bird seed?

Will it eat crisps? Jenny asked. There was a good mush of hard salty crumbs in the bottom of the packet that Jenny had been saving the whole walk home.

No, Jenny's dad said. Or yeah, but it's not good for him.

How do you know it's a him? Michelle said. Maybe she's a girl robin.

Jenny shook out the ends of her crisp packet on the grass. Here, girl, she said. Here, here.

Cate said, I kissed Tim McCarthy.

Jenny kicked the football for Max rather harder than she had intended.

Jenny, Cate said. Did you hear me?

Yeah, said Jenny. Max lolloped across the football pitch and caught the ball between his teeth. He looked delighted with himself.

I said I kissed Tim, Cate said.

Congratulations, said Jenny.

Cate stood with one hand on a cocked hip. That's it? she said.

I thought you were playing hard to get, Jenny said. She took the slobber-slick ball from Max's mouth.

I was, yeah, said Cate. But then I decided to just go for it.

Jenny put the ball on the muddy grass and swung her leg back to kick it. What was it like? she asked.

Cate shrugged. Okay, I guess.

Your first kiss, Jenny said.

My first kiss, said Cate. Are you jealous?

Jenny's heart did a little thud. Nah, she said. A bit.

Don't worry, Cate said. I'm sure lots of boys will want to kiss you soon.

Max returned the ball to Jenny and looked at her with eyes full of longing. Jenny made herself give a little laugh. That's okay, she said. I'm saving myself for Stephen Gately.

★

The ghost of Stephen Gately faded into view, pale and spectral, scratchy-chinned and short-haired, in the corner of Jenny's bedroom. He was barely visible behind Cate, who was sitting on Jenny's bed in front of her, blowing on the cherry red of her nail varnish.

Anyway, Cate said. I think they shoulda shown it.

Jenny stroked the tiny plastic brush over each of her toenails in turn. My dad says no, she said. It's a national soap opera, like. Jenny parroted her dad's words. People aren't ready for that.

Cate snorted. Ready for what? she said. It's just a kiss.

A gay kiss, Jenny said. Don't you think that's disgusting?

Yeah, said Cate. Who wants to see two boys kiss? Want a drink?

Unbidden, a memory of the man who'd shown Jenny his penis on two separate occasions flashed into her mind.

Huh? Jenny said.

Cate held out her can of Coke. Want some? she said.

Oh, said Jenny. No.

Cate said, Anyway if you're a boy why would you want to kiss another boy when you could kiss a girl? Girls are so much prettier.

Oh. Jenny blinked. Yes, she said. Yes, they are. She took a breath. And they smell nicer, she said.

I bet they kiss better, too, Cate said. Tim kissed like a washing machine. There was spit all down my chin.

Yuck, Cate, said Jenny.

Yuck, Cate agreed.

They fell about laughing.

★

The ghost of Stephen Gately faded in and out of sight. On a breeze, a robin red breast with crisp crumbs in its beak glided to her nest up in the neighbour's tree. Two small eggs lay on a bed of straight-edged jigsaw puzzle pieces. In the newly painted kitchen, Jenny's parents kissed over a stove full of rashers and eggs. The coffee was burnt. Michelle pasted a poster of a 1960s French actress in the space where a Spice Girls one used to be. The Barbies on her bookshelves looked on.

Some months later, when the ghost of Stephen Gately at thirty-three had stopped appearing to Jenny, now thirteen, she used the last of her dad's Palladian White to cover her bedroom wall. Some of her posters were stuck too fast to peel off before painting. The paint splashed the branch from which the hapless cat dangled. Hang in there, barely visible under the first base coat. The paint sprinkled the magazines spread across the floor. The real Stephen Gately smiled out at Jenny with his blue eyes, his white teeth.

The paint smeared across his floppy hair, parted in the middle. The paint dripped down over his smooth, unstubbled chin.

Break-up poem recited knee-deep in bog water

I take a Polaroid of my girlfriend naked

Phones don't have shutter snaps like this. When I rise from my knees on the floor they crack like this. The shush of the paper working through the camera is the bedsheets shifting underneath you. The whirr of it is the fizz of arousal between my breasts. The blank of the picture is your expression but when I snatch the photograph from the grip of the mechanism the tear of it is the smile spreading across your face.

Two of cups

We are not the lovers. There is no snake to tempt us. There is no enticing apple up on a tree between us. Instead, we are mirrors. Instead, you drink of my cup as I drink of yours.

How to transfer the soul of a woman onto watercolour paper in three easy steps

You will need:
Watercolour paper in warm water, soaked.
(I run you a bath, sprinkle Epsom salt like seasoning. The steam rises and I think of dumplings in a wicker basket. You sink to your chin and I lie against you. Your hands immediately meet between my legs.)
A Polaroid picture, not yet developed.
(I peel the back off the photograph like I peel off your clothes. You pose on your knees on the bed, arms behind your head. A smile like you could eat me alive. I click the button over and over. I can never take just one. You can never give me just one.)

Method:
Pull the image away from the negative and stick the darkness to the paper, let it soak in. You can heat it with your breath, soft words, the sounds you try to keep quiet, the sounds you bite back, the sounds of teeth biting down on a shoulder. You can press a tender kiss to the back of its neck as it sleeps.
(The negative is the black stain where the picture used to be. The shape of you marked in absences. In the picture, your hips. I rub the negative on a blank page and look, I've made you another shadow.)

Knight of cups

Wherever we go I ride to meet you. Under my
helmet my hair is shorn. This is no fairytale. We
are not two damsels in a castle. I hand you a
helmet and you straddle the bike behind me. My
gloved hands rumble the motor. Your bare hands
immediately rise to cup my breasts.

Break-up poems

The first time we met our shadows merged, separated,
merged again under the sunlight. You look nothing
like me, yet our shadows are identical. In bed we are
two mirrors reflecting endlessly.

I don't know when it started but one night I woke
to find myself alone, reflecting the bed onto the dark
ceiling. Hours later you returned, cold, with dirt under
your fingernails. Each night since, I stir and find you
gone, wake again to your cold hands, the smell of
damp earth in your short hair.

How else to keep you but inside a photograph?
How best but by keeping your soul between sheets of
Polaroid paper to ensure you never leave me?

In the morning I asked you to write me a poem.

I only write break-up poems, you told me.

Common objects for spell casting

Two coins. Rose petals. Earth and water. The
thorns of a blackberry bush, slightly bloodied. A
hagstone (the hole in the centre wide enough to

slip two fingers through).
I wonder would you slip your fingers through.
You may keep my soul transferred onto paper
but I wonder do you know the things I do to
keep you.

I pin a Polaroid of my naked girlfriend to my noticeboard

It is not online. It is only shareable to those who enter
my room, who can touch it. Feel the slick of the
soft plastic tab, the sheen of the ink. There is a tiny
hole in the top-right corner, now, enough to stick
a pin through, swift, and fix the photograph to the
corkboard. The pin has a round head, pearly-pink, and
you grin when you see it. When you are not there I
unpin the picture, bring it to my lips. When you are
not there it is the picture I take to bed with me.

The soul as a pink-headed pin

It hurts to touch a soul straight on. Like an
electric shock, we startle. Better to graze it.
Better to touch a soul indirectly. Better to circle
it. Better to apply pressure gradually, around,
beyond. Better to make a V of your fingers,
allow the apex of the flesh just above your
knuckles to pinch, just barely. Better to tease.
Better to wait until a soul is plump and ready.

I frame a watercolour transfer of my naked girlfriend and hang it on my wall

The image is warped and flimsy, like a photograph developed underwater. In it, you swim. Your hands behind your head, your knees spread, your mouth set. Your stance is strong: even on your knees you're standing. The room around you is the deep earthy water of the bog and you are not moved by its tugs and draws. You stare straight into the camera (you stare straight into my eyes through the lens) and although the image is ghostly your presence is solid. This is the small pink nub of the soul. This is the transfer.

  I want to tell you that although you may eat me alive I have trapped your soul and hung it on the wall above my bed so that no matter how far from me you wander, no matter how cold your feet or how wrinkled your fingers, you will always return.

How to take a transferred soul and slip it into a willing body in three easy steps

Do not touch the soul directly. Instead, circle it with something soft so it will not flinch. The best way to transfer a soul into another willing body is with the tip of your tongue. Summon the soul with a spiral, slowly traced. Wrap your wet mouth around it. Let the flat of your tongue touch it, firm and light all at once. When the round pink nub of the soul is ready between the gentle pressure of your lips let the insistent

255

rhythm of the tip of your tongue coax it into
the willing body. Watch as the soul's new home
convulses with pleasure. Watch as the body
welcomes the soul home.

*My girlfriend sends me a picture of her naked body in the
mirror*

In your family home you take a picture, snap it on
your phone, silently, so your mother will not hear
from her bedroom the noise of the fake shutter snap,
which only exists as an indulgence, as a reminder:
here, now, you have preserved a moment as if in
centuries of layered peat. Upload it to the cloud, now,
let it be amorphous, nothing like a real object at all.

In the picture steam rises. It is wet and warm. There
are beads of sweat or condensation at your collarbones
that require me to pinch the screen to zoom enough
to view.

In the picture: your phone. It is the closest thing to
the mirror, the closest thing to your naked body. It
partly obscures your face, although you tilt your head
so your expression – coy, in the blur of the steamy
mirror – is readable. You send it to me and I open it
like a present. The line of your hip just above the jut
of the sink. The press of one arm against a dark pink
nipple. I send a line of cartoon droplets in reply.

Into the bog (wet and warm, steamier than the
bathroom after a shower) I walk, every night.
I chain the wheel of my bike to the closest
walkway and follow the remains of an ancient
path. I go deep. There isn't silence; there are
birds. Rustles in the bracken. Sometimes, a damp
sucking noise I cannot identify. It doesn't scare
me. I walk further from my bike than I would
otherwise be comfortable, helmet under one arm.
My runners shuck into the sticky earth and I pull
them out each with a soggy squelch.
From somewhere ahead, or maybe below, or
maybe deep within me: this siren song:
Come to me, love, I've been waiting for a
good thousand years. Give or take. I bloodied
my fingers on blackberry bushes every autumn. I
buried one coin in soil, threw one into the lake.
I watched it splash, this sudden wet gush soaking
me to the wrist. I crushed rose petals against my
flesh until I smelled like someone entirely other.
I fingered every hagstone on the long lake shore.
They don't call me a bog witch for nothing. I
mean. Here I am in this wet aul bog. Here I am
under layers of peat and bone. Here I am with
my leather skin and my spells. The swirls of my
fingertips are wrinkled I've been waiting so long.
See them when I beckon. Can you smell the
salt of the bog on my fingers? Can you follow
me this far in? Can you come deeper? Can you
come deeper still?

My girlfriend returns from the bog

I do not know where you go to at night but I know that you go. When you are gone, I stroke your picture. The whirl of the print of my left little finger traces your biceps, your spread knees pressed into the mattress. I mirror the gesture with the first two fingers on the right between my own legs.

The picture is warm as a body, no matter how long it stays pinned to the noticeboard on the side of the bedroom closest to the cracked-open window. Warm as a soul, a breath in the cold bog.

When you return it takes an hour for your hands to thaw against my body in the bed. Your knees and feet are cold points of contact. Your nose when you press your lips to mine is a small stone left out in a chill wind. I ask where you have been and you say wandering. You do not mention the traces of peat muck in the cracks underneath your feet. You do not mention the tiny flecks of blood under your nails or how the tips of your fingers are wrinkled as if they have spent days under water. You only press those fingers between my legs and lick them. You only tell me I am delicious, delicious.

A song to call the bones

Come, come. Come wet and muddy. Come slick over the silky bracken. Come plump and bloody on the blackberry bushes. Come in the holes of hagstones taken from the lake shore. The world is the cloud and the bog is the Polaroid picture.

There is nothing more real than the smell of this
peat, the layers of earth that shift and kiss, the
bodies that lie beneath it. You want to keep this?
You want to capture the pink nub of the soul
between layers of sleek plastic? There is nothing
better than the bog for keeping. You will not
get away. Come bathe to the bone. You will
wade in to find me, Polaroid likeness in hand.
You will leave your phone with my bike on the
footpath. In here, there is nothing but time. In
here, there is nothing but bodies and bone.

The devil

My mother says any parent knows the feeling. She
sings it in her bedtime story voice: I'll eat you up I
love you so. She counsels caution, says I amn't ready
to be eaten. But I have already prepared my seasoning.

Knight of wands

We ride into love like a battle, side by side,
wands aloft. The tip of the stick is a flame that
won't go out.
It's this torch you take with you when you
follow me, finally, into the bog.

I follow my girlfriend into the bog

Finally, I follow. The rumble of your motor seems
distant but nowhere is too far for me to shadow.
Besides, soon I, too, can hear the siren song.

We leave the town behind and the lights leave us. At
the end of the walkway: your bike. Deeper in the bog:
your body. I cannot tell how far but the picture in my
pocket is a compass, pointing. I leave my phone, keys
and wallet in your saddlebag. All I take with me is your
photograph. My boots drop me quick up to the ankles.
Each step is a muscle strain, an effort, a demonstration:
here is how far I will come to find you.

There is a light up ahead. Two figures in the
swirling brown fog. Their hands are clasped: pale,
leathery palm to water-wrinkled fingers. How long
have you been sinking into the deep and the peat?
The mud sticks my feet. Each step is a labour of love,
each footfall heavier than the last. Ankles, shins, knees.
Soon my hands crawl me out, soon I slither over the
bog on my belly to reach you.

Deep ahead: your hands, outstretched. Beside you:
the bog witch. I know, all of a sudden. I know her
name. I know how long she has been waiting. I know
how the small pink nub of your soul transferred to
and then back from watercolour paper, from the cork
noticeboard in my bedroom, recognises hers. And it is
not so much that I know what she wants as I know
what you do.

Your hands clasp mine and you pull me into your
arms. Your tongue licks the bog moss from my
fingers. Into my ears you whisper delicious, delicious.

Under the layers of peat are bodies already.
Hooks stuck into their shoulders to string them
up. Throats slashed, necks bled, nipples cut off.
These bogs are brutal. There's no rest for those
who lie here. We stay preserved forever.
Tell me you want that, my love.
Tell me you want me to break up with you,
break you up. Break your heart, break your bones.
Suck the marrow from them. Take a bite outta
your hipbone with the meat still on: delicious.
When I break you up you break up with me.
Delicious.

My girlfriend the bog witch pulls me deep into her bog

I was wrong: there are not two figures in the
swirling brown fog. There is only the woman and
her reflection. There is only the Polaroid picture and
its negative. There is only the witch and her shadow.
One tight pink soul between them.

All this time I thought I was casting my Polaroid
spells to keep you and here you are: a witch and her
reflection beckoning me into the bog.

In my slick fist: the warmth of the photograph of
you. Tight around my waist: the grip of your arms.
Around me: the soft peat moss. Rising fast and wet to
meet me: the sucking deep of the bog.

Submerged somewhere between my chest and
throat, I realise I want this.

Of course you do, come close to me, there is room
for us both under the blanket of this bog.

Your mouth on mine, your hands insistent.

Do not wait until my skin turns to leather, do
not wait until all of me is preserved but my
hair, do not wait until my teeth stand stark
against the dry flesh of my gums.

We sink through layers of bodies and bone. There is
nothing better than the bog for keeping. Better than
the small pink nub of a pin against a soft cork board.
Better than the slick sheen of Polaroid plastic.

Better than a bath of rose petals, better than
bloodied fingers on blackberry bushes, better
than slipping two fingers through the holes
of hagstones wet from the lake shore.

If this is the end then I am the reverberations of the
last bass note. If this is the final footfall then I am the
echo. If this is a break-up then I am the poem written
six months later. My body and yours: preserved
forever in the bog.

Two truths and a lie

Truth:

She took the doll out of the plastic. Unwound the wire bows from between the doll's legs.

Truth:

The doll was beautiful. Blue eyes and long, synthetic hair in a shade of chestnut. It had a voice box that could be accessed from the middle of the doll's back. All that was required was a small screwdriver, for the four small screws. The flesh-coloured plastic square flapped back and inside was the voice. A throat inside your back, would you be well, her mammy said. Next one'll be talking out her arse.

Lie:

Her mammy didn't like the doll. Not from the start and not at the end.

Truth:

There were three things the doll's box said. Its voice was high but not a child's. It didn't look like a child, either.

Truth:

Let's play, it said. You're so pretty, it said. You're my best friend, it said.

Lie:

If she had wanted to stop the doll from talking, she could simply have removed the voice box.

Truth:

She was too old for dolls already.

Truth:

In the night with the bedroom door closed she pressed the doll down under her covers, rubbed the doll's hard body between her legs until the whole bed shook with it and she threw her head back, mouth wide, eyes on the ceiling.

Truth:

Sometimes she took the doll's hand and pushed it under her the band of her knickers and that was even better.

Lie:

The doll's hand didn't feel like a real hand at all.

Truth:

The doll's plastic eyes were independent of the rest of its plastic face. The lids, framed with coarse synthetic lashes brown as conkers, closed when the doll was laid down and opened when the doll was raised to sitting. The plastic pupils were like holes. The plastic irises were blue.

Truth:

When the doll blinked, its eyes clicked.

Lie:

The doll's eyes only blinked when someone was there to hold it, set it to lie, set it to stand. Otherwise, the doll's eyes stayed in the position they'd taken depending on where the doll was put.

Truth:

The doll came with a stand, like the porcelain toys the girl's great-grandmother had in her attic. The stand was half as tall as the doll and adjustable. It had a metal clasp that encircled the doll's neck. By the throat it was held up and displayed.

Truth:

Each night the girl placed the doll gently on the windowsill and tightened the metal around its throat. Perhaps the cold arm of the stand constricted its voice box, for she thought often that she heard the doll speak, although she had not squeezed the spot to make it talk. Let's play, it said. You're so pretty, it said. You're my best friend, it said.

Lie:

Those were the only things the doll could say.

Truth:

The girl told the doll her secrets as does a penitent in the confessional.

Truth:

A girl's secrets are confessions, admittances of guilt, although few girls have anything to feel truly guilty about.

Lie:

The doll, being a doll, had done nothing to feel guilty about either.

Truth:

Her mammy plugged the hoover into the one socket on the landing, pressed with her foot the pedal to make the machine suck. Dust from the landing carpet hissed through the tube into the paper sack.

Truth:

Dust is composed primarily of dead skin cells, flaked continuously from living bodies, light as snow. Each brush of a person against another, each hair fallen from a rapid morning brush, each microscopic fibre flicked from an item of clothing as it is discarded from a body into the laundry hamper floats softly to the carpet to be sucked into the vacuum the mammy hauls up the stairs – its long handle inevitably bumping the sloping ceiling above – every Sunday afternoon without fail.

Lie:

The doll's skin did not shed dead cells to mingle with the dust of the living. The doll was only plastic and not a moving, breathing thing at all.

Truth:

The girl had almost forgotten how to play. Her old dolls sat, hair unbrushed, gathering dust, on top of the book-shelves: displayed, out of the way. Some of their names the girl had already let slip from her mind. Years from then, she knew, when she had children of her own, she would have to dredge the depths of her childish memory. Perhaps, in her sorrow at having lost them, she would then give her old dolls new names. She would watch her own daughters (she could picture them, now, as ghostly pastel shadows: something like the memory of the small child she used to be) and their play would slowly, dawn-ingly, remind her of the games she once knew.

Truth:

The girl had new games now.

Lie:

The girl's doll was not part of her new games.

Truth:

The doll's lips were hard plastic, the same as the rest
of its face. They puckered, and were painted a dark
shade of pink. The doll's lips were plumper than the lips
of the girl's other dolls, less childish, more like the doll
was wearing lipstick, or had been wearing lipstick that
morning, which had faded into the creases of her lips as
the day wore on, becoming matte as a wine stain and
harder to scrub off.

Truth:

Occasionally, at night, the girl told herself she could
see the tiniest imprint of bite marks on the blush-toned
bottom lip of the doll's mouth.

Lie:

The girl's mouth remained unbitten.

Truth:

The girl sat on the floor under the window with three
of her closest friends. Between them, an empty bottle of
spirits. It spun on its side like a broken compass. Its north
changed based on the flick of the wrist of the girl who
turned it. Above them, the doll, from the choke of its
metal perch, watched with its blue plastic eyes.

Truth:

Truth, the first girl giggled. Truth, said the second.
Truth, the third sighed. The girl who owned the doll
chose dare and at her peers' request removed her polo
neck and bra before them. She stood in the centre of
the room, circled. Fingers pinched the flesh of her waist,

hands measured her breasts, knuckles poked each pimple and errant long, dark hair.

Lie:

The flush of the girl's face was pure embarrassment.

Truth:

When her friends left, the girl took off her clothes and stood facing the long mirror on her inside wardrobe door. From its perch on the windowsill, the doll watched.

Truth:

The girl traced her fat and flesh, her pimples and hairs with lipstick of the same colour as the doll's faint blush.

Lie:

She hated every second.

Truth:

The mammy made desserts for the girl's nana's birthday: trifle topped with custard and cream, the jelly soaking through the sponge; chocolate fudge cake dense as a dark night; little rocks of macaroons sprinkled with a snow of desiccated coconut.

The girl spoke to her closest friend on the phone. The friend said, do it, go on, I dare you. Would you do it? the girl said. I would, the girl's closest friend said. In a heartbeat.

Truth:

When the girl stuck the first two fingers of her right hand as far down her throat as she could she thought of her closest friend doing the same.

Lie:

The girl left the doll in the bedroom as she vomited. She did not want a witness.

Truth:

In the living room the girl's father opened brown card-board packages received in the post: files and manuscripts, shiny hardback books with his face scowling intelligently from the inside cover flap. He folded the boxes over, the card unyielding, and stamped on them in his slippers, hauling the flaps over to hear the satisfying cracks. He grinned as he shoved them into the green bin, arm sunk in to the elbow. On the living room coffee table: curls of card and thick brown tape rolled into sticky balls, the handles of scalpels weighing down address labels, their blades pushed to the top of the bookshelves, to be safe.

Truth:

The girl sat on the floor under the window with her closest friend. You first, said the friend. No you, said the girl. The friend inched her lips closer to the girl's. No, you, said the friend. On the floor between them, an empty bottle of spirits. The breath that mingled between their mouths was strong and bitter citrus. No, you, said the girl. From its choke-hold on the windowsill the doll watched.

On the floor between them, a silver blade from the girl's father's scalpel. No, you, said the friend. Her lips were a hair's breadth from the girl's. No, you, breathed the girl.

The friend took up the slanted blade and drew it across the skin of her inner arm. Blood beaded in a tiny, thin line. Now you, she said. The girl took the proffered blade and pressed it against the crook of her elbow. She dug the tip in, gave it a wiggle. A drop of blood grew, fat and round, before running all the way to her wrist. The friend watched as she licked it all the way, pink-mouthed, eyes locked.

Lie:

It hurt.

Truth:

The mammy dug through her daughter's laundry basket for the weekly wash. Drew out jeans and jumpers, crumpled uniform shirts with biros staining the pockets, odd socks, once-white knickers whose bloodstains never fully washed out. She paused over a tiny dress, too small to fit a baby. It was supple, synthetic, navy. Its static from lying wrapped around one of the girl's fleece pyjamas gave the mammy a small shock when she picked it up.

Truth:

When she jumped at the small static charge, she noticed the doll. The doll was naked, strangled by the cold metal of its stand, turned to face out the window. Its bare bottom aligned with the mammy's eyes. The two little dimples in the plastic of its lower back winked.

Lie:

The doll's dress was clean as if fresh from the plastic it came in, cool and crisp in the mammy's hands. The mammy did not look closely but she could tell it was not stained. There was no reason for the girl to have undressed the doll. There was no reason for the girl to have thrown the dress into the laundry basket to be washed.

Truth:

The girl sat on the floor under the window with three of her closest friends. The doll, still naked, was under the bed. It was lying on its back but its head was turned. Its long, chestnut hair splayed out like a fan around it. Its blue plastic eyes stared out of its beautiful plastic face. Between the four girls, an empty bottle of spirits. The neck of the bottle pointed like an open mouth at the girl's closest friend. The other friends said you first, you have to go first. The girl came onto her hands and knees, crawled across the space between her and her closest friend. She sat back on her heels and wrapped her hands around her closest friend's neck. Ready? asked the girl. Ready, said the friend.

Truth:

The friend's voice shook.

Lie:

The girl's hands shook too.

Truth:

The girl tightened her grip, thumbs pressing against the hollow of her closest friend's throat. The friend's voice made a horrible noise. The other friends said nothing, only watched with wide eyes. The friend's eyes rolled to the back of her head and she became so heavy that the girl's hands could no longer hold her, hands linked around her neck like the metal stand around the smooth plastic under the doll's plastic face. The friend fell, hard, to the ground, and her legs kicked out behind her. Thumps on the bedframe and scrapes along the floor.

Truth:

From underneath the bed, the doll spoke. Perhaps the friend's flailing foot kicked out and hit it. Let's play, it said. You're so pretty, it said. You're my best friend, it said.

Lie:

When the girl's friend came to she felt as well as she had upon arriving in the girl's room that afternoon.

Truth:

The girl found her doll's dress in the pile of folded laundry her mammy left on her bed. It was still warm from the iron; warmer even than her uniform shirts, her pyjama shorts.

Truth:

The girl remembered removing the doll's dress, but did not recall having put it in the basket to be washed.

Lie:

The doll didn't either.

Truth:

The girl sat on the bed with her closest friend. They took turns wrapping their hands around each other's thin throats. When one would lose consciousness and fall upon the eiderdown, the other would bend her head to her friend and breathe into her mouth a kiss: like a prince to a sleeping princess they woke each other, over and over.

Truth:

The girl sat on the floor under the window with her closest friend. They took turns tracing long lines on each other's skin with the blade of the girl's father's scalpel. Because their other friends had noticed the first few raised red lines on both girls' inner arms, they soon switched to flesh more hidden. On the floor under the window they pulled up their skirts.

Lie:

The closer the blade came to the tops of her inner thighs, the more uncomfortable the girl felt.

Truth:

The girl took the doll to bed with her. Its dress was still folded with the girl's clothes, transferred to a neat pile on the girl's dresser, not yet tidied away. In the dark of the bedroom, the girl pulled the doll's long, chestnut hair. She scratched the doll's beautiful face, smacked it so the doll's eyes clicked with blinking. She took her father's scalpel blade from the pink glitter notebook she kept it in and drew it deep along the doll's chest and legs.

Truth:

Plastic is both harder to cut into, and easier, than skin. A blade skims through plastic, creates deep scores like ancient glyphs. It is possible to cut a rune, a symbol, a word, a name into plastic. To do so in skin produces too much blood to be able to read until one washes it all off.

Lie:

There was no blood to bead in long lines across the plastic skin of the naked doll.

Truth:

The doll smiled with its pink rosebud mouth. The girl smiled with her pink bitten lips.

Truth:

The girl pressed the pattern of scars in the middle of the doll's plastic back, just above the winking plastic dimples.

Lie:

Let's play, the doll said. You're so pretty, the doll said. You're my best friend, the doll said.

Truth:

She tied the doll's dress around its mouth to gag it. Spread the doll's legs so it would sit unaccompanied by the metal stand. She pushed the doll to the back of her wardrobe, between two boxes of shoes, so that it would be accessible to her at all times, but hidden.

Truth:

When she closed the wardrobe door the doll fell over. Around its beautiful plastic face fell the doll's long, chestnut hair.

Lie:

The doll was lying down so its eyes were clicked shut until such a time as the girl saw fit to raise it.

Truth:

The girl sat on the floor under the window with three of her closest friends. The windowsill above them was empty of dolls. Between them, an empty bottle of spirits. The open mouth of the long neck of the bottle pointed right between the girl's crossed legs.

Truth:

All four girls were thin, their skin pale, their eyes bright, their faces flushed under the make-up. They felt beautiful: hard planes of soft plastic; long, straightened hair; rosebud mouths.

Lie:

The doll, being stationary at the back of the wardrobe, did not witness the scenes that followed.

Truth:

The mammy had always liked the doll. Girls should play with dolls, she always thought, up to an age.

Truth:

The girl was at that age, the mammy thought, although in truth she was well past it. The mammy was sad but also somewhat relieved to see the doll's metal stand empty every time she stepped into the girl's room. Only the innocent faces of her daughter and their friends sitting in an innocent circle on the floor under the window, no doubt playing one of their innocent adolescent games.

Lie:

The doll was, after all, only a relic of an even more innocent time, and more innocent games long forgotten.

Truth:

The girl took the doll out of the wardrobe. Unwound the navy dress from around the doll's mouth.

Truth:

The doll was beautiful. Blue eyes clicked open when it was raised to sitting, blinked shut when it lay down. It had a voice box that spoke when a particular spot on its lower back was pressed just so. The girl pressed on the scores and scars of the hard plastic and pushed the doll's hand down under the bedcovers. The girl's closest friend closed her eyes and opened her mouth.

Lie:

Let's play, the doll said. You're so pretty, the doll said. You're my best friend, was all the doll ever said.

Playing house

I wake up far from home. The house is inside me.

Roads stretch in four directions from the junction. There is nobody else. The earth is hard and red. Trees strain to reach the sky.

My face is in the dirt when I shake the last of sleep from my dry eyes. The taste of salt and silt on cracked lips. It cakes my hair, my clothes.

There are no powerlines, no pylons. There are no streetlamps to light the night. Besides, it's coming morning; the sun rises behind me and my shadow is the shape of the house.

The day we moved in we fucked on the hard floor and our knees were bruised for weeks. Her kneeling behind me, one hand reaching around. My cheek flush with the floor, mouth open, tasting dirt. There was no furniture, no carpet to burn our shins. Only the echoes of our grunts in the harsh light of the naked bulb on the ceiling.

There are no houses here but the one inside of me. No buildings, shops or cars. Only the red road running on and on into a hazy distance. It feels warmer than it should. If I took my shoes off the soles of my feet would not be uncomfortable on the dusty ground. I don't remove my shoes; instead, I walk.

The house is heavy. Inside me, furniture shifts, crockery clinks and cushions fall soft to the carpeted floor. Houses are not fast movers at the best of times, and in the heat of this wasteland my movements are laboured. Alone, I lumber. The large square of my shadow lengthens as the day goes on. The peak of my roof reaches far-off trees and still the road continues, straight and red, red and straight and on.

For weeks we ate with wooden spoons out of cardboard containers, grease glistening our chins. She tied a scarf around her head to protect her hair from dust and shook it out the stark bare windows at night, sending small clouds against the outside wall of the house. We bought a bin, a bucket, a mop. She poured equal parts water and white vinegar into a spray bottle and spritzed the surfaces so that the whole house smelled like a dusty chipper's. When she pressed me up against it and pulled my trousers down I could taste the malt.

Eventually, there is only one road; the junction far enough behind me that it no longer exists. In front of me, the road. Behind me, the road. To either side, the red and the brown and the scraggly trees, the tangle of shrub and the silence that should, in theory, be filled with the scurries of small birds. The sky is empty but for clouds. There are no insects that I can see. The lack of buzzing is louder once I realise this.

There is a ringing in my ears: the telephone in the house inside of me. There is nobody left to answer it. In its cradle, the receiver rings and rings.

Her hand grasped along the edge of the new rug from where she lay on the bare mattress, until it reached the phone. She swore softly, raised the receiver, and tried to push my head away. I only buried my face further up between her thighs, lengthened the strokes of my tongue. Her mother's voice came, tinny and distant, from the top of the mattress. I broke up her muttered hello with two fingers, crooked. Her breath was louder than the voice on the other line. She tried to speak but I sped up. The fingers of her other hand groped along the floor to push the black button on the shiny red receiver. She hung up mid-sentence on a long, low moan.

The sun rises and sets and rises again. At night I sleep in the shadow of the house inside my body cast by the light of a bright, fat moon. In the day, I walk. I encounter no other people (no other houses, either). No cars pass me by.

Before the kitchen was put in, we bought a car. The two of us in the used dealership, avoiding the pointed questions of the salesman in his stained striped shirt, his leering eyes. The car we bought was old, with dodgy electrics, but it was ours. It backed out of the driveway and we sped it far out of town, the windows stuck rolled all the way down and the sun halfway to set. Her hand on mine on the gear stick. Her hand on my thigh. Her hand pressing up under my skirt between my skin and the thin fabric of my underwear on the long, straight road. Her lip bit bloody, my mouth some open door, eyebrows drawn down like I was in pain. How hard it was to concentrate on the road with her hands right there, her mouth like that. Lips pressed against my neck, sucking.

I need a map. There is no one in the passenger seat to guide me. There is no passenger seat. No scruffy car with windows that won't roll up once they are down. Perhaps there is a map inside the house, but the house is so deep in my gut I cannot reach it.

The kitchen was gutted to make way for new plumbing. The attic was scooped out for insulation. The bathroom became a cave of cables and pipes. We'd barely been in the house and already it was a shell of the home it presumably once had been.

Out with the old, she said gleefully as mallets hit through plaster walls. Dust crumbled on the scarf over her hair. In with the new.

We christened the shower, which still smelled of fresh rubber and cement, together, arms crossed at the crook of the elbow, her fingers making the same shape as mine in her.

One morning I wake again, my face in dry dirt again, and I am not alone on the red road. Before me is a fox. Sleek and scrawny, brush of fur the colour of wet rust.

Did I dream you up, I ask. My voice is dustier than the scrabble of trees, creaks in the breeze.

Don't think so, the fox replies.

It sits in companionable silence as I stretch my limbs. Inside me, the house groans at each long movement. The sky is too covered in cloud for my shadow to show and for this I am relieved, and slightly sad. I had grown accustomed, as I walked, to the company of the house's shadow.

Now, though, there is this fox.

Do you, I ask, also have a house inside you?

Eh? says the fox.

A house. I try to mime the shape of a red-brick terrace, two-up, two-down.

Oh. The fox flicks its tail. You mean a den.

A den, I repeat.

A home.

Yes, I say. Yes. A home.

Oh, sure, the fox tells me. Yeah. Big hollow of earth deep in the guts of me. Sometimes I can feel it breathe.

Is it not uncomfortable?

We begin to walk together, shadowless, both. I try to imagine the house as empty space, a hole in the ground, but in truth, the house inside of me is as empty as the space around a fox's den.

A bit, the fox admits. Got some earthworms wriggling around up in there. Gets fierce tickly.

I let maybe half a mile go by before I ask, What about your family?

Eh?

Your family. I try to mime the shape of a couple with a baby on the way, the box room already kitted out in cribs and changing tables, twelve tiny onesies folded neatly in a drawer.

Oh, says the fox after a few minutes. You mean your skulk.

Do I?

Your kin, says the fox.

Yes, I say. Yes. Your kin. Your skulk. Are they in the den inside of you?

The fox is silent a long time. Ahead of us under cloud, a new junction approaches. We are almost upon it when my companion speaks again.

No, says the fox. It stands on the crossroads. I kept the den, says the fox, but there is no one left there.

We fucked on the hard floor, on the flimsy kitchen table when the dust cleared, against the shining tiles of the shower, on the bare mattress and then on the soft bed with boxes covering the rug we'd laid down before the furniture.

In each room, the trace of our breath. In every corner, a weaving of the web of us. This, I thought, not bricks or plaster, rubber or cement, this is how we build a home.

I wake up alone, the taste of silt and salt on cracked lips. The sun is high in the red, dusty sky. There has been no rain.

The red road stretches in front and behind me. To either side, the cross of the junction. The trees are thin. The fox is gone.

Inside me, the house grumbles. I can hear air in the pipes that sounds like the banging in the night we got used to, finally, each winter, the central heating firing up like some belligerent ghost.

My back cracks when I stand. Somewhere far inside me something crashes. There are broken things here that no one can see and only I can feel. Some of them are too deep for me to ever piece back together.

When is a house finished? she asked me.

We'd just hung the last print. For weeks we'd measured walls and frames, created miniatures to scale and rear-ranged them two-score times and ten on the bedroom floor. This, we said, this was the layout. Now just move this one half an inch to the right. The framed dictionary page should be under the Van Hove print. The commis-sioned illustration of the house should be hung between both our parents' wedding photographs. On the wall, it had to be perfect.

And, she reminded me, there needed to be ample space for the family photographs to come.

Again, I leave the crossroads. There is nowhere to go but straight, whichever way I turn. Once my body is pointed in a direction, it can only move ahead from there.

This road is as straight as the last one. As red and dry. As warm. The house is as heavy, but no heavier. As though it has reached capacity deep inside the guts of me.

I walk, I sleep. My shadow stretches as a house with a roof, a chimney, the hint of a thin porch in the dark space around the front door.

Inside me the telephone rings. Inside me the pipes clank and bang. Inside me the insistent drip of the shower head makes a groove around the drain. Inside me the ghost of her breath whispers my name.

We slept in the middle of the big bed, the crown of her head under my chin, my left leg over her right, both our elbows tucked in to allow us the smallest possible space between our bodies. At the flimsy kitchen table we ate side by side. We crowded into the car, kicked aside the shopping bags and chargers, the cardboard coffee cups and crumpled receipts and kissed over the gear stick.

The house was this big but no bigger. Two-up, two-down red-brick terrace with a garden the size of a postage stamp. Inside it were webs of breath and body heat, of love and routine.

On another day, many days after the first day, I awake believing myself to be alone, only to sense another body not far from mine. My face is pressed into the road like every morning, the sun gently rising, the air warm as breath. In my mouth the customary dirt. By my feet when I turn to sitting is a squirrel. Tufty-eared and rotund-bellied, its fur red as bright dry rust.

Where did you come from? I ask. Inside me, the cistern of the house belches, sends a wave of nausea through my throat.

The squirrel rubs its nose with a tiny clawed paw. Some tree, it says. Same as you, I suspect.

Around us, the trees are sparse and bare.

Okay, I say. The house is particularly creaky today. The lights flick on and off. If I pull up my shirt I can see the intermittent glow through the thin skin of my navel. If it sends a signal it is not one I know how to read.

It has been so long since I have listened deeply, though, I am not sure there is any signal I could now understand.

Here, though, is this squirrel.

Do you, I ask, have a house inside you too?

My voice is thin from ill-use, high as a kettle whine.

What's that? says the squirrel.

A house. I try to mime the shape of a kitchen with a rickety but aesthetically pleasing table, a living room with a wall full of carefully placed framed prints, a small bathroom with a large shower, a bedroom and a box room without a bed.

Ah. The squirrel blinks a few times. You mean a drey.

A drey?

A nest, says the squirrel. You know. A home.

Yes, I say, yes. A nest, a home. Do you have one of those deep in the guts of you?

Sure thing, says the squirrel. Of course. Big bundle of twigs and leaves and moss. Some leftover eggshells from the birds who lived there before we built on top of the structure that was once their home.

Isn't that painful?

We walk together, the squirrel matching my steps seven skips to one. I try to imagine the scratch of twigs, of branches and buds. I try to imagine the ghosts of the long-hatched chicks of the birds who once nested in the same small space. It occurs to me that the house inside my gut is just as cluttered. Just as tangled through with long-weaved patterns of bodies that don't live there anymore.

Ah, yeah like, says the squirrel. Scratches me up something fierce. The wind keeps whistling through the branches, keeps me up at night. Sounds like screams at times, if you get me. Sounds like I'm not alone in there.

I don't know if my heart sinks or lifts at this. I let a few of my steps elapse on the cracked dry ground before I ask, So there is nobody else left inside your nest?

What you mean? says the squirrel.

I mean, I say, as the sun washes my shadow long across the ground. What about your. Your mate. Your young. Are they inside the nest inside of you?

Eh? says the squirrel.

I try to mime the shape of her body pressed close to mine, of the swell of a belly straining the buttons of a winter coat, of the greyscale printout of an ultrasound scan stuck to the fridge of the kitchen we fucked in so many times.

Ahhh, says the squirrel with what I can only interpret as a smile. You mean your scurry.

Is that what you call it? My treads are long and heavy. A scurry sounds like something fast and light.

Obviously, says the squirrel. What the fuck else would it be?

Inside of me, the magnetic letters on the shiny white fridge rearrange themselves to spell the word *family*, but there is nobody there to read the word, there is nobody there to see.

The squirrel hops ahead, bush of a tail kicking up small clouds of dust. In the distance, a junction approaches.

Nah, says the squirrel. My belly nest is empty of the aul drey. Nobody there now, not any more. You stay behind if you like, love. I've to just keep moving.

In the back of the car, the baby carrier clicked into a large plastic base. We had to fold the front passenger seat to fit it and she complained that each time we carried the baby in or out of the car we would hit our heads on the roof of it.

We'll change the car, I said. Get a five-door, a hatch-back. Buy it new. Electric windows with those suction sun shades in the shape of cats and bears.

She had visions of emergencies, not being able to access the back seat in time, I knew this.

Yes, she said. Yes. Let's.

In the new car she never touched more than my hand.

Is there even such a thing as a map of this place? Ahead of me, the road. Behind me, the road. Any map would only be two straight lines and a red dot: you are here. You are on the red road in the wilderness with a house inside of you and you are all alone.

This time I barely touched the junction. Only enough time for the squirrel to scamper away, the light nest made of twigs and moss hardly slowing it at all.

My house is heavy. I thought it could not weigh me down any harder and yet it seems to have settled somewhere at the crux of my hips. Instead of lumbering, I waddle. My centre of gravity is now somewhere in the region of the narrow stairs that lead from the small hall to the smaller landing.

If there is space for a whole house inside me, I think before settling into sleep by the side of the long and dusty road for one more night, face in the dirt, alone, then there was space for us all in the house. Empty space filled with light and shadow. Empty space filled with webs of breath and patterns in the shape of the bodies that inhabited it before. Our bodies. Future bodies filling the spaces we made for them.

Her hands stroked my temples in the dark, cool room. The window was open and the air drifted in to mingle with whatever quiet song she had playing from the speakers. The whirl of warm oil at her fingertips traced patterns along the sides of my face, into my hairline, down the back of my neck. I breathed deep into the belly of me and down there something answered in a language I did not yet know.

I wake up far from home. It is not so much that the house is inside of me as I am inhabited by the house.

I come to with silt in my eyes and dirt in the cracks of my mouth. Dust coats my hair without a scarf to cover it. The groans of the home in my guts send waves of nausea through what is left of the body I once owned.

Slowly, I sit. Slower, I stand. Behind me the road stretches, long and red, red and long and on and on. Before me the road stretches and on it is a hare. Long-eared and lanky, fur the colour of silty rust. It is tall as the ground to the middle of my thigh. Its eyes are wise and wide.

Oh, I say, not another one.

The hare flicks its ear. Seen a lotta hares around here? it asks.

I mean, I say, and I begin my journey forward, terribly slowly, the entire weight of me bearing down on my knees. Not really.

Figured as much, says the hare.

My companion lopes ahead of me, doubles back so I can keep the pace. The warmth rises through the shoes I have not yet discarded. Sweat mists my brow. Beside me, my shadow is boxy, wavers in the morning heat so that it looks as if there is a steam of smoke rising from my chimney. I know, though, that there is no one home to stoke the fire. There is no one left at all.

Except this hare, long-eared and loping, doubling back to match my laboured steps.

Do you, I ask, my breath short, my words pushed out on each exhalation, steps long and weighty, have a whole fucking house inside of you too?

The hare stops for a moment and cocks its red head. A house?

Yeah. My dizziness spins the scraggle of trees in the distance, the rusty shrubs that border the endless road. A house. I try to mime belonging. I try to mime safety, security. I try to mime the feeling of returning from a long journey and knowing that there is a place for you in the world.

The hare's expression is full of questions; it does not understand.

A den, I say. A nest. A burrow, a lair, a hive. A roost, a sett, a stable. A warren, a web.

I have none of those things, the hare tells me, inside me. I have, the hare says, only the road.

In the distance there is a junction. My feet trudge the miles between now and then. The road? I ask it.

The road, the hare says again.

And. My voice cracks like the dry earth around us. What about your family?

My family? asks the hare.

Your skulk, I say, your scurry, your swarm, your pack, your kin?

Oh, sweetheart, says the hare. I gotcha. You mean your form.

Your form? I repeat, the daze of the day lying heavy across my eyelids.

Your form, says the hare. Your kind.

Yes, I whisper. What about them?

The hare laughs a little laugh, sends its ears to flicking. What about them? it asks me. They don't have a home inside them either. They just make a space on the ground around them when they're tired, just like me.

It jumps up and gives my belly a little pat. The house likes that. Then, hop, hop, lope, the hare leaves me to the road, where, again, I make space on the ground on which to sleep in peace.

The house wants out. It convulses and shakes. Furniture falls, glasses break. Somewhere has sprung a leak. I soak the dry ground with it. It leaves a long trail behind me until even that is hidden by another cleansing night.

The road does not end. There is always another junction, another red road stretching into the dusty distance.

Eventually, again, I awake with my face in the dirt and rise to realise I am not alone.

Before me is a woman. Her dress and hair are red as the rusty road. Her shadow is long and hard. Whatever way the sun lands above us makes it look as though her shadow is my own. Square and gabled, small flick of chimney rippled up against a scraggle of trees.

I know you, I tell her. Do you also have a house inside of you?

The woman opens her arms. No, she tells me, no, my love. My house is inside of you.

The house comes out in a slick of blood and fluids. The house has its mother's eyes. The house was built of breath and bodies. The house is a map. The house is a home. The house is all we need on the long red road.

Acknowledgements

To Elsa and Luna: you are all I ever need on the long red road.

To Maman, Dad, Claire, Kevin and Thomas: in a million lockdowns you were and always will be home. Thank you for everything.

To Carmel, in loving memory.

To Jess: your friendship is threaded through these stories in the raths and houses and hangovers.

To Emma, who asked for a story about a bog witch and got a poem about love and bone marrow instead: I'll eat you up I love you so.

To Claire: I wouldn't have a career without your support and expertise. Thank you for not blinking an eyelid when I said something along the lines of 'You know how I'm supposed to be writing a YA novel? How about I send you a bunch of horror-adjacent adult short stories instead?'

To Fede: thank you for your gorgeous editing, for understanding exactly what I was doing with this collection, and for bringing it screaming and bloody and beautiful into the world.

To Alexa, Frankie, Javerya, Alice and the teams at W&N and Hachette Ireland: thank you for taking such good care of me and my horrible creature.

To the Arts Council of Ireland for their generous funding, which meant I could abandon a novel in the middle of a global pandemic and write this horrible creature instead.